THE GREY GATES

OUTCAST

VANESSA NELSON

OUTCAST

The Grey Gates - Book 1

Vanessa Nelson

Copyright © 2023 Vanessa Nelson

All rights reserved. This is a work of fiction.

All characters and events in this publication are fictitious and any resemblance to any real person, living or dead, is purely coincidental.

Reproduction in whole or in part of this publication without express written consent is strictly prohibited.

For more information about Vanessa Nelson and her books, please visit: www.taellaneth.com

For Mum and Dad,
With much love.

Contents

1. CHAPTER ONE — 1
2. CHAPTER TWO — 9
3. CHAPTER THREE — 20
4. CHAPTER FOUR — 29
5. CHAPTER FIVE — 38
6. CHAPTER SIX — 46
7. CHAPTER SEVEN — 60
8. CHAPTER EIGHT — 72
9. CHAPTER NINE — 79
10. CHAPTER TEN — 84
11. CHAPTER ELEVEN — 95
12. CHAPTER TWELVE — 107
13. CHAPTER THIRTEEN — 112
14. CHAPTER FOURTEEN — 117
15. CHAPTER FIFTEEN — 126
16. CHAPTER SIXTEEN — 131
17. CHAPTER SEVENTEEN — 145
18. CHAPTER EIGHTEEN — 154
19. CHAPTER NINETEEN — 165

20.	CHAPTER TWENTY	169
21.	CHAPTER TWENTY-ONE	174
22.	CHAPTER TWENTY-TWO	193
23.	CHAPTER TWENTY-THREE	207
24.	CHAPTER TWENTY-FOUR	219
25.	CHAPTER TWENTY-FIVE	227
26.	CHAPTER TWENTY-SIX	232
THANK YOU		238
CHARACTER LIST		239
ALSO BY THE AUTHOR		241
ABOUT THE AUTHOR		243

Chapter One

Max got out of her pick-up, the cool night air flat and dead against her skin and in her nose and mouth as she started walking across the cracked and worn road surface. In this part of the city, there were no little bits of magic here and there to keep the air fresh and the buildings clean despite traffic passing by. This was the Barrows, where the residents were more concerned with putting food on the table and keeping the lights on than such luxuries as clean windows. The buildings around her were squat and square, made for function with no attempt to also make them beautiful. A few of them had boarded-up doors and windows, suggesting that they were empty.

Districts like this were common working arenas for Max and the rest of the Marshals' service, and the lack of magic in the air was more reassuring than anything else. It meant that whatever it was she had been called to deal with wasn't powerful enough that its presence had seeped into the air. She kept going, wondering what had panicked the city police so much they needed to call in a Marshal.

She spared a moment to wish that the police had chosen another night to summon help, as she'd spent most of her day using her limited magic to reset the protective wards around her own home, and now had a mild headache along with the phantom taste of stale beer in her mouth. She didn't know why overuse of magic should leave her with a hangover that tasted like old beer, but it did. She'd been looking forward to a quiet evening to rest and recover from the magic use, but part of the job was being available to be called in even on her days off, so she had answered the phone and brought herself here to see what was needed. As she had on many other occasions, she reminded herself that she would have hated an office-based job with regular hours. Assuming anyone would have been prepared to hire her. A Marshal's work was varied, interesting and had a clear purpose, all of which she liked more than she disliked the irregular hours.

The patrol vehicles' blue and red lights flickering off the surrounding buildings turned the bare spaces of packed earth between the ugly concrete structures into a poor man's disco. All that was needed was some uncoordinated dancing and a thumping bass beat. At least the first responders on the scene had cut their sirens so she wasn't having to listen to the two-tone wail as well as see the lights. The flickering was bad enough, causing the foul taste in Max's mouth to sharpen.

There was a rookie standing between the furthest-away cars, her dark blue uniform so new that Max could smell the dye from several paces away. The shirt and trousers had creases that Max suspected had taken an age to achieve. The rookie had her thumbs tucked into her belt, sleek blonde hair tied in a tight knot at the back of her head. Even in the unflattering, ever-changing light, she looked pale, as if she might be sick.

"Can you turn the lights off?" Max asked as she reached the rookie. "I think everyone knows we're here now." The straight, wide length of the street might be deserted, but she would bet good money that there were eyes watching them from the windows of the occupied buildings around them. Police were a reasonably common sight in the poorer quarters of the city, like this one. But on a night like this, when the city's communication network was still being repaired after the storm that had blasted through the city the day before, watching the police do their work was a cheap form of entertainment.

"Ma'am." The rookie stuttered over the word, looking Max up and down with wide eyes, clearly trying to work out who she was. Max hid a smile. She was used to the reaction and had chosen to feel amused by it. She was taller than a lot of human men, and dressed head to toe in tough, casual clothing, from her leather jacket to her close-fitting trousers and calf-length boots, with a squat, snub-nosed gun in a thigh holster. Red-toned, mid-brown, jaw-length hair was tucked behind her ears, revealing a trace of scars across one cheek. She had more weapons, and more scars, but not many people got to see them. Even without all her scars on show, she did not look like a government agent.

"Max Ortis," Max said, lifting the chain at her neck so the badge showed. The rookie's eyes widened as she saw the seven-pointed star that was only carried by one agency. Max dropped the chain back, hiding the badge again. The shining metal made an excellent target for the things she hunted. "Who's in charge here?"

"That's Sergeant Williams, ma'am, er, Marshal. The tall man over there," the blonde said, turning to point and almost tripping over as she seemed to have forgotten she had her thumbs tucked into her belt. Or perhaps that was the effect that Sergeant Williams had on her. From this distance, Max could tell he was tall and had an athletic build.

"Alright," Max said, and stepped past the rookie. "Remember to fix the lights, yeah?"

She didn't wait for an acknowledgement but kept going, heavy leather boots making no sound on the cracked tarmac.

Sergeant Williams turned as she approached. He was a square-jawed man, perhaps a little over thirty, with dark stubble on his jaw and a tousled hairstyle that, unlike Max's, had probably taken hours to achieve. From a few paces away she could smell the cologne he used. It was marginally preferable to the ghostly fermentation in her mouth, but not by much. The prominent jaw tightened as he looked her up and down. Head to toe. Surprised and displeased.

It didn't matter what he thought of her. She wasn't there for him. She lifted the badge again

"Max Ortis. You called?" she asked.

"Sean Williams. Sergeant Sean Williams," he said, and half-extended a hand, returning it to his side before Max could react. "Yeah. We found something in the building we thought your lot should see."

"Be more specific," Max requested.

"What looks like a nest made out of, well, out of torn up sheets. It's covered in some green goo that smells awful. Not normal." His lips pressed together. He looked as out of place here as the rookie did, both of them too starched and clean for this area of the city. They'd be far more at home in one of the tidier inner districts. It might be the first time he or his team had come across something unusual enough to warrant a call to the Marshals. Every law enforcement officer across the city carried the Marshals' contact number. And almost all of them hoped to never have to use it. Calling in the Marshals meant acknowledging that whatever the police were dealing with wasn't human. And most city residents, the police included, didn't like to think too much about that.

Max nodded, cataloguing the details he'd provided. It sounded like a Harridan nest. Nasty things. A full-grown Harridan was an all-hands-on-deck crisis, which would need more than one Marshal, but she should be able to deal with a nest on her own. Assuming that's what it was. Harridans were rare in the city, usually kept at bay by the magic barrier holding back the Wild. But that barrier failed from time to time, most recently about ten days ago, which was more than enough time for a Harridan to make its way into the city and lay some eggs.

"Any movement outside the nest?" she asked, drawing her weapon and checking the clip. Fully loaded. As it should be. Good. She was going to need it. And possibly the spare magazines tucked against her back. And, if she was really unlucky, the small back-up gun she had next to the spare magazines, or the knives she also carried.

"Ah. No. Don't think so."

"No, or you didn't check?" Max asked, looking back at him.

"No. We cleared the room," he said. "My people know their jobs." The rookie had killed the red and blue lights, so his face was in sharp shadow with the headlights of the cars lighting one side. He looked annoyed and embarrassed. Max was used to that, too.

"Alright," she said. Her calm acceptance seemed to surprise him. She took a step past him, heading for the main door of the low, angular building behind him. Even from this distance she could smell the faint trace of Harridan bile. They liked to build their nests in disused buildings, sicking up a sticky substance to hold the layers of the nest together. She had cleared out a half dozen of them since she had joined the Marshals' service about seven years before. More than enough. But the creatures didn't seem to get the message, and kept creeping back into the city from the Wild.

"Ah. Ma'am. Marshal. Are you going in alone?"

Sergeant Williams was hesitant. Not wanting to go back into the building. Not sure he should let her go alone. It was almost funny.

"Yes. Stay here, and shoot anything that comes out that isn't me," she told him.

"Shoot?" he repeated.

"That's what I said. You know how to use that thing?" she asked, pointing to the gun at his hip.

"Ah. Yes, ma'am. I do. And so do my people."

"Well, then," she said, and turned back to the building. It was unlikely that any of them would actually hit a Harridan moving at full pace, but they might prove her wrong. And it would give them something to do while they were waiting for her to come back.

Lifting the gun with both hands, its worn surface as familiar as her own skin, she made her way forward to the dark opening of the door. The Sergeant might be surprised she was going in alone, but Max preferred it that way. There was no one next to her who could get hurt.

The door itself was mostly gone, either torn by the law officers or by the Harridan looking for somewhere to nest. The bright lights from the vehicles showed her a mass of some kind on the other side of the room. Bedsheets, as the Sergeant had said, glowing faintly green in the poor light. And moving. A gentle undulation that told her the nest was full. And close to going active.

She thumbed the selector on her gun to rapid fire and took another step forward, crossing the threshold.

And stopped.

There was something else there. Another smell. Sharper, more acidic than the Harridan's nest and its bile.

She glanced up just as something vivid yellow and with too many legs dropped off the ceiling and landed on her shoulder. An ice-cold pain stabbed into the exposed skin at the open collar of her jacket, digging into the flesh at the join between her neck and shoulder.

She yelled, using her gun to swat the thing away, pain going white hot as the serrated edges of its stinger tore her flesh. It was about the size of a domestic cat. It slammed against the side of the door and hung there for a moment, rows of tiny eyes staring back at her until she shot at it, careful to aim away from the police outside, rapid fire tearing through the door frame as the creature fled.

She heard cries of alarm from outside. A few scattered gun shots. They would be useless. She'd yet to meet someone who could shoot a crow spider running at full pace.

She staggered, numbness spreading from her shoulder, arm hanging useless, gun still in her grip as she scrabbled in a thigh pocket with her other hand. Where was it? Where? There. Her fingers, shaking as the venom coursed through her body, grabbed hold of the cylinder. She barely had enough grip to shove it against her thigh and press the end, feeling another slice of cool pain as needles shot through the tough material and into her skin, sending a jolt of anti-venom into her body.

She sagged against the door surround and focused on her breathing. Better. The wound from the serrated stinger was painful, raw and bleeding. But she was functional. More or less. And with the anti-venom doing its work, she wasn't going to die from the sting. Not tonight.

At the corner of her eye something moved. The impression of something dark and sinuous curled against the bile-covered sheets.

The nest. The damned thing was hatching. Now, of all times.

Adrenaline surged through her, breath harsh and fast in her ears. She wasn't ready to deal with the nest. Not yet. But she didn't have a choice. She couldn't let the larvae loose, not even one of them.

Bracing her back and shoulders against the wall, she managed to get her gun up, needing both hands to hold it steady. She fired, pouring the rest of the magazine into the writhing mass of linen and green spit.

The shrieks reassured her that the bullets had hit home. Most of them, at least.

When the magazine was empty, she fumbled with the release, grabbed another magazine from her back, reloaded, and repeated the process until the mass was completely still and there were no more shrieks.

By that time, the anti-venom had done its work and she was shaking in reaction to it, the various different poisons fighting with each other in her blood. It was like a coffee and sugar rush all run together and did not help her magic hangover in the slightest. She shouldn't have tried to renew all her protective house wards in the one day, but she hadn't been sure when she'd get another chance. And she was paying for it now.

Her shoulder hurt like hell. Too sore. Something grated in her flesh when she rolled her shoulder. That creature must have left part of its stinger in her flesh.

A pox on it. That meant a doctor's visit. And she'd almost rather face another Harridan.

The nest was gone, though. That was the main thing.

"What the hell?"

Human. Not a threat.

Her mind registered the basic details, keeping her weapon at her side, away from Sergeant Sean Williams, who was now standing in the doorway, shotgun in his hands, staring open-mouthed at the remains of the nest. Bits and pieces of black creature had spilled out onto the floor. None of the bits were moving. That was good, as far as Max was concerned. Harridans, even the baby ones, were only still when they were dead. None of the Marshals - Max included - liked killing things. Harridans were one of the exceptions.

"Sergeant, next time you and your people clear a room, make sure to check the ceiling," Max said, and pushed away from the wall. "Some of the division's cleaners will be along shortly to tidy up. Stay out of here. Don't touch anything and keep your people back. That stuff is toxic."

He looked like he wanted to argue, but held whatever he had to say in that firm jaw. Max put her gun away and bent down, slowly, to collect her empty magazines, tucking them into her jacket pocket. The division's armourer got more than a little tetchy when Marshals didn't return equipment for reuse.

That done, Max left the building and Sergeant Williams, who still looked shaken. She pulled out her phone as she walked, trying and failing to keep walking in a straight line as she headed towards her own vehicle. Her head was heavy, her feet light, her stomach churning with the after-effects of the injector. And the stale beer in her mouth had bloomed into something truly foul.

"It's Max," she said when the call was answered. The civilian communication network might still be under repair. The law enforcement one was working. "There's a Harridan nest that needs cleaning up and someone needs to go looking for a crow spider in the Barrows."

"We can do the clean-up, but there are no spare Marshals to go after the spider," the cool voice at the end of the phone said. "You'll need to get it."

Max checked in her stride, the wound at her neck stinging, and thought about telling the dispatcher that she was injured. It didn't take long to decide that the information wouldn't help. Therese had already called Max in from her day off. That meant that there were no other Marshals to spare. And if Max was walking and talking, she'd be expected to work.

"Oh, alright," Max said, sounding surly in her own ears. "But that's it for the day."

"We expect you back on duty as normal the day after tomorrow," Therese said, still in that cool voice, and hung up.

Max glared at the blank and unresponsive screen before she put the phone away. She had never met a human with less human warmth than Therese. The dispatcher ran the department with precise and finely calculated efficiency and, as far as Max could tell, the fact that no one really liked her did not bother the woman in the slightest.

A slight whine from ahead of her, coming from the back of her battered pick-up, reminded her of the job she still had to do. And she would have some back-up this time.

Chapter Two

The various dents in her pick-up were obvious, even in the poor light. The vehicle worked, though, and would take her most places she needed to go. It was also big enough to hold her, her equipment and the two giant dogs standing in the open back, leaning over the side panel, their eyes fixed on her as she came closer. Her shadow-hounds were little more than blots of darkness against the battered metal pick-up bed, their short, silky coats perfectly adapted for the night. Superb hunters, the natural magic they carried was almost undetectable, but their presence brushed her senses, easing some tension out of her.

One of the dogs whined slightly, sniffing at the wound at her throat. The venom that had almost felled her human body would have had little effect on her dogs.

"Yeah, Cas, I got stung. Too slow." She raised a hand and patted the dog on his head, stroking his silky soft ears. Then had to repeat the process with the other one, Pol, both of them wanting the reassurance. The familiar feel of short hair under her fingers soothed her as much as it did them. She wanted nothing more than to go home and settle on the sofa with them, warm and safe. But there was work to do first. "Shift over a moment," she said, leaning over the side of the pick-up to the locked box. The dogs moved back at once, eyes fixed on the box. She opened it up, tossed in the spent magazines and empty injector, then reloaded her gun and the ammunition slots on the belt at her back and pulled out a fresh injector pen, tucking it into her thigh pocket. It was a tight fit along with a field dressing and painkilling patches. She thought about using one of the painkillers, but she didn't know how it would interact with the anti-venom. Besides, the pain was more or less bearable.

She frowned into the lock box in the pick-up. That was her last spare injector, and she was running low on magazines, too. She would need to restock. She picked up her spring-loaded crossbow and one of the weighted nets, tucking them under her arm, wincing as the movement reminded her that part of the crow spider's stinger was still inside her. That done, she opened the tub that had been the dogs' almost exclusive focus, pulling out a handful of biscuits for each of them, scattering the treats on the bed of the truck.

Giving Cas and Pol some time to chase down every last biscuit crumb, Max leaned back against the side of her truck and poked a finger into the wound, wondering if the stinger was close enough to the surface for her to simply pull it out. Just touching the entry point was enough to make her eyes sting and her vision waver. That answered one question. She wasn't going to be able to get the stinger out on her own. She couldn't operate tweezers while she was passed out. She definitely needed a doctor.

Later. Right now, she had to deal with the crow spider.

The dogs were hanging over the side of the pick-up bed by then, one nose on each of her shoulders, dog slobber and biscuit crumbs scattering down her jacket. She didn't mind. Marshals' clothing had to be hard-wearing and the deep red leather jacket was scuffed and marked from years of hard use, as were her dark trousers. She gave each of the dogs another pat. She couldn't have risked them near a Harridan nest. The Harridan young would have swarmed her dogs. But the pair would be only too happy to hunt a crow spider for her.

"Want to go hunting?" she asked them.

They gave almost identical soft barks. They knew that word.

"OK. You run, and I'll follow in the car," she said. She gestured for them to come out of the pick-up. They landed noiselessly on the ground beside her, their shoulders almost as high as her waist, nudging her with their soft noses as she double-checked that the trackers on their collars were secure and active. That done, Cas and Pol bounced on their paws, eyes gleaming as they stared back at her, waiting for her command. "There's a crow spider. Go find it."

The pair sniffed the air for one or two breaths each, then took off, silent shadows in the night, slipping between the law enforcement vehicles without disturbing any of the officers still there.

Max got into her vehicle, docking her phone in the cradle next to the steering wheel, opening the tracking app that would let her follow her dogs. Before she drove off, she took a moment to rummage in the glove compartment, fingers eventually closing around a chocolate bar. It wasn't her favourite kind, and had been in there for a while, but it would hopefully take the edge off the taste in her mouth. Chewing on the stale food, she followed her dogs, the phone screen showing the dogs' location. Despite its battered appearance, the Marshals' mechanics kept her vehicle running smoothly, the engine quiet, and Max turned the headlights on low. Just enough light for her to see the road ahead, but not too bright to attract unwanted attention.

She turned from the wide, straight street she had been on to a narrower, curving road that snaked through what might have been a green, welcoming space at one point but which was now as run-down as the street she had just left, with low-growing, tangled weeds to either side of the worn and buckled road surface. All the buildings here, smaller than the ones she had just been in, were boarded up, windows and doors covered.

A mile or two away from the battered building that had housed the Harridan nest, her dogs came to a stop, signalling that they had found their target. Relieved that the spider hadn't gone all that far, and was still in one of the run-down parts of the city, Max parked the vehicle as close to her dogs as possible, the anti-venom still making her light-headed. She needed something more to eat than an ancient chocolate bar. And someone to remove the stinger. But first, she needed to take down the crow spider before it had the chance to attack someone else with its remaining stinger. Even with only one stinger, the creature could still do a lot of harm.

They were almost at the edge of the city here, the dark mass of the Wild less than a mile away. There was, of all things, a children's play-park. Probably a relic from happier times, when the edge of the Wild had been many miles away and the city had been expanding rather than contracting.

The fencing around the play-park had gaping holes from neglect, what had once been a large swing set missing most of the chains and swing seats. There was an ancient see-saw, and a rusting climbing frame, with a darker shadow at the top of it.

Her dogs were pacing around the base of the climbing frame. Too clever to go up and get the spider, which would be far more agile than they were on the metal bars. But they were keeping it there.

Max lifted the crossbow, checking in her stride as she went from cracked concrete to a softer surface. Glancing down, she realised that the playground had been floored with heavy sponge. A safer landing than concrete for children and their fragile bones. Satisfied that the ground would stay firm under her feet, she kept going, loading the specially adapted net onto the crossbow.

She looked up at the crow spider when she got to the edge of the climbing frame. It glared back down at her with its too-many eyes, waving its remaining stinger in the air, doubtless ready to lose that one, too. Crow spiders seemed to have no instincts apart from *attack* or *run away*. And those instincts didn't always work well for the spider.

Max fired the net, the compact load from the crossbow spreading open in flight, landing on the crow spider, which was still trying to stare her down. The weighted edges of the net fell, the hidden magnets snapping together, capturing the creature.

Only when it was caught did it try to wriggle free, and succeeded in falling off the top of the metal frame, falling to the spongy ground. The net held, as it was meant to, the too-many legs and its remaining stinger safely contained.

Max bent to pick the thing up, surprised as always by how little they weighed. The dogs came towards her, wise enough to keep their distance from the net as the spider wriggled.

"Well done," Max told them. The dogs rubbed their heads against her and she gave each of them a pat, made awkward by the net in one hand, crossbow tucked under her other arm. "Come on. Let's get this into holding."

The dogs' ears pricked up as they looked up at her.

"Yes," she said, smiling, "you'll get biscuits, too."

The two gave small, happy sounds and bounced away from her into the back of the pick-up so that they were waiting for her when she joined them. She put the spider into the back, throwing a heavy tarpaulin over it, then put the crossbow away and got a few more treats out for the dogs. Shadow-hounds were supposed to be terrifying, fierce and ruthless hunters and killers. She was sure that some were, but her pair - for the most part - were gentle and silly with no concept of personal space. It was maddening to find dog hair on every surface in her home, but she wouldn't have it any other way.

As she got back into the driver's seat to the sound of the dogs crunching their biscuits, she wondered for the hundredth time why she didn't also remember to stock the pick-up with her own food. Particularly on days like this, when she was light-headed from magic use and now woozy from the anti-venom still working its way through her body.

The Marshals' division's base of operations in the city was not housed alongside the police headquarters in one of the tall, gleaming buildings at the city's centre, surrounded by smooth roads and pavements and smartly dressed people rushing to and from their very important business. Instead, the Marshals' base was contained within a tall, chain-link fence that had seen better days, taking up an entire quarter of a run-down industrial estate. The division sprawled across a series of low buildings, each one squarer and plainer than the last, no matter which way they were viewed. This far out from the city's centre, no one had bothered to make the buildings pleasing to look at. They had been designed to serve as weatherproof spaces to work, and no more than that. The buildings here had been patched and repaired over the years, and in daylight the walls were a chaotic mix of different colours of white, grey and sand, depending on what paint or plaster material had been available. At one end of the complex was a much larger, equally square and ugly building with a range of reinforced steel-and-concrete pens behind it that could provide temporary housing for creatures that the Marshals captured, before they were returned to the Wild.

Max parked outside the larger building, glancing around the complex on reflex as she got out. There were a few other vehicles there, all of which belonged to the people stationed here. There was not one other Marshal's vehicle, which was unusual. She wondered for a moment what was so big and important that the entire Marshal's service apart from her was needed. And then decided she was too tired and sore to care right now.

Cas and Pol were already out of the pick-up when she peeled back the tarpaulin and picked up the wriggling net.

"Thinking of deserting me again?" Max asked her dogs as she approached the building's door. "There would be no hunting or chasing if you stayed here, though."

The door opened before she reached it, a waft of bitter smoke and chemicals washing over her. The dogs gave happy yips of excitement and ran past the person at the door, headed into the building.

The man at the door, a wiry human as tall as Max's shoulder wearing an old, faded blue sweatshirt that was too big for his slim frame and a pair of khaki trousers with a hole in one knee, head covered with wispy grey hair, a cigarette hanging out of his mouth, looked Max up and down before saying, "You look awful."

"Thanks," she said with no sincerity, and stepped into the building as he moved back.

His pale blue eyes moved to the net she carried and his features sharpened. No longer a harmless-looking vagrant, there was keen intelligence in his gaze. "Now, what do we have here?"

"Crow spider," Max said. "It's missing one of its stingers, but I figured you could still use it."

"Indeed, indeed. Wait. Where's the other stinger?"

"Still in me," Max said. "You can have the stinger if you want to take it out of me?" she asked, trying not to sound too hopeful. The Marshals' chief scientist knew his way around all manner of creatures. Pulling a stinger out of a human should not be beyond his skill. And if he would do that, she could avoid a trip to the clinic.

"Oh, no," the man said, in evident disgust. Apparently handling humans was far worse than the supernatural creatures he dealt with.

"But you do want the spider, yes?" Max asked with forced patience. Raymund Robart had one of the sharpest minds she had ever come across, but occasionally needed to be reminded to focus on something outside his own head.

"Bring it for me," Raymund said, turning away. He paused and glanced back at her, a faint frown pulling his brows. "You should get that stinger out as soon as possible."

Max bit down several hasty replies and followed him further into the building. Raymund operated on the assumption that everyone around him was significantly less intelligent, and he was usually right. The comment had probably been his version of being helpful. Max normally found him interesting, but right now she was short-tempered from pain.

The chemical smell grew worse as they went into the building. It was a familiar back-drop from previous visits to the science building, but she never quite got used to it.

They went past the armoury, the door closed as usual, and the glass-walled weapons manufacturing space. There were only a pair of workers in there just now, working on one of the bullet presses. At the end of the weapons workshop was an open door with the fresh scent of baking wafting out into the corridor. As they approached, Max could see her dogs winding themselves around another human, tails wagging furiously.

"Leonda, they've had snacks and they've been fed already," Max called through the open doorway. At odds with the wonderful scent of baking, the room itself was a stark, utilitarian space. One side of the room was a toughened glass wall and door with a clear view into the weapons workshop. The rest of the space was an office, meticulously neat and tidy.

"Oh, I don't know how you can say that," Leonda answered, looking up with a smile, teeth bright against her deep brown, cool-toned skin. She had changed her hair again since the last time Max had seen her. It was now a shocking, vibrant pink colour, cut short to frame her face. She was dressed with far more care than Raymund, in a long-sleeved, dark green top and slim-fitting jeans that were practical in her role as the Marshals' chief armourer. Despite her ready smile and now pink hair, Max knew the appearance was deceptive and Leonda was just as intelligent and passionate about her work as Raymund. The woman laughed as Cas head-butted her hand, looking for more pats. "They are clearly starving."

Max shook her head slightly, smiling, and moved on. The monster she was carrying had no place in that room. Besides, she did not begrudge her dogs the visit. Her dogs had loved Leonda Parras from the first moment they had met her, and the feeling seemed entirely mutual. It was impossible not to like Leonda.

Raymund stopped a little further along the corridor at a reinforced door, opening it with a key held on a chain around his neck.

Max took a slow, deep breath before she followed him inside. She did not like this room. Not one bit.

The room itself was brightly lit, full of boxes made of bullet-proof glass. The boxes had grilles fitted to let air in, and a pair of round apertures to one side to allow the scientist to reach into the boxes. Almost every one of the boxes contained a monster like the one she was carrying.

"We're due to make another harvest tomorrow," Raymund said, opening one of the empty boxes. "So your arrival is timely."

Raymund and his assistants would milk the venom from the various creatures around the room, he meant. And then use that venom in the weapons the Marshals carried. Crow spider venom, in particular, made an excellent tranquilliser for many of the dangerous creatures that the Marshals hunted.

Max's mouth was dry, so she just shoved the net inside, stepping back to let Raymund shut the box. He slid open the cover at the side, putting his arms into a pair of heavily armoured sleeves and gloves before reaching through the heavy rubber sponge apertures into the box, unclipping the magnets that held the net shut.

The crow spider left the net in a whirl of legs and eyes and fury that made Max want to take a step back, even though she was safe behind the reinforced glass.

Raymund pulled the net away from the spider and carefully out of the box through the heavy rubber, sliding the glass cover back in place over the apertures. "I suppose you'll want this cleaned before you take it back?" he asked her, dropping the net into a nearby hazardous materials bin.

"Yes," Max confirmed.

Even though all the monsters in here were safely contained, she had to resist the urge to draw her gun, her skin crawling. Most of the things in here couldn't kill her. Not on their own, with one bite or sting. But there were far too many of them for her peace of mind, and she could all-too-easily imagine them swarming over her. "I need to resupply," she said, remembering the empty magazines and injector in her pick-up.

"There's not much left. The others took most of the ammunition," Raymund said. He set the sleeves and gloves on hooks at the side of the box, looking at the crow spider. The creature stared back at him. "Don't worry, I'm not going to hurt you. I just want some of the venom you have," he said to the creature, seeming to forget that Max was still there.

"I'd best be going," Max said, taking a step back towards the door. She still had to get to the clinic. The way her night was going so far, she might not make it to her bed and some much-needed sleep until sunrise.

"Don't forget your beasts," Raymund said, as she was leaving the room. He was frowning slightly. "They disrupt our work."

"I won't forget them," Max promised.

She left her dogs with Leonda while she went to the armoury room near the front door. Raymund had not been exaggerating when he said there was not much left. It looked like every Marshal had stocked up with as much as they could carry. Max managed to find a pair of magazines for her gun and a replacement net for the crossbow, but that was almost everything that was left. Leonda was going to need to call in every member of her team over the coming days to fill the shelves again.

Max glanced at the empty trays on the table outside the armoury with a stab of guilt. She had forgotten to bring her spent ammunition from the pick-up. The huge surge in the Wild a decade before had swallowed up most of the quarries and mines and other natural resources that the city had relied on. Re-using and re-purposing was required, and Marshals had been sent back out into the field more than once to collect their spent equipment. At least Max had hers in the pick-up, ready to be brought in next time she was at headquarters when, hopefully, she wouldn't be so tired and sore.

With nothing more to find, Max went back to Leonda's room to find the armourer kneeling on the floor, Cas lying down with his head on her lap, Pol standing beside her with his head over her shoulder.

"You are such good boys, aren't you?" Leonda was saying in a low, crooning tone as Max came into the room. "Did you get what you needed?" she asked, in a quite different voice.

"Some," Max said. "It looks like you're going to have a busy few days re-supplying."

"Yes," Leonda said, her normally cheerful manner absent. She stroked Pol's ears with a gentle hand, the dog half-closing his eyes in bliss. "I've no idea what's going on, but almost every Marshal apart from you turned up at sundown to restock. If we'd had some warning, we could have been prepared for it."

"I'm sorry," Max said reflexively, even though it was not her responsibility. Leonda and Raymund, along with their separate teams, worked hard to make sure the Marshals were well-equipped with weapons and information to help in their work. They took pride in being prepared. They would both have hated being taken by surprise.

"Well, it's a lesson learned," Leonda said, shaking off her melancholy and getting to her feet. "We just need to make three times as much as we think we'll need rather than just two times."

Max managed a smile.

"Gosh, you look terrible. Are you alright?" Leonda said, a crease appearing between her brows as she stared at Max.

"Got stung by a crow spider," Max explained. "I'm heading to the clinic now."

"Good idea. Here, take something for the journey," Leonda said, picking a paper-wrapped object from her desk. Cas and Pol came on alert immediately, eyes glued to the paper packet as Leonda carried it across the room to Max. "It's some of my mother's cheesy bread."

"That's very kind of you," Max began, then her stomach growled. Loudly. "Thank you," she managed, heat spreading across her face. "I think I forgot to eat earlier."

"Words I will never say," Leonda said cheerfully. "Thanks for bringing the boys to visit. It always makes me happy to see them."

"They love you, too," Max said, smiling at her dogs who were fawning around Leonda, sensing the visit was coming to an end. "No, you do not need any more treats," she told her dogs as they looked hopefully up at the scientist.

"If you give me some warning next time, I'll make sure to have some meat pie for you all," Leonda said.

"You are too good to us," Max answered.

"I like to cook. I get that from my mother. And it's a small thing when you're all keeping us safe," Leonda said. "Now, off with you, I've got ammunition to make."

"Yes, ma'am," Max said, smiling, and took her dogs with her, Cas and Pol almost tripping over their own feet in their eagerness to stay close to the paper packet in Max's hand.

Max had to bribe the dogs back into the pick-up with more biscuits before she had a bit of space to get into the driver's seat, spending a happy few moments wolfing down Grandma Parras' famous cheesy bread. It was heaven to her taste-buds, finally chasing away the last of the magic hangover taste and putting her in a much better mood for facing the doctors at the clinic.

Chapter Three

The clinic was a few miles from the Marshals' headquarters, tucked close to, but distinctly outside, one of the better areas of the city. It took up half a city block all on its own, a single storey building that was rarely dark and empty.

Still, Max was surprised to see that this late at night, the car park was almost full, stuffed with big, shiny vehicles that looked like they belonged either to one of the elite divisions of the police force or to one of the city's Five Families. Even with the food from Leonda, Max was heavy with exhaustion, her shoulder sore, and in no mood for dealing with members of either of those groups.

She abandoned her pick-up where it should be out of the way and left the dogs to guard it, heading towards the front of the clinic. She stopped almost as soon as she had started walking, noticing the eight people standing around the awning and the lights that marked the entrance to the clinic. All eight were wearing body armour under their coats and carrying a variety of lethal-looking weapons. That meant that the occupants of the vehicles were definitely in the clinic, and that one or more or their number was injured badly enough that they needed immediate treatment and no one had wanted to risk the delay in getting to one of the large hospitals closer to the city's centre. Which, in Max's experience, generally meant that the people around the injured were on edge and more aggressive than normal. The last thing she felt like dealing with just now. But she still needed to get her wound treated, and the stinger removed before it caused a worse injury or infection.

Despite their vigilance, the eight guards hadn't seen her, so she turned, making sure to keep her movements easy and unhurried, and went down the wide access road along the side wall, following the road around the side of the building to a back entrance where there was a loading area and a reinforced steel door.

The security light above the back door was on, the harsh white making her eyes sting. She pressed the buzzer beside the door, pulling her badge out and showing it to the camera lens next to the security light. That done, she waited. And waited some more. Plenty long enough for her to question and question again the wisdom and necessity of being here. The doctors here were all more than competent, but most of them treated Max as a nuisance rather than a patient. On her last visit, the doctor had somehow forgotten to add painkiller before stitching up Max's arm.

Max forced herself to wait. She might be lucky and get one of the friendly doctors.

At length, there was the faint sound of a key turning. The door opened a crack to reveal a nurse. A human woman who Max recognised from previous visits. Her luck was definitely on the turn for the better. The nurse was an experienced practitioner with a calm, unhurried manner. She had a halo of wispy white curls and a face meant for laughter. Her normally pale skin looked washed out with exhaustion, her scrubs bearing a variety of stains that Max didn't want to think about too much.

"Marshal Ortis," the nurse said, brows lifting in surprise. Glenda. That was the name. Glenda Martins. "We haven't seen you for a while. What's up?"

"Nurse Martins. Encountered a crow spider. I need some help to take the stinger out," Max said. "And a refill for my anti-venom injector."

"Oh." Glenda hesitated, looking behind her at the corridor Max couldn't see. "Well, you might have a bit of a wait. It's been a busy night."

"So I gathered. It's alright. I need this thing out. If you can give me some forceps and a quiet space, I can have a go."

"Nonsense," the nurse said firmly, opening the door wide to let Max into the building. "We'll get you seen to. Come on, there's a free room you can wait in. This way."

Max waited until the heavy door was shut and locked before following Glenda down the wide, dimly lit corridor. There were various closed doors on either side. Store rooms, a staff room and a locker room, Max knew from previous visits. Close to the back door, there was also a refrigerated room that could store the dead before they were collected, if need be. And everything, from the rubberised floor to the ceiling lights overhead, was coated with magical warding. This was a neutral building, its sole purpose to heal people, and yet they didn't take any chances. Max approved. She might not like coming here, but she knew that the building was as safe as the operators could make it.

They reached a T-junction. The corridor they were on ended, crossed with another, better lit, corridor that also had several doors leading off along one side only, all the doors having narrow windows built in to allow a glimpse into the rooms. The doors mostly led to treatment rooms. The only exception was the one just to their left, which led to the reception area. Max catalogued all the exits and possible incursion points with automatic reflex, making sure that the layout hadn't changed since her last visit. There shouldn't be any trouble here, but she had long ago learned to be cautious.

"If you go to room eight, at the end there," Glenda pointed, "I'll get a tray and come and see you when I can."

"Thank you," Max said, trying not to look too relieved. Glenda was more than capable of treating the wound, and had never made Max feel less than welcome.

Max headed along the corridor, past the closed doors. The rooms inside were all lit, and all of them occupied. She caught glimpses of bloodstains on walls and medical professionals in stained scrubs. The patients were all screened from view by sheets hung from rails on the ceiling, but one room she passed had two armed guards inside the room with a doctor and patient.

The sight of the guards made her head spin and her throat close up, panic choking her.

She stopped and leant against the wall of the corridor, out of sight of the room, heart thumping, mouth dry. She knew the insignia that the guards were wearing. She hadn't seen the patches on the people outside, thanks to the distance, but in here, at closer quarters and with the room brightly lit for medical treatment, she knew exactly who they were. Warriors of the Order. Or, to give its full name: the Order of the Lady of the Light. The magical and military operation dedicated to the service of the Lady Herself. The warriors provided military protection for the magic-wielders of the Order. But if a warrior had been injured, they would be here alone, the rest of their team staying on task to protect the magician. Which meant that the patient was probably a Guardian, one of the powerful magicians sworn to Her service to combat dark magic and the dark lord Himself.

This was the closest Max had been to any member of the Order, warrior or Guardian, in eight years. Eight years in which she had done her best to ignore them, to stay out of their way, to be invisible. Whatever worked to keep her away from them. The Order had rejected her. Cast her out. And she wanted nothing to do with them. Not now. The feeling seemed mutual, as they had ignored her, too. And now there were warriors and possibly a Guardian nearby. Just through the wall from her. She wondered who it was, if she knew them. If she might have called them a friend once.

She was older now, and with far greater exposure to the world and far less trust in people. The good memories she had of the Order - the feeling of being part of something bigger than herself, working towards a common purpose - were tarnished with cynicism, wondering if anyone there had truly liked or valued her at all. Still, she hated the way her throat closed up and her eyes stung. Eight years' distance and she had tried to fool herself that she didn't care. She had changed a lot since then. She didn't need them, and they had made it perfectly clear that they didn't need her.

She wanted to go back into the night, collect her dogs and drive home. Far away from here. Far, far away. She must have at least one pair of pliers at her house that could get the stinger out. She had survived worse.

Testing her theory, she put her hand on the wound, and almost blacked out from the pain of it. She held in cursing with difficulty, not wanting to draw the attention of the warriors. She needed another pair of hands to get the thing out of her. And she was here now. If she kept quiet, and the nurse was quick, then she could be out of here before the Order even knew she had been in the building.

So she forced herself to move, to keep walking, along the corridor to the last door. It was the only empty room, dimly lit by a desk lamp. There was another door, leading to the reception area. The room itself felt crowded with a single bed and wheeled chair, presumably for use by the physician. Max let herself in and struggled out of her jacket, hissing with pain as the stinger dug into her flesh, dropping the jacket onto the bed and letting herself sit on the edge, facing the door to the reception area. Just for a moment. Just until the room stopped spinning.

Stripped down to her sleeveless black t-shirt, she glanced down at the part of her shoulder she could see. Her pale skin was veined with trails of venom, dark and foul, that had worked their way along her flesh before the injection had stopped them. By morning, the trails should be gone and her skin back to its normal pale tone. The trails had almost reached her elbow, though. Even in the few moments it had taken her to grab the injector and get the anti-venom into her. If she'd been a bit slower, or hadn't had the injector with her, she would have been dead. Another Marshal lost to the city's service. Instead, it was another hard-won piece of wisdom for her. Always check the ceilings.

With the wound open to the air, she felt exposed, and hated it. She might need to be here a while, too. A noise through the wall reminded her of the Order's warriors and Guardian nearby, prompting a closer look around the room. If there was some anaesthetic to take the edge off and some forceps, she might not need to wait for the nurse.

There was a mobile trolley with a tray of medical instruments on the top layer, and a locked medicine cabinet. Max sighed. No luck. Even if the cabinet had been open, she wasn't sure which one of the drugs in there was what she needed. And there were no forceps on the tray, not even a scalpel to help her cut the thing out.

So she would have to wait. She looked at the clock on the wall and scowled. It had stopped a long time ago. She dug her phone out of her pocket, wincing as the movement made the stinger dig deeper into her flesh, and checked the time. Nearing midnight. She would give the nurse until midnight, she decided, and then head home. If she put some ice on the wound, she might be able to get some rest, and come back the next day when presumably there would be no Guardian and no other members of the Order.

Even as she thought that, the door at the back of the room opened and the nurse appeared, a metal tray balanced on one hand. She flipped the light switches, bathing the room in harsh, white light, which woke up the magic hangover Max had all but forgotten about.

"You're in luck. We managed to get someone else to come in on their night off," the nurse said, "so I have time to fix you up." She put the metal tray down on the space on the trolley and wheeled it over to beside the bed. "Let's have a look."

Max glanced at the door to the reception area. The nurse's entrance and the lights going on should have drawn attention. Nothing. She stayed on the bed, gripping the side with her good hand to stop herself reaching for her weapon. She hated feeling so exposed.

"I've got you a new injector, some antibiotics and fresh dressings in here," Glenda said, holding up a large paper sack. She put it on the bed next to Max's discarded jacket.

"Thank you," Max said, surprised and touched that Glenda had remembered.

"If you can drop the empty injector in at some point, that would help," Glenda said.

"I will," Max promised, thinking of the empty magazines along with the injector in her pick-up. She would have to do some clearing out when she was properly back on duty.

"That looks nasty," the nurse commented, snapping on a pair of bright blue gloves. "I've got a numbing spray, but I can't give you an injection. I'd need a doctor to sign off on that, and they're all busy. You seemed like you might be in a hurry," the nurse added, to Max's surprise.

Max's mouth curved up at the unexpected understanding. "It was supposed to be my day off, too."

"Ouch," the nurse said in sympathy, and aimed a small spray can at Max's shoulder. The liquid hit Max's skin and blissful numbness spread around the area, followed moments later by fiery pain as the nurse put the forceps into the wound.

Glenda was quick and skilled, though, and got the stinger out with minimal fuss. Max released the breath she had been holding, her eyes watering, and held the gauze pad to the wound as requested while the nurse dropped the stinger into a bio-hazard container.

"It's going to take a few days for the wound to heal properly-" Glenda said. Whatever else she might have said was interrupted by the door to the reception area opening without notice.

A young man scowled into the room. He looked barely old enough to be carrying the automatic rifle strapped across his chest. Despite his youth, he wore body armour and the insignia of the Order, a patch with a double-headed axe, over dark, close-fitting clothing. He had blond hair crafted into an array of spikes across his head, and a tattoo snaking down from behind one ear. Doubtless he thought he looked tough, but to Max's eyes he looked too young and out of his depth, an overgrown child playing dress-up.

"Who's this? How did she get in?" he demanded, lifting his weapon. "No other patients, you were told."

"And we told you that this is an open clinic and that we don't close our doors to anyone in need," Glenda Martins said calmly, staying where she was, peeling the back off a wound dressing and pressing it to the wound on Max's shoulder, discarding the blood-soaked gauze into the bio-hazard container. "This Marshal was wounded on duty," she added over her shoulder.

"She's not supposed to be here," the young man said, chin jutting out.

"Go and find your supervisor," Glenda said, still in that calm voice, getting up and stripping off her gloves as the warrior disappeared. "I'm sorry, Marshal. Everyone is a bit on edge."

"That's quite alright," Max said. She remembered just how seriously the Order's warriors took their duty. None of them would be happy that a Guardian had been injured on their watch. And she didn't want to be here longer than she had to be, not with so much tension in the building. She tried to get up from the bed and found that her head was still spinning.

"I'd advise getting some food and plenty of fluids soon, too," Glenda said, putting a hand on Max's bare arm, her touch shockingly warm, making Max realise just how cold she was.

"I will," Max promised.

Before she could try to stand up again, another armed body appeared in the doorway. A senior member of the Order. Max could tell that simply by the way he stood, with quiet self-assurance. He was dressed in similar clothing to the boy, but even on a dark night no one would ever mix the two up. The man in the doorway had close-cropped dark hair that looked like he cut it himself, a firm jaw coated in the suggestion of a beard, a face that had seen one too many fights, and a displeased expression.

And Max knew him. Bryce. No last name, or not one that she knew. He might look human, but she was quite sure there was something else in his heritage. That was relatively common in the city, with its mix of peoples. He did not seem to have aged a day since she had last seen him, about ten years before. He had been one of the toughest instructors in the Order and had thrown her across the training room in practice the one time she had been in his hand-to-hand combat class, dismissing her as entirely useless when she could not master the moves that he was trying to teach her. Moves that every other student in the class seemed to adapt to with no difficulty. And when she had tried to attend his class the following day, he had not let her into the room. The humiliation still stung, ten years later.

Apart from those brief encounters, she could not remember exchanging any words with him. It was possible he might not recognise her. She had changed since then. Grown up, in more ways than one, her appearance quite different now.

"What's going on here?" Bryce asked, breaking into Max's tumbled thoughts. It was said with the quiet authority of someone used to getting the answers he sought.

"As I told your junior, the Marshal was wounded on duty," Glenda said, facing the warrior. "And our doors are open to those who need us. You agreed to let us work without hindrance. That includes having guns pointed at us."

"We did agree. But she didn't come in through reception," the man said, glancing at Max. She stiffened, wondering if he would recognise her. His brows lifted and he took a longer look, eyes tracing the evidence of venom down her arm. "Crow spider?" he asked.

"Yes," Max said, voice clipped.

"Perhaps she didn't feel like being interrogated by all the armed muscle you have hanging around the reception area?" Glenda suggested, her calm tone edged with a touch of acid that made Max bite back a smile.

Bryce's brows lifted, but he didn't seem offended. And Max realised that although he was armed, he was not holding a weapon. He was dangerous enough without one in his hands, though. She had the urge to huddle into her jacket, as if the old leather would protect her from the warrior. She held herself still. Bryce could be lethal, but he was not threatening her.

"A fair point," he conceded. "She came through the back door?"

"Yes," Glenda said. "Marshal, you'll need to change that dressing twice a day, and the instructions for the antibiotics are on the bottle. Come back if it looks infected or doesn't start to heal soon."

"Thank you," Max said. She made it to her feet and picked up her jacket and the paper bag. She thought about putting the jacket on and decided against it. The numbness was wearing off and she didn't want to pass out from pain in front of Bryce.

He was frowning now, taking a closer look at her.

"Have we met before?" he asked.

"No," Max said, forcing the word out, trying not to make it sound like a lie.

He was still frowning. Not entirely convinced. But he didn't press her further.

"I'll walk you out," he said, stepping back from the doorway, clearly meaning for her to go through the reception area.

"I'll go out the back," Max said.

He lifted his chin, clearly displeased at not being obeyed.

"I'll walk you out," Glenda said, just as more noise erupted from one of the other rooms. To Max's ears, it sounded like a spoiled child having a tantrum. It was probably the Guardian. For people who were supposed to be the most powerful magicians in the world, some of them were notoriously afraid of pain. "It sounds like you are needed elsewhere," the nurse pointed out to Bryce.

With a frowning glance between Max and Glenda, Bryce nodded, then turned and left, heading out into the reception area.

Max found she had to lock her knees to steady herself before she could walk with Glenda back along the corridor to the back door, shivering slightly in reaction. He had not recognised her. She felt light and almost giddy with relief. He had not recognised her. She was safe for a little while longer at least.

On that happy thought, she left, stomach growling in protest, reminding her once again that she needed food.

Chapter Four

Having food in the house was a rare luxury. Max had forced herself to stop at an all-night grocery store on the way home and spend a few minutes picking up some essential supplies, including some snacks to keep in the pick-up for both her and the dogs. She was glad of it when she opened her fridge door the next morning and marvelled at the shelves full of things she could eat, trying to focus on that bit of wonder rather than the remnants of the nightmare she had woken from. Nightmares were common. Fresh and edible food in her house was not.

She made a mug of tea with her only clean mug, and settled at the kitchen table, eyeing her surroundings. The fridge might be tidy and full of goodness. It was far more than could be said of the rest of the room. She had worked more days without a break than she cared to remember, and it showed. The place was filthy. Dirty dishes piled high, takeaway containers and used mugs and glasses scattered here and there. It was enough to make her want to crawl back into bed. But she'd had some sleep now, and knew that all that waited for her between her sheets were more nightmares. Besides, if she went close to the bedroom it would just remind her that she needed to tidy up in there, too, and do some laundry.

In the meantime, there was the miracle of actual food in her house, and she opened the bag of chocolate-chip banana bread she had bought the night before. It would do for breakfast. Besides, she didn't have a single clean plate or cooking utensil to make anything more complicated.

The banana bread was perfectly fine as a fuel source, washed down nicely with two mugs of tea. She managed to ignore the untidiness around her by staring out the kitchen window. She was close to the Wild here, the great forested edge of it visible from her kitchen, on the other side of a band of grass that was almost waist high on Max. If she concentrated, she could feel the magic that formed the barrier between the city and the Wild, keeping the worst of the Wild at bay and allowing the residents of the city, particularly those who lived in the more central areas, the illusion of safety. Closer in, she could feel the pattern of her own wards, the spells she had renewed the day before strong and clear in her mind. A very necessary precaution this far out from the city centre, even if the effort of maintaining the wards had left her with a magic hangover that had only just faded.

Within the protective wards, her garden was so overgrown it could almost pass for the Wild with its varied shades of green, a few vivid splashes of pink and red here and there the only hints it was actually a garden. Even the Lady's altar had been neglected, and Max usually tried to ensure that, at least, was tended. The simple wooden bench with the metal bowl of water on the top of it didn't look like much, but the Lady's priests and priestesses taught that it was the intent that counted. Max could only hope they were right, as she needed all the goodwill she could get from the Lady.

There were plants overgrowing the bench and the water was choked with leaves and insects, as neglected as the rest of the garden. There had been no time to tend to it for weeks, and unlike in the central city, there was no one around to help out with chores. Even if she paid them well above the rates charged in the inner city, very few people wanted to come this close to the Wild, let alone live or work here. It suited Max. There were no neighbours to keep an eye on her, or for her to be responsible for if the worst should happen and the Wild should breach or surge forward again.

Some people might find the place lonely. Hers was the last house at the end of a dirt road, but she loved the space and the quiet. Her earliest memories were of being crammed with other children into a dormitory room at one of the city orphanages. There had been no privacy or quiet spaces there. She hadn't understood why it had been so difficult, not then. Moving into the Order's buildings had been marginally better - at least she had been given her own room, barely big enough for a bed and a desk to study. But even there, the building had always been full of people. It hadn't been until she came back to the world and found this house outside the city that she had been able to truly relax and breathe freely and realised just how much she needed space to herself and quiet to think. She might have to deal with crowded spaces and people all day in her work, but she always had this place to come back to. There were no street lights, and almost no services operated this far out of the city centre. Just driving up the road to the gates soothed her.

She dug into the packet and frowned as her searching fingers met empty air, realising that she had finished the banana bread. And her second mug of tea.

Just as she was facing the awful prospect she would actually have to do some housework, her phone rang. She picked it up, brows lifting at the caller ID. It seemed that Therese was interrupting another day off. All Marshals were required to answer even on their days off and Max reminded herself, once again, that she would have hated an office job as she brought the phone to her ear.

"Yes," Max answered the phone. She had long since learned that Therese's reactions didn't change whether Max was friendly or polite or not. The woman simply did her job.

"You're needed at a crime scene in the Barrows," Therese said.

"I was just there last night," Max observed.

"This is a different address." Therese gave Max the address in the same flat tone.

Max memorised the address out of long habit. Therese hated to repeat herself. Then asked the obvious questions, "What crime scene? Why am I needed?"

Max waited, half expecting Therese to simply hang up.

To her surprise, the woman answered. With a loud, put-upon sigh, but she did answer. "Some dead body. The local cops think there might be something strange. And you're the only one available. Again."

Max glared at the phone as Therese simply hung up. Then she looked at the disaster that was her kitchen and decided that viewing a dead body might not be the worst thing she had to face today.

Cas and Pol were more than happy to get into the back of the pick-up and go for a drive. Then again, Max thought, they were generally happy whatever she asked them to do, whether it was chasing a crow spider or keeping watch on the house and grounds whilst she re-set the wards. They were the easiest companions she had ever had, and she gave them extra pats before she settled into the driver's seat.

She arrived at the address, which turned out to be the remains of a garden next to the local community centre. The garden had not been tended for some time, the beds of what might have been vegetables overgrown with stinging plants. The fruit trees that must have been planted in better times, when the Wild had been further away, were growing into each other now as no one had trimmed them for several years.

There were a few police vehicles parked around the garden's perimeter. The nearest one had a familiar-looking rookie cop standing next to it. There were no lights this time, which Max was thankful for.

"Ma'am," the rookie said as Max approached. "Sergeant Williams is over there, with the medical examiner." Her blonde hair was in the same sleek bun as it had been the night before, the dark blue uniform just as crisp and new, even in daylight, making Max realise just how battered and worn she looked by comparison. The rookie had her thumbs out of her belt this time and managed to turn and point without stumbling.

"Thank you," Max said, making her way between the cars and heading across the garden to where the Sergeant was standing next to a tiny woman in white coveralls.

"Max Ortis, as I live and breathe," the woman said, a grin splitting her face. She was barely taller than Cas and Pol, but had a force of personality that made her seem much larger. She was also one of the oldest beings that Max had ever come across, the weight of her years a burden she generally carried so lightly they were almost invisible. She looked to be a human woman somewhere in her thirties with mid-brown, riotous hair scraped back into a haphazard knot at the back of her head, pale brown eyes bright as she looked up at Max. "I haven't seen you for ages, honey. How are you?"

"I'm well. And you?" Max asked. The last time she had seen Audhilde had been at least a year before, when someone had decided it was a good idea to bring a predator to a birthday party. Audhilde and her team had collected the human bodies. Max had been there to deal with the predator.

"Oh, can't complain. Did Sean call you in?" Audhilde asked.

"I think so," Max said, and nodded to Sergeant Williams by way of greeting, not surprised that Audhilde would refer to the square-jawed young man by his first name, not his rank. "At least, I had a call to come here."

"That was her idea," Sergeant Williams said, in clipped tones. He was standing in a rigid posture, clearly unhappy about something.

"Alright," Max said. "Why don't you tell me what you found?" she asked the Sergeant. She knew Audhilde well enough to know that she was not going to be offended by the man's rudeness. She was probably finding it quite amusing. Max wondered if the Sergeant had realised just who he was dealing with, or even if the woman standing next to him was not human. Audhilde was legendary among the city's law enforcement as the longest-serving medical examiner. She had served through the careers of better men than Sean Williams would ever be. And she was almost always right.

"Some kind of a knife fight. We have one dead body and a lot of blood," Sergeant Williams said, jaw tightening. He glanced down at Audhilde. "It's definitely a murder. But it looked gang-related to me." Max's brows lifted. The city had its fair share of violent humans, which the police kept watch on, and fighting between gangs who had claimed different territories was reasonably common, as far as she knew. But they were far out of the city's main streets here, far away from any areas which Max thought were claimed by any particular gangs.

"Let's take a look," Max suggested. From the tightening of Audhilde's face, she was quite confident there was nothing gang-related about this murder. And confident, too, that Audhilde had already expressed that to the Sergeant and been ignored.

Sean Williams turned on his heel and stalked a few paces away. There was a crime scene technician already there, who scuttled out of his way in a manner that suggested the Sergeant had already shouted at the tech once today. Max frowned. While he seemed impatient and had been rude, she had not realised he was also quite that stupid. The techs were there for a reason, after all, and if he trampled over evidence, he would be held accountable for it.

Still, this was not her jurisdiction and catching human killers was not her job, so she stayed quiet and followed the Sergeant to a narrow band of vivid yellow tape that marked off a large area of the garden.

In the middle of the tangled undergrowth there was a body lying on its back. What looked like a human man, somewhere between thirty and fifty, with long brown hair tangled around his head, eyes open and staring up at nothing. He had been stripped to his waist, and there were knife wounds across his bare chest and stomach. A series of straight cuts that did not form any pattern that Max could recognise.

"See, some kind of knife fight. There's no need for you to be here," Sean Williams said.

Max decided that she did not like the man. She glanced at Audhilde. "I'm assuming you've told him this wasn't a knife fight?" she asked.

"Several times." The petite woman drew her lips back from teeth that, if Sergeant Williams had cared to look closely, would seem far more pointed than they had a few moments ago.

"You can't possibly know that," Sergeant Williams said, his prominent chin set.

"Well, all the wounds are on his front. There are no defensive wounds on his hands or arms that I can see. I don't know anyone who would just lie there and let someone carve them up like that," Max said. Those were all remarkably obvious signs, and she couldn't help but wonder how the Sergeant had got to his current rank. He may well have connections within the Five Families that had helped him get to Sergeant. However, unless his conduct improved, he wasn't likely to advance further. Even the Five Families liked their police to be competent.

"We'll do a tox screen," Audhilde said, "but I'm thinking some kind of drug was used to keep him still."

"Definitely not a fight. This was a murder," Max said. She moved sideways to view the body from a different angle. "I don't understand the purpose, though." She looked at Audhilde and lifted a brow.

"Very good," Audhilde said, the hint of a dimple showing. "That's why you are here."

"Alright," Max said, continuing to walk around the outside of the tape, keeping an eye on where her feet were going, then glancing back to the body. "The body is crossways with the sun's path," she noted, not knowing if it was significant or not, but the body was lined up straight north to south, and amid the chaos of the garden that did not seem an accident. "Some kind of ritual, I am guessing," Max said slowly. It had been a long time since she had taken classes in dark magic, and she had tried to forget them entirely, along with everything else about the Order and the Guardians.

"That was my guess, too," Audhilde confirmed.

"There's nothing here to suggest it was anything other than a human killing another," Max said, and looked across at Audhilde. The medical examiner knew, as well as Max did, that human crimes were outside the Marshal's jurisdiction. Which made Max wonder just why she had asked for a Marshal.

"If it is a murder, that's our job," Sergeant Williams said, sounding thoroughly annoyed by the idea.

"That's true," Max said cheerfully. "I'm sure that Audhilde will give you her usual detailed report and you'll have plenty to work on from that. Do we know who the man was?" she asked.

"No. His pockets were completely empty," Audhilde said.

That was unusual enough to catch Max's attention again. Even the poorest of the city's dwellers carried something with them, even if it was just the ID cards that the city's rulers required all citizens to carry, no matter their species. The human population might protest against the requirement to carry ID, but then most of them didn't know that the cards were coded to let law enforcement know just who and what they were dealing with. It wasn't a perfect system, but it was one that the major species had learned to live with.

"So someone brought him here, probably drugged him, took everything out of his pockets that could be used to identify him, and then killed him in this really odd way," Max summarised.

"Odd?" Sean asked, sounding less defensive than he had.

"If you have a knife, and you want to kill someone, then surely you just stab them as deeply as possible? You don't make all these shallow cuts," Max pointed out. She had completed her circuit of the body and was back at Audhilde's side.

"The cuts should not actually have killed him," Audhilde said. "I don't have a cause of death yet."

"No cause of death? The twenty stab wounds didn't kill him?" Sergeant Williams was back to being arrogant.

"The twenty-three shallow cuts in his skin may have bled a lot and look terrible, but they would not be enough to kill him," Audhilde said, not looking at the human. Standing close to her, Max could feel the tension in Audhilde's small body and wondered if Sean Williams had any idea of just how dangerous the petite woman really was. If he provoked Audhilde further, he might find out just how lethal she could be. And then there would be something here for Max to deal with. Even though none of the Marshals were properly equipped to deal with a powerful vampire, if the vampire went rogue then the Marshals would be the ones expected to deal with it.

Max shifted her weight. Just a little bit, just enough to draw attention to the weapon at her side. The human did not notice, but Audhilde did, her eyes gleaming with mischief as she glanced at Max. The mischief let Max relax a fraction, enough to turn her attention back to the Sergeant.

"The community centre should have security cameras," Max said. "And it would normally be open into the evening. So you might get lucky with witnesses."

Sergeant Williams blinked, as if it had not occurred to him to actually seek out witnesses and investigate the crime.

"I'll need to call in a detective," he said, and moved away.

Left alone with Audhilde, and with the human out of earshot, Max lifted a brow. "What is it? You didn't have a Marshal called to look at a human crime."

Audhilde was silent for a moment, lips pressed together, then looked up, her eyes shading darker. "I have a bad feeling about this one," she said at length, perfectly serious, "and someone in the Marshals needed to know this had happened."

Max absorbed what Audhilde was saying, and not saying. "You think there will be more?" she asked, a chill running over her skin.

"This looks like a mess," Audhilde said candidly, "but the wounds are in a pattern of sorts, even if we can't see it. Yes, I think there will be more."

"But the Sergeant, and whatever detective he manages to bring on, won't believe that," Max said slowly. It was her turn to press her lips together. "Alright. I can make some enquiries about blood rituals, and I'll put an alert out to the other Marshals."

"Good," Audhilde said, as the Sergeant came back to them.

"Detective is on his way," he told them, and eyed Max, hesitating.

"Well, it seems you have matters in hand," Max said, "and I've got other things needing my attention." Like her revolting kitchen. "Audhilde, it was good to see you again."

"And you. We must get drinks sometime," Audhilde said, with a gleam in her eye.

Max grinned and waved goodbye, heading back to her pick-up, knowing that none of the people around her would understand Audhilde's barbed humour. Drinks, indeed. With Max as Audhilde's beverage of choice. Probably not one of the humans knew that they had a real-life vampire standing in their midst, under the sun and wearing baggy white coveralls.

Chapter Five

Having promised Audhilde that she would make enquiries, Max headed to the most likely place she knew of to start finding answers.

The Hunter's Tooth didn't look like much from either the outside or the inside. It was a long, low building sitting between the edge of the Barrows and one of the nicer city districts. The once-pristine paint on the building had long since turned to an indeterminate dirty cream colour, great patches of it chipped or stained, the pitched roof missing several tiles. There was what looked like a vast, run-down warehouse attached to one side of it and a ten-foot-high wall running around the back of the warehouse to join up with the Hunter's Tooth. The building to the other side - probably another warehouse, or commercial building - had been knocked down years ago, the space now taken over by parking for the Tooth's customers. On any given day, and at any time, there was usually an extraordinary array of vehicles there ranging from sleek, incredibly expensive bits of metal and chrome to rugged all-terrain vehicles with even more dents in them than Max's pick-up.

Even in the late morning, the parking lot was still a quarter full, including a pair of vivid pink convertibles tucked next to what looked like little more than a metal frame on giant wheels.

Cas and Pol barked their excitement as Max parked in direct view of the bar's front door. She grabbed a double handful of biscuits from the box in the back, stuffing them into her pockets, and then made her way to the Tooth's door, the dogs pacing ahead of her, stopping now and then to sniff at something in their path.

The interior of the building should have looked seedy and run-down, with mismatched chairs and tables, old posters with curled corners on the walls along with age-flecked mirrors. It had never seemed run-down to Max, not since the first time she had found her way here, still raw and shaken. It had always felt like a home from home. The large floor area was divided with patterned silk screens and ceiling-high plants, breaking the space up so that many of the tables had the illusion of privacy. There were pool tables at one side, the lights carefully directed down to the table surfaces and not glaring out into the room.

The horse-shoe shaped bar was dimly lit, only one person working at the moment. Max took a look around the room as she headed across to the bar, noticing a pair of near-identical scantily clad women in serious conversation with a dark-suited man in one of the rounded booths. Settled a distance away from them were a couple of burly men, wearing stained overalls, working their way through the pitcher on the table in front of them. The burly men had Wild magic around them, the heady and untamed power that saturated the Wild. The trace was strong enough that they had to have been inside the Wild recently, but that was reasonably common in this bar.

Her hounds ignored everyone else in the room, heading straight for the bar, putting their paws up on it, tails wagging madly as the bartender turned towards them. He grinned, white teeth brilliant against his mid-brown skin, and gave them each a pat on their heads.

"Cas. Pol. How many times do I have to tell you, no paws on the bar?" he asked, and tossed each of them a bit of food. The dogs jumped down, scrabbling on the floor for whatever it was. The man turned his grin on Max. "Good to see you, Max."

"And you," Max said, smiling, and glanced down at her dogs. "What did you give them?"

"Just some cooked chicken. I keep some handy," he said easily, leaning across the bar to greet her.

Max accepted the light kiss on her cheek, breathing in his scent. Whatever he might look like, Malik was not human and had a rare ability to change his scent. He always smelled delicious, no matter what scent he was wearing. Today he was a heady mix of fresh baked bread and the finest coffee, bitter and dark with a touch of sweetness. She settled on a bar stool, folding her hands together, taking stock of Malik.

He seemed just the same, which was no surprise. As well as being extraordinarily beautiful, he was the most easy-going person she had ever met in her life, always friendly, always warm. He had had a haircut since she had last seen him, his thick black hair curling around his head, the shorter cut showing off his striking bone structure. In all the time she had known him, he had never tried to play up his good looks, and today was no different, the t-shirt and jeans he was wearing worn and comfortable.

Looking at him now, she remembered, as she often did around him, lying next to him tangled in crisp cotton sheets, feeling lazy and content and safe for the first time in a long, long while. She gripped her hands together more tightly to avoid reaching out to him again. He would not turn her away, she knew that, but she had long ago come to the conclusion that he was not what she needed. And that was still true.

"What can I get you?" he asked.

"Just coffee, if there's any ready?"

"Always," he said, turning away to get her a mug from the pot brewing at the back of the bar. He brought two mugs back, and then a plate of what looked like home-made cake. "Grandma Parras stopped by the other day. I think she's trying to fatten me up."

"You and everyone else she meets," Max said, pouring plenty of milk into her coffee. Without diluting, Malik's coffee was almost lethal.

"It's been a while," Malik commented. He leant a hip against the bar, his own coffee mug cradled in his hands. No milk for him. Of course not.

"Work's been busy," Max said, wrinkling her nose as she remembered the disaster zone that was her kitchen, which would still be waiting for her when she got home.

"I heard there was trouble last night," Malik said.

"Really? I wasn't there. Supposed to be off duty finally. Like today," Max said, picking up some of the cake, and ignoring Cas and Pol, who were staring at the plate as if they had never eaten in their entire lives.

"Hm," Malik said, taking a sip of his coffee and staring at the black liquid for a moment before he looked up, his deep brown eyes unusually serious. "The trouble was big enough to involve the Marshals and some of the Order. But no one is talking about what actually happened. Not right now."

Max finished her cake. Marshals and the Order rarely worked together, as Malik had implied. Only in extreme circumstances, where the threat was serious enough that it might spill over into the civilian population. Trouble that bad could easily have resulted in a Guardian being injured. Max half-closed her eyes, focussing on the flavours in her mouth. Not even the thought of that sort of trouble could make Grandma Parras' baking anything less than delicious.

"There was a significant breach of the Wild about ten days ago," Max said. It was the sort of thing that would likely be common knowledge among the community by now. Despite the best efforts of the Marshals and magicians in the employment of the city, the barrier between the city and the Wild did fail from time to time, allowing creatures from the Wild to venture into the city. Such breaches usually kept the Marshals flat-out busy for weeks afterwards. "We've been seeing a lot of predators within the city limits. I had a Harridan nest and crow spider to deal with last night."

"Somehow I thought that breach had been contained," Malik said thoughtfully. There was no edge to his tone. There never was, not with Malik. He was the only individual that Max had not one single bad memory of. Even when she had broken up with him, he had been calm and understanding. Doubtless it helped that he was never short of company if he wanted it. But there had been no bitterness, just a quiet acceptance and a heartfelt wish for her good health and well-being. And he had always welcomed her back to the Hunter's Tooth, as warm and friendly as the day they had first met.

"The breach was sealed," Max said. She hadn't been there, one of the few Marshals held in reserve to deal with any emergencies. While it had grated to be on the sidelines, she knew it was sensible. Her magic wasn't strong enough to make a difference to the effort, and she had been better used in keeping watch for any creatures that might have slipped through the breach.

It had taken almost every Marshal using all of their magical abilities several hours to close the gap in the perimeter wards again, sealing the Wild behind its barrier once more.

"But we don't know how many creatures got through," Max said. Or how many more they might have spawned in the time they had been in the city, she added in the quiet of her own mind, remembering the Harridan nest. A fully adult Harridan, or a mated pair of them, could easily have caused the sort of trouble that required most of the Marshals and some of the Order to deal with.

"You've done a good job. I haven't heard any rumours," Malik said. Then he frowned, the crease between his brows unfamiliar. "Did you say you were supposed to be off duty yesterday and today?"

"I did," Max agreed, taking a long drink from her mug. With the contents about half-and-half milk and Malik's coffee, it was perfect. "Audhilde called me to visit a dead body earlier."

"One of hers?" Malik asked, surprised.

"No," Max said, a ghost of a laugh escaping her. "I think she's more discreet than that."

"Ah, Hilda. I could tell you some tales," Malik said, mischief on his face.

Max laughed. "I don't think anyone else dares to call her that."

"She loves me," Malik said, with no false pretence or vanity. Everyone loved him.

"No, not one of hers," Max said, shaking her head. "This was a human male." Max described the human, as best she could remember him, and the cuts on his torso.

Malik stayed still and silent while she talked.

Before he could answer, there was a heavy tread on the floorboards behind her. The dogs, who had settled at Max's feet, lifted their heads, eyes gleaming in the shadows of the bar, low growls sounding.

"Marshal, is it?"

It was the two burly men she had seen earlier, drinking their way through the pitcher. One of them had the empty pitcher in one hand.

"Yes," Max said, not moving.

"We don't want your kind in here," the man on the left said, something other rippling under his skin.

"You're new here, aren't you?" Max asked. "Just got back from the Wild?" They both wore faded metal disks on their right shoulders, the sort that a magician might use to provide an individual the ability to pass through the magical barrier against the Wild. A lot of the non-human residents of the city liked to visit the Wild from time to time, and as long as they used an official pass, and didn't bring back anything, the city's council was happy to let them.

"What's it to you?" the man on the right asked, jaw jutting out. He held the empty pitcher like a potential weapon.

"This is neutral ground," Max said in the same, conversational tone.

"This is the Hunter's Tooth," Malik said from behind the bar. He wasn't speaking loudly, his voice full of peace and promise. Max saw the two men leaning slightly towards him, the tension and anger seeping from their bodies. "Let me refill that for you, on the house," Malik went on. He reached past Max's shoulder. The talkative man handed him the pitcher, Cas and Pol alert at Max's feet. "Why don't you go and sit down again? I'll bring the drink over in a moment. And some of Grandma Parras' baking."

"That's mighty generous of you," the man on the right said, all the anger and tension gone from him. The two men turned, bumping shoulders with each other, and headed back for their table.

"I'll just be a moment," Malik promised, going to the side of the bar and digging into one of the cupboards under the bar top for some noxious looking liquids that he poured into the pitcher.

"Forest ogres?" Max guessed. The trace of magic had been much stronger close-up, and she had been able to see the trace of something *other* in their faces.

"Yes. They don't come in that often, but they are often slightly feral if they've been in the Wild," Malik said. Max nodded her understanding. The magic in the Wild affected even non-sensitive humans, so she could only imagine how much more powerful it was for the forest ogres, who carried their own magic.

Malik got another plate of cake and the pitcher and left to serve the two men.

Turning to follow Malik's movements, as he was always worth watching, Max noticed that the little incident had drawn the attention of the smartly dressed man and the two women he was with. The man was staring at her with a fixed, hard look. The women were pouting, perhaps not liking the attention being taken away from them.

Max turned back to the bar. If they were regulars, they would leave her alone. If they were newer, like the forest ogres, then she might need to deal with them.

Malik came back and picked up his coffee again.

"I can think of a couple of humans who've been here and might fit the description of the dead man," he told her, then smiled at her obvious surprise. "We're famous, don't you know?" he asked, grinning. "A lot of wannabe magicians come here."

"Oh, I can imagine," Max said, wrinkling her nose. And she could. All too easily. She had met a few from time to time. There were whole swathes of the human population, who made up most of the city, that wanted to deny or ignore the existence of the other-natured beings, and even the Wild itself. But then there were those who were fascinated by the *other*, who wanted to get close and see what all the fuss was about. She had seen a lot of them on Audhilde's table over the years, eyes open and staring in death.

The Hunter's Tooth was actually as good a place as any for the curious to visit. Thanks to Malik's influence, there was almost no violence inside its walls, and his open-door policy meant everyone was welcome unless they started trouble. The few people who had been foolish enough to start a fight in the Tooth had found themselves barred for life, the doors magically coded to stop them even coming inside. Max didn't know how Malik managed it. He used whatever power he had in a way she had never come across before.

"Any idea of names?" she asked, not wanting to hope too much.

Malik shook his head. "But the two I'm thinking of both commented that they normally drink at the Sorcerer's Mistress."

"Lovely," Max said, nose wrinkling in distaste. The bar was in one of the more upmarket parts of the city, and a hang-out for even more wannabe magicians. She had been there once, many years ago, when she had first joined the Marshals, and had hoped to never go there again. Then a happy thought occurred. She didn't need to go. She just needed to pass the information on to Audhilde and let the human police follow up.

"Can you tell me anything else about them?" she asked, thinking that might be helpful for the human police.

Malik thought for a moment before answering. He always wanted to provide the best answers he could. It was one of the many things she liked about him.

"There was a lot of drunken talk," he said, eyes half-closed as if he was replaying something in his mind. "A lot of boasting, as I remember. You know how much magicians like to gossip," he said, a smile tilting his mouth. Max resisted the urge to roll her eyes. "They were quite low-level magicians, as I recall. But they were hinting they'd been involved in great things. So nothing really unusual there," Malik added, opening his eyes and giving her another smile.

Max nodded, absorbing the information. Low-level magicians boasting was nothing new, and they seemed to gravitate towards each other, trying to outdo the last tall tale. They also loved to gossip. She could only imagine what stories were circulating about the latest breach of the Wild. Anyone with magic sensitivity would have been able to feel the trickle of Wild magic into the city. Of course, the truly powerful magicians would not be involved in such conversations. They had no need to talk about their exploits. Still, knowing that the men had been lower-level magicians and prone to exaggerating was a little more information she could give to the police. She thanked Malik.

"My pleasure," he answered.

"I also need to look into dark magic. Specifically, blood rituals. Know of anyone dabbling in that just now? Or where I might find out?" Max asked.

"Maybe. Let me think on it a little. You still have the same number?" Malik asked.

"Yes." Max looked at her empty mug. "I guess I've got no more excuses to ignore my housework now."

Malik laughed. A gentle sound that invited her to join him. "Cas and Pol aren't good at housework?"

"Not unless it involves chasing vermin," Max said, smiling back.

She said her goodbyes and headed out into the day with a lighter heart, Cas and Pol skipping along beside her. A visit with Malik always did her good, even just drinking coffee and exchanging information. It almost put her in the mood to work on her house. Almost.

Chapter Six

The corridor stretched out in front of her, impossibly long with an impossible number of doors. The doors were everywhere. They appeared and disappeared at random. On either side, above and below. The air was too hot to breathe, her lungs screaming agony with every inhalation. Her skin had blistered and healed and blistered and healed more times than she could count in the hours or days or weeks that she'd been walking down this corridor. The door on her left opened slowly, tendrils of grey smoke emerging. She froze, desperately looking for somewhere to hide. She knew what that grey smoke meant. Something was coming. Something terrible. The grey smoke swirled and danced, punctuated by the deep, urgent bark of a dog.

The barking dog dragged her out of another nightmare and back to the daylight world. She woke alone in her bed, covered in sweat, the covers tangled around her, gun already in her hand, as the perimeter wards lit up in her mind, warning her of the visitor that the dogs had already sensed.

Max stumbled out of bed, not bothering with shoes, and made her way through the house, the feel of bare floorboards under her feet and the cool air on her skin reassuring her that even though it was dark in the house, she was awake and in the daylight world. Far away from the nightmare world.

She had barely made it out of her bedroom before someone started pounding on the front door. Hard enough that if Max and the dogs hadn't already been awake, they would have woken up.

The dogs were just outside the bedroom door, on alert, eyes towards the front door. They hadn't gone very far from her, which probably meant she'd been crying out in her sleep. They tended to stay close when she had a bad night.

Waking to their solid warmth around her eased some of the after-effects of the nightmares, and let her know she was back in the waking world.

The pounding came again. Whoever it was seemed determined to get her attention.

Now that Max was on her feet and armed, the dogs barked, close enough to Max's head that the sound echoed in her ears, and took off through the house, heading for the front door, barking madly, leaving Max to follow them at her much slower pace. It had been a rough couple of days, and last night she had spent far too long clearing out a nest of crow spiders in the Barrows. Cas and Pol had taken great delight in chasing down any of the creatures that got away. Raymund had been inordinately pleased at receiving another half dozen guests for his harvesting project. Max never wanted to see another one of the yellow monsters again in her life.

The security light outside her front door was on, the glass top of the door showing her a face she hadn't seen for a while. A surprising and unwelcome visitor.

Feathered blonde hair stood out in an artfully arranged style around a face that most supermodels would kill for, complete with wide-open, vivid blue eyes. Ruutti Passila looked like a porcelain doll come to life. The appearance was a lie, Max knew. The woman was one of the sharpest, toughest characters Max had ever met. On the surface, she was a detective with the human police force, a job she carried out with some skill. Underneath, Max was quite sure that the woman was not entirely human. She was potentially dangerous, whatever she was. Although Max had never caught her openly using any magic, she managed to close more cases than most of her colleagues.

"Hush now," Max told her dogs as she opened the door. "What do you want?" she asked the woman, not bothering with manners. Ruutti used her delicate appearance to get under people's skin and was accustomed to the most deferential treatment. It made Max irritated just thinking about it and she took a perverse pleasure in going against Ruutti's expectations.

"Well, good morning to you, too," Ruutti said, mouth curving up in a smile as she eyed Max head to toe. "Rough night? Why wasn't I invited?"

"I was dealing with a crow spider nest. If I'd known I was going to be tangling with crow spiders, I would definitely have considered calling you," Max said, the lack of sleep and remnants of her nightmare making her surly. "I'm sure you and the spiders would have had a lot to talk about."

"Ouch," Ruutti said, her smile widening, eyes bright.

"So, what do you want?" Max asked. She hadn't realised that Ruutti even knew where she lived, let alone that the detective would make a house call. Not when Ruutti could have phoned or got someone else to pass on a message. Max pointedly glanced outside. The sun hadn't even tried to make an appearance yet. "It's way too early."

"It's morning," Ruutti contradicted, then wrinkled her nose. "Oh, alright, it is early. There's something I want you to look at. Your office said you'd be home. Come on."

"No," Max said, not moving. "I was promised a day off," she said, sounding childish in her own ears. She had managed to wrangle a promise from Therese not to call her in today. But it seemed Therese had already broken that promise by sending Ruutti here. It would be just like Therese. The woman never seemed to sleep or take a day off herself, and had no sympathy for Max's wish to have a day to herself.

"Oh, dear, did you have to do some work? Poor little girl. Come on, woman up. There's a dead body, and it's weird."

That was enough to get the rest of Max's attention. Ruutti was an experienced detective. It was not like her to ask for help. Or to refer to dead bodies as weird. It was almost enough to make Max curious enough to want to help. Almost.

"I've worked over twenty days straight and got called in on both my days off," Max said, still not moving. "I need sleep. Does no one get the concept of time off?"

"No," Ruutti said, smile peeking out again. "At least, not when it comes to anyone else." The surprising honesty made Max want to smile, an impulse she squashed. It was never wise to give Ruutti any advantage.

"By the Lady," Max said, scrubbing a hand over her face. "There are at least twenty other Marshals. Why do you have to pick me?"

"Because you're the only one that's halfway competent," Ruutti said easily. "I mean, sure, the others can take down a crow spider. But anything more difficult? Nah."

"I haven't even had coffee," Max protested. It was a token protest. She knew she was going to help, and Ruutti doubtless knew it too. Ruutti asking for her help, and the bare information she'd passed along so far was enough to get Max's full attention.

"I brought coffee and muffins," Ruutti answered, pointing to her feet. Max looked down to see a giant-sized takeaway coffee cup and two large paper bags sitting on the stone front step to the house. "I got extra muffins. I assumed the hell beasts would want some, too."

No wonder the dogs had been so pleased to see the human. Max looked down at her two supposed hell beasts, who were watching the paper bags with single-minded focus.

Max looked back up from the coffee to the detective's face. The woman was trying to seem outwardly calm and confident, but there was a nervous tension about her that Max had never seen before. She had come to Max's house, well outside Ruutti's normal jurisdiction and closer to the Wild than most sane people wanted to be. Not just that, but she had brought bribes in the form of food and drink. Something had shaken the normally callous detective. And Max found she was curious to know what that was.

"Dead body," Max said, tucking her gun under her arm, then bending to pick up the offerings. "Alright. Let me get my gear."

"And clean up a bit. I think you've still got spider venom on you somewhere," Ruutti said, nose wrinkling again. "I'll wait by the cars."

Max closed the door in her face and turned away, sniffing cautiously at the coffee. It smelled delicious. As irritating as Ruutti was, she did know her way around the city's cafés.

Sniffing the coffee also told Max that Ruutti was not entirely wrong about her smelling. As well as the delicious scent of coffee, Max caught a whiff of cleaning fluids and, yes, the faintest trace of the acid spider venom. There was no time to shower before Ruutti would be back, hammering on the door.

Luckily, one of the services the Marshals' division provided for its operatives was supplies of cleaning spells, coded into ordinary-looking strips of paper.

With a pair of cleaning spells - one for her, and one for her clothes - it didn't take Max long to be ready, the dogs hard at her heels as they left the house. Max did not mistake their attention for anything other than greed. She was carrying the paper bags and coffee, all of it unopened.

Ruutti was leaning against the side of Max's pick-up, looking like she was modelling for a fashion shoot. Max's irritation spiked again.

"Are they coming with us?" Ruutti asked, looking at the dogs.

Max ignored the question. "You said weird. What did you mean?"

"Human male. Killed sometime last night. Looks like a knife. Lots of blood missing."

"None of that sounds too weird," Max said, frowning.

"You need to see it. They're holding the scene for us, but they won't for long. Come on, I'll lead the way," Ruutti said, glancing down at the dogs. She didn't have to look down too far as the dogs' heads were almost at her shoulders. "Do they know how to behave at a crime scene?"

"Better than most law enforcement," Max confirmed, temper bristling at the implied insult to her dogs.

Ruutti said nothing, heading over to her own vehicle which was, of course, utterly perfect, gleaming with polished metal and not one single speck of dust, despite having driven the dirt road to Max's front gate.

Muttering under her breath, Max sent the dogs into the back of the pick-up, fed them a muffin each and then got behind the wheel. She had long ago mastered the art of eating and drinking while driving and she had a feeling she would need the energy for whatever it was Ruutti wanted to show her.

The first light of day rose as they drove, the light dull and flat and the sky heavy with the promise of rain later. A perfect match for Max's glum mood.

The functional blocks of the buildings on the outskirts of the city were as dull as the sky overhead and Max spotted a few more boarded-up windows and doors, signifying more empty properties, as they drove. More people moving out of the suburbs into the city proper, most likely. Although the Wild seemed to have settled where it was, it was still too close for comfort for a lot of people.

The place Ruutti led them to was closer to the centre of the city than Max had been for a while. A far cry from the Barrows, or the run-down industrial area where the Marshals' division was head-quartered, or the tangled green wilderness that surrounded Max's home. Instead, they were in a residential area, with large, well-maintained buildings built of soft red stone, surrounded by vibrant green parks and gardens, the plant life all carefully maintained. The rows of houses were bisected by the occasional service road, discreetly tucked away between tall hedges, mostly out of sight.

The jarring note was the pair of patrol cars at one end of a service road, with two uniformed officers standing nearby. The officers looked like middle-aged street cops, the sort that were reliable but had no real ambition to progress further up the ranks. Their greetings to Ruutti were respectful and slightly star-struck. Max resisted the urge to roll her eyes.

"Er, ma'am, our orders were only law enforcement and the crime techs past this point," the younger one said, eyeing Max and her dogs with suspicion.

"This is Marshal Ortis and her helpers. I've asked them to view the scene," Ruutti said, breezing past the officers.

"Yes, ma'am," the younger one said, still wary of Max, and even more wary of the two giant hounds pacing at her side.

"It's alright, they don't bite unless I tell them to," Max assured the officers in her most cheerful tone and strode past them, following Ruutti.

The detective was pacing ahead, not waiting for Max, her back straight. She seemed to have grown more tense on the drive here. And she had been on edge when she had arrived at Max's door.

Ruutti walked along the side of the nearest building up to the point where the service road was crossed with another service road that ran behind the property, in between it and the next row of houses. It all looked perfectly ordinary apart from the very large white canvas tent that was stretched across the junction, another uniformed officer standing guard at the half-open entrance.

The dogs both lifted their heads, noses twitching, staring at the tent, the hair along their backs lifting.

"Wait here," Max told them. Their noses were far more sensitive than hers would ever be. All she could smell were chemicals, and the faint trace of old blood. None of that would have unsettled her dogs. There was something else there. Apprehension slid over her skin, wondering what could have unsettled her dogs at a crime scene that had been gone over already by technicians and police.

Ruutti went past the officer on duty, and flicked her hand, beckoning Max forward. Max paused to pull her Marshal's badge out, the seven-pointed star gleaming, and then went past the officer into the tent.

The other woman had taken a step to the side, hands tucked into her pockets. Waiting.

With no help or prompts from Ruutti, Max looked around the space for herself.

The first impression was chaos. They had stepped from an ordered, neat road with no debris or hint of an uneven surface in sight to a scene that would have been more at home outside the abandoned buildings Max had visited the night before.

As well as the chemical smells and old blood, there was a damp, rotten stench in the air. It sent a chill across Max's skin. There were a lot of things that could cause that smell, but they were nowhere near a body of water, which left the most likely explanation as being that someone had been working dark magic in this place, the remnants of it trapped under the sheets of the tent.

The road surface was cracked, as if something had hit it hard, the cracks radiating out from the point of impact.

In the middle, at the point of impact, was a body. A male, stripped to his waist, his jeans in tatters. There were pools of blood on the ground around him, and more traces of blood further away. And they were not random patterns. Even from where she was standing, Max could see that the blood had been worked into symbols. There was at least one stylised eye that she could see, and something else that might have been a serpent. Or a crude drawing of one.

She traced the radius of the cracks, and her brows lifted. It took a lot of force, or a lot of power, to make an impact that large. And with the damp stench in the air, she was going with power. Someone had cast a spell here, using the dead man's blood.

"Some kind of ritual," Max said, looking across at Ruutti. "But you knew that already."

"Yes. One of our magicians is working on it."

The woman was still tense, and still trying to cover it.

Max made her way closer to the dead man, using the path that the human technicians had marked out using metal slabs. She stood near his feet and looked along the length of his body, tracing the wounds in his flesh, and had a flashback to a few days before, standing in the tangled community garden with the hostile Sergeant Williams and Audhilde. This man could have been a twin to the one who had been left there.

There were differences. The wounds on this man were far more extensive. Whoever the killer was, he had taken his time. There were deep and shallow cuts on the man's legs and arms, and more symbols carved into his chest. Max didn't know enough about dark magic to even guess at the purpose for the cuts, or in what order they had been made. She still hadn't heard from Malik with the promised information.

The worst part was his face, frozen in an expression of horror, eyes staring up at the tent above them. There were traces of tears on his cheeks.

"He was alive when this was done," Max concluded, her stomach turning. She would never get used to the awful things that people did to each other.

"Yes. Our medical examiner thinks he died of blood loss. Or a heart attack brought on by blood loss. At any rate, none of the wounds themselves actually killed him."

"Not Audhilde?" Max asked, knowing the answer before Ruutti shook her head.

"It's her day off," Ruutti said, baring her teeth in a smile.

"And no one wants to disturb her," Max concluded. She did not blame them. Even though Audhilde exuded charm, even humans could sense the core of steel will in her. Max wouldn't want to irritate the ancient vampire, either.

Max tilted her head, looking at Ruutti. The woman sounded rattled. And Max still wasn't sure why. This would hardly be the first awful death the detective had seen. And it wouldn't be the last. There was something else. Something that Max was missing.

She turned back to the body, looking at the symbols on his chest and on the ground around him, and saw what she had missed earlier. Tucked into the symbols on either side of his shoulders was a pair of stylised doors, a glyph that Max was all too familiar with.

"A follower of Arkus did this," Max concluded, voice flat and grim. She could not imagine anyone else using that symbol. Not even foolish children. Most people would not even speak His name, but Max was not one of them. She didn't believe the old superstition that simply speaking the word would draw His attention, no more than she believed calling on the Lady would draw Her attention. One was dark, one was light, and they were both immensely powerful, with far better things to concern themselves than someone speaking their names, Max was sure.

But whoever had set this ritual out on the hard surface, whoever had cut into the victim, had wanted to draw the dark lord's attention. And had generated forceful magic to do so, if the after-effect was anything to go by. Enough to penetrate the barrier between the daylight world and Arkus' underworld? Max hoped not. A phantom trail of scorching fire seared across her skin along with the ghostly, acrid stench of burning. She could not imagine why anyone would want to draw Arkus' attention. But there were plenty of foolish people in the world.

"Yes," Ruutti said, the tension leaving her body along with the trail of heat on Max's skin. "Now do you see why I wanted you here?"

Max held her words in for a moment, touching two fingers to her forehead and bowing her head to the dead man in a mark of respect. "I'm not sure what help I can give you," Max said, moving back to join Ruutti. "Unless you think something non-human did this, it's outside the Marshals' jurisdiction. Dark magic is the provenance of the Order," she reminded the detective. Not that Ruutti would need reminding, as she was perfectly well aware of the separate jurisdictions that the police, Marshals' division and Order held within the city. From the stubborn expression on Ruutti's face, Max guessed that she didn't want to turn the matter over to the Order. And Max had no intention of speaking to them, either. But there was something else she could do. "You need to get Audhilde to see the body, though."

"What do you mean?"

"There was another death in the Barrows a few days ago. Similar knife wounds, but no markings around the body."

Ruutti's attention had sharpened to a knife edge. "I didn't know about this."

"The Sergeant at the scene thought it had been a knife fight," Max said, keeping her voice neutral.

Ruutti snorted. "Idiot. Alright. Did you get an identity for the other victim?"

"No. Not my case," Max said, jaw set. "And neither is this." The dark magic wasn't enough on its own to pull in a Marshal. There were humans who dabbled in dark magic, and they were definitely a concern for the Order and not her.

"Too bad," Ruutti said. Whatever unease and tension she had been carrying had been bottled up again and she was back to her forthright, blunt manner. "My boss has agreed with your boss that this is going to be your case."

"Oh, really?" Max asked, brows lifting. "Just me?"

"I'm to be your liaison," Ruutti said smoothly. Max did not believe her. The woman lied as easily as breathing, and it was often hard to tell. But in this case, she had overplayed her hand. There was no possible world in which the human law enforcement would simply hand over the death of one of their own to the Marshals' service without wanting to keep track of the investigation. And if Max did eventually find the killer, Ruutti would want credit for the arrest.

"I'll need to check with the head Marshal," Max said. It was a stalling tactic. Assigning her to work on something like this would be just like him. The head Marshal, Faddei Lobanov, might have reluctantly agreed to let Max work alone, but he had made no secret of the fact he did not like it at all. Working with Ruutti wasn't the same as another Marshal, of course. Which meant that it didn't technically breach the agreement Max and Faddei had reached when she had joined the Marshals' service.

"Of course. Do you want to use my phone?" Ruutti asked.

"No," Max said, glancing back at the body. She hesitated a moment. It really wasn't her business. But there were those ritual markings, a hint that the killer had been trying to achieve something far more dark and twisted than a simple murder. The memory of heat and smoke crossed her skin and her breath again, along with a sense of obligation to the dead. The killer needed to be found. Max wanted him found. And whatever else Ruutti was, she was a good detective, who would also want to catch the killer. "What have you learned so far?"

"Less than I would like," the woman answered, taking a step so she was shoulder-to-shoulder with Max, arms folded across her stomach as she stared down at the dead man. "There was nothing on him to give him a name. No one local recognised his photo."

"You woke up the neighbourhood to show a head shot of him to the neighbours?" Max asked, startled. "I'm not sure his own mother would recognise him like that."

"We made him look a bit less dead," Ruutti said, a sparkle in her eye. "But he wasn't carrying any photos from when he was alive, so that was all we had."

"Alright," Max said. "So, none of the neighbours recognised him. Anyone not answer the door?"

"Only one. But she's eighty-five, and, according to the neighbourhood gossip, she's in hospital for a hip replacement," Ruutti said. "So I don't think she's our dead man."

"No," Max agreed.

"And she doesn't have any young male relatives, either. Not as far as we can tell, anyway," Ruutti added, perhaps anticipating Max's next question.

"So if he's not local, then why here?" Max asked, mostly to herself.

"Is the death being on a crossroads significant?" Ruutti asked. It was a sensible question.

Max paused, a flood of memories rising. Other crossroads, in other places and other times. "It might be," she forced herself to say over the memories. "If you believe the old legends that there's power in crossroads."

"It doesn't matter what I believe. It's what the killer believes," Ruutti said. A piece of wisdom that sounded like she had learned it from someone else and was repeating it.

Max made a non-committal sound and began walking slowly around the tent, mapping out the symbols as she went. "The ritual was not complete," she observed.

"It was complete enough to shatter the road," Ruutti threw back.

"I don't think that was the intent," Max said, remembering those doors drawn in blood. "Of course, it's possible there was no ritual at all and the killer just drew a bunch of random things on the road."

"You don't believe that for a moment," the detective said. She was still standing by the body, watching Max pace around the room. "More like the killer made a mistake somewhere."

"It's possible. But you don't just start with a human at the middle," Max said, half to herself.

"No?"

"No," Max said, shaking her head, crouching down again where she could see the line of the body, the man's dark, curling hair drifting slightly in an unseen breeze.

"You know something about rituals," Ruutti said.

"I am a Marshal," Max answered. It was as much as she was prepared to say. The Marshals got a lot of training and knowledge that regular law enforcement did not. It went with the territory. If a Marshal was expected to hunt down a supernatural, they had better have some understanding of how their prey operated and how to stop them.

The badge gleamed, silver flaring in the shadows under the tent.

"What is it?" Ruutti asked. It would be easy to forget she was intelligent and ruthless underneath the carefully arranged hair and big blue eyes. Perhaps she had seen a Marshal's badge flare before. Or perhaps she was just very observant.

"There's residual magic in this space. You need to get your magician to clean the space before you try and move the body," Max said. She glanced at Ruutti and saw an unusually serious expression on the detective's face. Satisfied that her warning had been taken to heart, Max turned back to the body. "This was not a quiet death. Did none of the neighbours hear anything?"

"No," Ruutti said, in a way which told Max that the detective had already thought of that particular issue. "Hardly anyone uses these streets, though, so they would have been deserted. And there was some kind of a party happening further down the block. A lot of noise from that."

Even a party wouldn't have covered the sound of the man's screams, Max knew. The killer must have used some kind of spell to mask the sound.

Which brought her back to the question of why here? The killer seemed to have brought his victim here, to this particular spot in the middle of one of the city's nicer districts, with the risk of being seen. She glanced up, as if the sky could give her some answers, and saw only the stretch of canvas from the tent.

"We have pictures before the tent went up," Ruutti said, following Max's gaze. "But now that the neighbours know there's a body here, they don't want to see it." Her nose wrinkled. "Apparently they've already been calling their representative, demanding that the rubbish be removed."

Max lifted a brow.

"Well, perhaps not those exact words, but that's what they meant," Ruutti said. "So, what do you think?"

"I think this is going to be a difficult case to solve," Max said slowly, taking another look around the space. "Do we know the orientation of the body?"

"No. Is that important?"

"The first body was oriented north-south," Max said. "Quite deliberately placed. It would be helpful to know if this body is the same. They might not be connected."

"I'll find out," Ruutti promised.

"And I think we should wake up the neighbours again," Max said.

"They didn't see or hear anything," Ruutti repeated, frowning. "My team know their jobs."

"The victim might not be local, but the killer might," Max said.

"People don't usually kill close to their homes," Ruutti objected.

"I'm sure that's true. But this place has some meaning for the killer. We should rule out the neighbours," Max said.

"Fair point. Alright. Let's go," Ruutti said, striding out of the tent.

Left alone in the space, Max took a final, long look around, opening her senses a little. Just a little. Places of violent death could be overwhelming. She could see the remnants of the spell in the air above the symbols, the air coated with the residue of death. And something older. Much older. There was too much on top of it for her to get a clear picture, but she made a mental note to research the history of this place. Crossroads of themselves might not have power, but certain places did, depending on their past. And she would put good money on there being some dark history to this particular point in the road which had led the killer to bring his victim here. Finding out that history might help find the killer. She hoped.

Chapter Seven

Questioning the neighbours with Ruutti was at once frustrating and amusing. Despite having law enforcement at their door for the second time in the space of a few hours, everyone - man, woman, young and old - seemed dazzled by the detective, focusing almost exclusively on her, and all but ignoring Max and her silver badge. Which left Max free to observe the neighbours' reactions, but also meant that if she wanted to ask anything, she had to get Ruutti to repeat the question before anyone would answer. Max could not work out how the detective managed it. There was no obvious magic in the air around her, and yet everyone practically fell over themselves to help.

It didn't take long to work out that, despite their proximity to the crime, none of the neighbours had anything to do with it. Or at least, as far as Max could tell. The neighbours all seemed both horrified and fascinated that such violence had happened close to them. And none of them had enough magic in their houses to suggest they would know one end of a magic ritual from the other.

Max also took note that none of the neighbours to the crime scene seemed to find it odd that questions were being asked by a police detective and a Marshal. Of course that might have been Ruutti's influence. Max wasn't sure that any of the neighbours would even remember that there had been a Marshal there. But in normal circumstances, if the neighbours had possessed any sensitivity to magic, they would have felt something wrong with the killing and would surely have expected one of the police's magicians to be on the scene rather than a Marshal.

By that point, Max was tired and hungry and her dogs were bored. One of them - most likely Cas - had found a piece of old rope from somewhere and they were playing tug and chase with each other along the street, weaving in between passing cars and the crime scene vans that had arrived to remove the body and take down the tent. Max envied her dogs their ability to live in the moment, to forget about the grim reason they were all here.

There was a slender, black-clad figure among the white coveralls of the crime techs, walking beside a quartet of people carrying a stretcher with a zipped-up body bag. The duty magician, Max assumed. She wasn't sure why most human magic users seemed to feel the need to wear head-to-toe black, but it was almost a uniform. She wondered if this one had a crystal on a string around his neck as well, like the last magician she had come across.

Even as her mind provided a sarcastic critique of the magician and his outfit, Max had to hold back a sigh. Doubtless the magician was far more competent and practised in his craft than she would ever be. It always felt to Max as if magic should be so much easier than it was, that she should be able to wield power much more easily, but she struggled, every single time, with the formal magic that the Order had taught her.

"There's nothing more for us to do here," Ruutti said, breaking through Max's unhappy thoughts. "Unless you want to wait for the tent to be removed?"

"No," Max said. She needed to come back after dark, when there was no one else around. Not with Ruutti at her shoulder and over a dozen witnesses. Before then, she needed to visit Malik again. He had promised to look into dark magic users for her, and it wasn't like him to stay silent.

"Where to next?" Ruutti asked.

Before Max could answer, one of the white-clad crime scene techs approached, carrying what looked like a clipboard and a bundle of papers. "You wanted a copy of the inventory, ma'am?" he said to Ruutti.

"Yes. Thank you." Ruutti nodded, taking the papers from him. She flipped through the pages, brows lifting. "This is comprehensive. Good work."

"Thank you," the tech said, a faint smile on his mouth, before he left. Max suppressed an urge to roll her eyes. Even the crime scene techs were not immune to Ruutti's influence.

The detective lifted a brow at Max. "Well, where are we going?"

"Don't you have reports to write?" Max asked, waving to the papers Ruutti was holding.

"Not just now," the detective said, grinning. "You're not going to get rid of me that easily."

Max glared down at the petite woman, and wondered just what it would take to shake off the detective. Even as she pondered various scenarios, her phone rang. She checked the caller ID and her brows lifted. Malik.

"Hey, what's up?" she said as she answered the phone.

"Can you stop by the Tooth?" Malik asked.

"Of course." Max paused and eyed her unwanted companion. "I might have company with me."

"All are welcome," Malik reminded her, a smile in his voice.

"We're on our way," Max promised.

"Who was that?" Ruutti asked, as Max headed for her pick-up. "His voice sounded delicious." She had far sharper hearing than she should, Max noted.

"You'll find out soon enough," Max promised. "Come on, we're going to the Hunter's Tooth."

"Really?" Ruutti's nose wrinkled. "Is that your idea of a classy place to hang out?"

"Or you can go and write your reports," Max said.

"I suppose I could rough it for one day," Ruutti said, still sounding appalled at the idea. Doubtless Ruutti preferred places with white tablecloths and fresh flowers on the tables, and where uniformed waiters would bring her order across on a silver tray. Max had seen those places from the outside, and never been tempted to go inside. Always assuming that the staff would let her inside, and not call the police to have her thrown out onto the street.

The same two pink convertibles were in the parking lot when Max drove in. They seemed a good match for the two women who had been in the bar during Max's last visit. She wondered if the women had left at all, or if they had been at the Hunter's Tooth for three days straight. It wouldn't be the first time a supernatural being had decided to have a prolonged drinking session. And with Malik's influence on the bar, there was surprisingly little trouble.

There was also a large, sleek black vehicle that screamed of wealth and power, its windows heavily tinted, taking up a full four spaces by some truly inconsiderate parking. There was magic around that black vehicle that made Max's skin crawl, so when she got out of her pick-up, she left Cas and Pol on guard in the back of it. There wasn't much worth stealing in her pick-up, but it would be difficult to replace. And she didn't want to walk home.

Ruutti was already out of her vehicle, eyes travelling around the area, expression hard to read. Max waited for her to say something cutting, but the detective simply lifted a brow at Max.

Wondering what Ruutti was thinking, and then deciding it might be better not to know, Max led the way into the bar.

There were a few more people scattered around the internal space, including the two women and suited man she remembered from a few days before. There was a chattering group of youngsters by the pool tables, sounding like they were having harmless fun. And there was a still figure shrouded in shadow in one of the horseshoe-shaped booths that gave Max the same uneasy feeling as the black vehicle outside.

She headed to the bar. Malik was dressed in a similar manner to the last time she had seen him, although she thought he had changed his t-shirt.

"Twice in one week. I am blessed," he said, smiling.

She accepted the kiss on her cheek and returned the smile, but she had lost his attention. His eyes had travelled past her to Ruutti.

It was the first time she had seen Malik unsettled. He froze completely, staring at the petite detective.

"Little cousin. It's been a while since I've seen your kind in here. Be welcome," Malik said at length, voice conveying seductive, caramel-coated warmth.

"I had no idea there were any pure blood males left," Ruutti answered. It was one of the most unguarded things Max had ever heard the woman say, and she took a closer look between the two.

"Ah, so that's what you are," Max said, half to herself. She had always known that Malik was something *other*, and after seeing Ruutti's effect on people, had suspected the same of Ruutti, despite the woman appearing to be completely human. It had not occurred to Max before now that they were made of similar material. It explained a lot. Malik used his influencing abilities to keep the peace in the bar and make sure everyone was welcome. Ruutti wielded her abilities like a weapon to get what she wanted. And Max could not sense when either of them were using their powers.

"There are a few of us," Malik said, staring at Ruutti. "More than you might think."

"How would you know? Aren't you tied here?" Ruutti asked, still seeming to be shaken.

Malik smiled, and even though it was directed at Ruutti, Max still found herself leaning forward, wanting to be closer to his warmth. As soon as she realised what she was doing, she straightened. He normally kept his innate magic subtle, untraceable to her, and although she had witnessed its effects, she had never been caught in it. She had never realised just how powerful he was. "This is the modern age, little cousin," Malik said, laughter in his voice. "We have many ways of keeping in touch."

For once, Ruutti seemed at a loss for words. And Malik was not his usual self. Max had never seen him less than self-assured, surrounded by his personal charm.

Max folded her arms, waiting for them to recover. When they simply stood and stared at each other for a long moment, and neither showed signs of moving, she cleared her throat, catching their attention. "Malik, you called?"

"I did. You'd asked about dark magic and blood rituals," Malik said. His eyes slid past Max and Ruutti to the shadowed figure in the booth. "Someone is here to answer you."

"That's-" Max began, and broke off, not quite sure how to finish that thought. *Impressive* didn't seem to be the right word. Not with the chill of the dark magic seeping into the air. *Dangerous* was the next word that occurred to her, but she had absolute confidence that Malik would not harm her, or risk the neutrality of the Hunter's Tooth.

"I can't take credit," Malik said, almost back to his normal, easy manner. "He insisted. I'll bring some drinks over, if you want to go and introduce yourselves."

"Sure," Max said, turning towards the booth. She took a step towards the shadowed figure and her feet dragged on the floor, abruptly too heavy for her to lift. She could feel magic coiling around her. A test. She hated this kind of game playing. She pulled out her Marshal's badge, the silver gleaming, and the weighted spell lifted, letting her walk across the floor, Ruutti beside her.

"You'd best have a fabulous reason for that little bit of nonsense," Ruutti said, each word bitten out. The detective was as furious as Max had ever seen her, glaring at the shadowed figure.

"Not really." The voice was dry as desert sand, containing a crackle that might have been rusted amusement. "But I so rarely venture out, you must permit me my little indulgences."

"I will—" Ruutti began. Max stood on her foot, earning a glare from the petite woman.

"Malik said that you came in person to speak to us," Max said, moving away from Ruutti, hoping the detective would get the hint. "What do you want to tell us, Lord Kolbyr?"

As Ruutti hissed a breath that seemed to be genuine shock, there was another crackling sound that Max identified a moment later as laughter. The shadows lifted and she almost took an involuntary step back as Lord Kolbyr was revealed.

He was a delicately made man, who would be not much taller than Ruutti if they stood next to each other. He had pale skin that looked like he had not seen sunlight for decades, or perhaps more, and sleek black hair that was brushed back from his forehead, emphasising his pallor and the vivid green of his eyes. He was also quite beautiful. For a vampire.

It was not his outward appearance that made her want to run away. It was his power. He was coated in magic so dark it made her skin crawl. The shadows he had held, disguising himself, and the weighting spell he had cast on her and Ruutti were just the tiniest bit of the power he wielded.

"You are every bit as clever as dear Audhilde reports," Kolbyr said, lips peeling back from his teeth in a smile.

Before Max could find a suitable reply, Malik had arrived at the table with a tray of drinks. Coffee for Max, something cloudy in a tall glass frosted with ice for Kolbyr and a round glass full of a lemon-scented drink for Ruutti. Malik, an experienced and expert bar-tender, left as silently as he had arrived.

"Do sit, please," Kolbyr said, waving to the booth around him. "The young siren tells me that you have questions." Young siren could only mean Malik. Max had always thought that Malik was past his first century, so not exactly young. But then, she supposed that when someone was as old as the vampire, everyone else must seem young.

"I do," Max confirmed, settling to one edge of the booth, silently amused when Ruutti mirrored her position. If Lord Kolbyr decided to cause trouble, there was not much either of them would be able to do, but they were both of the same mind that they each wanted to be close to an exit. Just in case. "I am curious what warranted your personal attention," Max said. With some of the older vampires, it was dangerous to ask them direct questions too often.

The vampire took a sip of the drink Malik had brought him, his eyes gleaming as he looked at Ruutti and then back at Max.

"One of my people told me that questions were being asked. An expert sought. I was curious," Lord Kolbyr said. It was a more direct and comprehensive answer than Max had expected.

With Ruutti unusually silent, her attention skipping between the drink Malik had brought her and the ancient vampire, it was left to Max to make the next move.

"Audhilde called me to a body with knife markings," Max began bluntly, not touching the coffee in front of her, even though Malik had mixed it half-and-half with milk. "A human male. Someone had carved him up with what looked like ritual marks. I wanted to consult with someone versed in dark magic and blood rituals, so I asked Malik if he knew anyone."

"And then word reached me," Kolbyr concluded. "So far, it's very dull."

"Earlier today, the detective here called me to another death scene. Another human male. Only this time, he had survived longer and whoever killed him had made markings on the ground around him using his blood. They included the symbol of Arkus," Max said, the name flat on her tongue. It didn't feel right speaking the name here, in this place which Malik worked so hard to keep neutral and welcoming.

But she had sparked Kolbyr's attention, she saw. The old vampire was leaning forward, listening to her every word.

"Describe the markings," he said.

"We can show you," Ruutti said, drawing a small, sleek device from her pocket. An electronic tablet. The Marshals had tablets, too, except theirs were about three times as thick and twice as large. But then, Max did not suppose that the one in Ruutti's hands had come from law enforcement supplies. Ruutti liked the best of things, and wasn't afraid to treat herself to new toys.

The screen lit up, and Ruutti flicked it to a photograph. "If you swipe left, it will take you through the markings," she told the vampire, putting the tablet on the table between them.

"Swipe left?" Kolbyr asked, sounding genuinely confused.

"Like this." Ruutti demonstrated.

"Ah. A mouse click without the mouse," Kolbyr said, and bent his head to the tablet. "And does it go bigger?"

"Pinch to zoom," Ruutti said, and demonstrated that as well. Max wasn't sure if the detective realised she had gotten closer to the vampire until Ruutti sat back, posture stiff, and picked up her drink with a white-knuckled hand.

Kolbyr ignored them, although Max was quite sure he was fully aware of their nervousness. He would almost certainly be able to hear Max's rapid heartbeat, for one thing. He might be dressed in a hand-made suit and look like a harmless man, but vampires were master predators and none of them survived as long as Kolbyr had without being aware of their surroundings.

Max picked up her coffee while Kolbyr looked through the photographs. Sitting drinking coffee while watching an ancient vampire scroll through pictures from a crime scene was certainly one of the stranger experiences of Max's life. As Kolbyr scrolled through, she went over the images in her mind. The careful placement of the symbols. The cracked concrete. The stench in the air.

"Most interesting," Kolbyr said, settling back and picking up his drink. He was old enough to be able to mask his feelings very well, but Max had the impression he was unsettled. "Someone has been studying things they should not be meddling with."

"What makes you say that?" Ruutti asked, taking her tablet back and tucking it away.

Kolbyr did not answer her, turning instead to Max. "Audhilde called you, you say? You, of all people?"

"She called for a Marshal. I was given the assignment," Max clarified. She had no clear idea of the vampire hierarchy in the city, as most of the old, powerful ones tended to stay within the heart of the city, living among humans and not causing the sort of trouble that required the Marshals. But she had the sense that Audhilde was among the higher-ranked of the vampires. And Lord Kolbyr was a law unto himself, from everything she had heard about him. He apparently owned an entire city block, complete with parkland. He lived in an enormous house, with a hundred empty rooms and a dozen silent servants. Or so the tales told. Max was never sure how much truth there was to bar gossip, but having met the vampire, she could easily imagine him owning at least one city block, and possibly more.

"And she did not call me herself," Kolbyr said. It was the same, rasping tone he had used before but ice slid down Max's spine.

"She has not seen the second crime scene or body," Max pointed out.

"Ah. Yes. A detail I had missed," Kolbyr said. Max did not believe him. He had been testing her. Seeing if she was loyal to Audhilde? Or seeing if Max would stand up to him? She couldn't tell.

"You know the ritual that the killer was trying to effect," Max said.

"I suspect so," Kolbyr confirmed, although it had not been a question. "There are a few possibilities. None of them are widely known," he added, expression pinched for a moment, clearly displeased.

"What are the possibilities?" Max asked bluntly.

"The most likely one is someone trying to connect to the great lord's domain," Kolbyr said. The reverence in his voice made Max's skin crawl again.

"Connect? You mean, someone wants to talk to Him?" Max asked, mouth suddenly dry. She would never understand the fascination some people had with Arkus, or the lengths that those people would go to in an effort to speak to Him, or break into His domain. The tales of the torment and damnation in the underworld should be more than enough to put people off, as far as Max was concerned. But, year after year, more idiots tried dark magic in the hope of catching a glimpse into the world below. The idiots seemed to think that there was power and wealth to be had there. They seemed to ignore all the other stories. The ones of endless pain and torture. She shivered, remembering the searing heat burning her skin, lungs full of acrid smoke, blind from the smoke and the fire. She blinked, clearing her eyes, and hoped that the vampire had not noticed her distraction.

"As if He would respond to a mere mortal's request," Kolbyr said, back to being displeased. "As if such a ritual was like making a telephone call."

"So, the first possibility is someone trying to get in touch with Him," Max said, forcing the words out. That was not good. The daylight world survived because He was safely trapped away, locked behind the Grey Gates, unable to break free.

Arkus had broken free once before. Long, long before Max or anyone else in the city had been born. The world had nearly been destroyed by Him and His legions of demons crawling out from the underworld, bringing fire and smoke and pain and death and destruction with them. Thousands had died in the first attacks. Thousands upon thousands had died while Arkus walked on the surface of the world. What had once been a daylight world, with the possibility of light and joy and hope and love and laughter, had been twisted, corrupted into something more like the world below. There had been no Order then. No organisation to stand against the darkness. The entire world had almost fallen to Arkus before He had been caged, set back behind the Grey Gates, the Lady Herself creating the Gates out of Her own power, sealing them behind Him.

Or so the tales told. No one alive today knew for certain what had happened, just that Arkus had been sent back into his own realm and had never re-emerged. Max's palms itched with the memory of molten metal burning her skin away. The Grey Gates had not remained closed. Arkus tried to breach them from time to time, building up His power. Even though His realm was outside the daylight world, the effects of His activities were felt in the daylight world. The Order called those effects Portents, signalling that the dark lord was attempting to rise again - attempting to break free of his own realm and take over the daylight world, and perhaps even try to reach the Lady Herself. The Order's records showed that the Portents showed up around every hundred years. His last efforts had been stopped eight years before. The Portents that had warned of His efforts had started two years before that, around the same time as the Wild had surged forward, swallowing vast swathes of land that the city had once relied on. Max wasn't sure if the two things were connected or not. What history told her, though, was that after Arkus' last attempt to break free, He would need time to gather His energy to try again.

But that assumed that Arkus was trying to break free through His own efforts. Not that He was being aided by fools in the daylight world.

With the smell of smoke in her nose and her ears ringing with the echoes of screams, Max picked up her coffee, her hand trembling. She cradled the mug between both hands, not wanting to show weakness in front of Lord Kolbyr, but not able to completely hide her reaction.

"There are other possibilities," the vampire said, drawing the words out. "Someone could be trying to bring one of the inhabitants of the deep through to this world."

She was going to be sick. Seeing the damage and destruction that creatures from the Wild could cause in the city was bad enough. Anything coming into the daylight world from the world below would be far, far worse. Arkus' court in the underworld was supposed to be home to a host of powerful, dangerous demons, any one of which could cause chaos in the daylight world.

"That's not all, though, is it?" Ruutti asked unexpectedly. The woman was staring at the vampire, all colour drained from her face.

"No," Kolbyr said, with another rasping sound that was his version of laughter. "The other possibility is that someone is trying a ritual of opening."

The words hung in the air between them for a long, long moment, Max trying not to be sick, trying not to think about the implications of what he had said. All the worst nightmares and memories threatened to surge back up again, and it was all she could do to sit still and breathe for long, long moments.

"Opening," she said at length, the word too big for her mouth to hold.

Kolbyr rose to his feet and she stumbled to hers, making room for him to leave the booth. He stood barely as high as her shoulder, but his presence coiled around her, the miasma of darkness making her skin crawl again. He twitched his cuffs into place, then glanced up at her, eyes bright.

"It has not been attempted for several hundred years. Before my time," Kolbyr said, a smile curving his lips. "But it is said that with the right key, the Grey Gates can be opened."

Chapter Eight

Max stumbled out into the daylight, her stomach churning, head spinning. Having made his awful pronouncement, Kolbyr had left. She had been held, frozen in place, for too long, and then had not been able to stay one minute more next to where Kolbyr had been, surrounded by the cloak of dark magic and with the words he had spoken still hanging in the air.

The Grey Gates. Someone might be trying to open the Grey Gates, dropping the barrier between the daylight world and the dark lord's realm, letting the horrors of the underworld loose on the world.

Memories flooded her mind, holding her in place. She had seen things she had no name for, but which dragged her screaming from sleep most nights. Bad enough to know that those nightmares existed in the world below. Worse - far worse - to imagine that they might be set free on this world.

She drew a long, ragged breath and tried to calm herself. It was a possibility, not a certainty, that someone was trying to open the Gates. The other possibilities were not much better, but at least didn't involve a waking nightmare.

The memories faded a little and she was able to look around, take stock of the here and now.

Kolbyr was long gone, the sleek black vehicle vanished. Cas and Pol were standing in the back of the pick-up, both of them watching her with their ears lifted. Cas gave a soft whine. Knowing something was wrong. Not knowing what it was.

Max looked up at the heavy sky above. Clouds so grey they were almost black, the air thick with the promise of rain to come. As if the weather itself could sense something wrong in the daylight world. The possibilities that Kolbyr had referred to.

A footfall nearby drew her attention fully back to the here and now with a snap. She was outside now. Away from Malik's influence. Vulnerable. She could not afford to be distracted.

She blinked, sure she had imagined it, but, no, there was Bryce standing a few paces away, wearing the same tight expression he had in the clinic a few days before. He was wearing more casual clothing than he had been, jeans and a faded, worn jacket that didn't hide the shoulder holster or knives he carried.

"What are you doing here?" she asked, the demand out before she could check it. Her Marshal's badge was still out, the silver gleaming.

"When Lord Kolbyr leaves his house, we pay attention," Bryce answered.

Max was so surprised he had actually answered her question that she couldn't think of anything to say. It made perfect sense that the Order kept track of powerful people like Kolbyr. There were a few people in the city with the genuine ability to shape the world, and he was one of them.

"What was he doing here?" Bryce asked her.

"I can't discuss that," Max said. The sort of reflexive response she had practised over the years. She was quite sure it would not impress Bryce. And it didn't.

"Try," he invited, shifting his weight slightly in a way that drew attention to the weapon he carried at his side.

Max laughed. She couldn't help it. She had just been terrified by one of the city's most powerful vampires, a magician steeped in dark magic, and her mind was ringing with the news that some idiot was possibly trying to open the Grey Gates, and here was Bryce trying to intimidate her? "Or what? You'll shoot me? Honestly, I think that would improve my week. Good luck keeping track of Kolbyr," she said over her shoulder as she headed towards her pick-up.

"Miscellandreax," Bryce said.

The name rang through her. She had not heard it spoken aloud for eight years. Not since she left the Order.

She checked in her stride, skin prickling. She stopped and turned, lifting a brow, trying to appear confused. "Sorry?"

"Miscellandreax T'Or Orshiasa," Bryce said. There it was. Her full name in the Order. Miscellandreax, apprenticed to Orshiasa. The Guardian's name was venerated in the Order. One of the oldest and most powerful of the Guardians.

Being trained by any of the Guardians to follow in their footsteps had been an honour, but it had been a particular honour to be accepted as an apprentice by Orshiasa. Or so she had been told, over and over. It had just felt like a lot of hard work from her perspective. And she didn't have any right to that name. Not now. Not for eight years. The head of the Order had told her that Orshiasa himself wanted nothing to do with her.

While she was distracted, Bryce had taken a step towards her, frowning as he looked at her. "I knew I recognised you the other day. You've changed a lot."

Despite the circumstances, she was impressed. He had barely known who she was when she had been in the Order. The warriors mostly trained and lived separately from the apprentices and Guardians. Yet he had recognised her despite the years and the changes in her appearance. Her long, dark hair was gone, her style now shorter and more practical, the colour different. And the things she had lived through and their memories had thinned and shadowed her face, making her look far older, far different, to the girl she had been. As impressed as she was by the recognition, it was also irritating. She had worked hard to stay away from the Order. "I don't know what you are talking about," Max said. "Now, if you'll excuse me, I have work to do."

She spun on her heel, heading for the pick-up. She hadn't gone two strides before he was next to her, a silent shadow. She stopped and faced him. He was within arm's reach. Too close for comfort. Her fingers twitched, wanting to reach for her gun. She held herself still with an effort. He was a fully trained, seasoned warrior. Apprentices were not schooled in advanced physical combat, and she had failed the magical teaching she had been given. He could overpower her with barely a thought. It would not be a fair contest.

"What do you want?" she demanded, temper flaring. She thought she had escaped. Thought she had left it all behind. And here he was, digging up old names and old memories she did not want to carry.

He looked surprised by the question. Or maybe it was her tone.

"You left the Order. Ran away. A lot of people think you are dead. Is this where you've been hiding this whole time?"

"I ran away?" she asked, voice rising in pitch. She remembered the day she had gone back to the Order. Standing in the familiar office with its dark wood panelling, the faint ticking of the clock loud in the silence. Until Kitris, the head of the Order, had spoken. *You are not welcome here.*

She had known, even then, that she would not be welcomed back with open arms and celebration. That had not been the plan. The plan had been her sacrifice, although that little detail had been hidden from her. Most likely, Kitris and Orshiasa had considered it unimportant. She had been expendable to them. The cold dismissal still stung all these years later. And stung again as she realised that Kitris must have told the rest of the Order she had fled. Run away from her training and responsibilities. It made her wonder, not for the first time, just how Kitris had explained the fact that the Grey Gates were closed and Arkus safely locked away. But she was not going to go back to the Order to ask him.

"What happened to the warriors that went with you?" Bryce demanded. From the way he was standing, and the deepening of his voice, Max realised that was the question he really wanted answered. He didn't really care where she had been for the past eight years or what had happened to her. But he did care about the team that had been sent with her. Which made sense. He had not known her, but the warriors who had gone with her would have been comrades, perhaps even friends.

"They are dead," she told him, words clipped. She couldn't meet his eyes, throat closing as the memories rose up again. Nine highly trained warriors of the Order. All of them dead within moments of each other, dying in screaming agony as trails of fire rose from the underworld, with her unable to do anything about it.

"Did you kill them?" he asked.

"What? No! How can you even-" she bit the words off before she could finish. Of course he could think it. He, and doubtless many others within the Order, believed she had run away. Turned her back on her responsibilities and duties and saved herself. Killing the team sent to protect her was a logical next step if he thought so little of her.

He was frowning at her. Not satisfied with the answers she had given, she was quite sure. She told herself that she did not care. It did not matter what he thought of her. Not one bit.

Somewhere behind her one of the dogs whined. A low, plaintive sound. Most likely Cas again, sensing something was wrong. But Max was not under direct threat, so the two shadow-hounds stayed where they were.

The noise had caught Bryce's attention, though, and he looked past her shoulder to the pick-up and the dogs. His brows lifted. "Shadow-hounds? How did you get them?"

She could understand the surprise. Shadow-hounds were rare, and notoriously picky about who they lived with. The Order had had a few pairs when Max had been there, and she had always thought they were ferocious creatures, trained for war. Quite unlike the comedians that her pair could be.

"They chose me," she answered Bryce honestly, glancing over her shoulder at the two faces staring down from the side of the pick-up. Warmth bloomed in her chest. The hounds didn't care that she'd been dismissed from the Order, or what her reputation was. They accepted her and loved her just as she was. "I have work to do," she told him, heading for the pick-up again.

This time he didn't follow her, which was just as well as her hands were shaking so badly it took three tries to get the key into the ignition. The last sight she had of him was standing, still frowning, next to the empty space where her vehicle had been.

She just drove, with no destination in mind, barely aware of her surroundings. Miscellandreax T'Or Orshiasa. She had been an eager student, taking her lessons seriously, doing her best to fulfil her teachers' expectations at all times. She had loved the learning, but somehow she had kept failing to meet whatever standards they had set for her. She had kept trying. The other students seemed to manage, and she was sure she could do the same, if only she worked hard enough.

That girl was long gone. Burned away along with nine warriors of the Order. That naive youngster would never have survived the antechamber to the world below. Would never have done the things she needed to do to survive. Max thought that girl had been left behind a long time ago, but she could feel her again now. Could feel the searing hurt of betrayal. The loss of all she had thought she had known and trusted. Raised in one of the Lady's orphanages because - as her teachers told her - her birth parents had surrendered her there rather than look after her themselves, she had hoped to find a welcome and a home in the Order.

It had felt right. And being turned away had hurt almost worse than the fires of the underworld.

Miscellandreax had come back into the daylight world with her whole body on fire from the world below, her hair and clothes incinerated, lungs choked, landing in a fresh water lake and boiling the water around her as she cooled. She had swum to shore, somehow, through hundreds of dead fish, the blackened outer layer of her skin peeling off to reveal new, pink skin underneath so that by the time she had reached the shore and crawled out of the lake, whole body trembling with exhaustion, she was mostly healed, bare skin covered in mud as she made her way on her hands and knees to higher ground. When the mud had washed off, there were still traces of burns on her skin. The heat had scorched her to her very bones. She still did not know how she had survived. She had faced the same fires as the warriors, and yet she had lived.

But she had lived, and ended up on the muddy shore of a lake full of dead fish.

There had been an old sheet of tarpaulin there. Big enough for her to use as a makeshift blanket, the fabric harsh against her new skin as she huddled into it. There had been an old fallen tree to sit on and she had rested there, shaking and crying, as the lake cooled, the dead fish washing to shore and attracting predators. The creatures of the Wild were never ones to turn away easy meals.

But every one of those predators left her alone, shivering and defenceless on that log.

The wheels of the pick-up bounced over an obstacle in the road and she came back to the here and now with a skip of her heart, wondering if she had hit something. But, no, it was just a rough road.

Her pick-up stopped apparently of its own accord and she blinked, finding her face wet with tears, somehow not surprised that she had ended up back here. The lake stretched out in front of her, serene in the late afternoon sun.

She got out of the pick-up and released Cas and Pol, both dogs rubbing themselves against her, seeking reassurance and a few biscuits before they ran off towards the water's edge.

Putting off the moment she had to look at the lake, Max turned back towards the city. She was on a small hill, and the city stretched out in front of her, sprawling as far as she could see to either side. To one side, the buildings were more spaced out, with large patches of open land between them. The city's farms, charged with keeping the citizens supplied with enough food after the Wild had taken away much of the farmland the city had depended on. Ahead of her, in the midst of the more densely built-on parts of the city, between the taller buildings that housed offices or flats, she could see the wide strip of different shades of green that ran almost the entire length of the city. The city green, a carefully curated bit of land available for all residents to use. Beyond the city green were several more blocks of buildings before the city tapered to a blunt wedge before disappearing into the mists that formed the edge of the world.

Max drew a breath in, squaring her shoulders, facing the lake. There was nothing to show what had happened eight years before. Nothing to tell anyone passing by that she had burst from the underworld into the lake. She had left the Grey Gates closed behind her, her palms and fingers itching again at the memory of the molten metal. Legends might say that the Gates could only be opened from the outside and closed from the inside, but when she had found the Gates, she had also found a latch on the outside, sealing Arkus and all of His demons into the underworld.

She had not been back here for a long time. She returned from time to time, somehow worried that the gate hidden underneath the lake would open again and spill the horrors of the underworld out into the daylight world. But the gate had stayed closed. Whatever Kitris had told the rest of the Order, and whatever Bryce might think, Max had done her job. The Grey Gates had been closed.

Chapter Nine

It was fully dark when Max got back into the pick-up and headed home. Cas and Pol had thoroughly enjoyed their few hours by the lake, chasing each other in and out of the water. Just as Max was enjoying the sight of their play, they found some old bones and she was reminded of the predators they really were. Still, it was better than thinking about Lord Kolbyr or Bryce or the Order or the Grey Gates.

As if on cue, her phone started ringing as soon as she reached the city limits, vibrating in its cradle by the steering wheel. She glanced at the caller ID and frowned at the unfamiliar number, then answered.

"Marshal Ortis," she said.

"Max, my dear, you have a knack for finding trouble," Audhilde's voice echoed in the pick-up cabin.

"What's happened?" Max asked.

"I was called to a second body today by Ruutti. She said you had an interesting conversation with Lord Kolbyr."

"More like a terrifying conversation," Max said.

Audhilde laughed, the sound warm and human, inviting Max to join her. "That is a common experience."

"You're not calling just to chit chat, though, are you?" Max asked. She was almost certain of it, but could never be sure with older vampires. Sometimes they grew bored and needed entertainment, and with a lifetime of power behind them, thought nothing of disturbing anyone who crossed their mind. And Audhilde was more sociable than most. She seemed to genuinely enjoy human company.

"No. I have completed my examination of the first body and started on the second. There are some things you should see. Can you come by the mortuary?"

"Now? Yes. I'm about ten minutes away." The city's mortuary was on the outskirts of the inner city, and it was late enough that Max wouldn't have to deal with too much traffic.

"Good. I will see you then," Audhilde said, and hung up.

The mortuary's examination room was lit with stark, white lights and smelled of cleaning fluids and decay. There were four bodies covered in white sheets lying on the cold metal tables, Audhilde standing near the foot of one of the tables, a tall metal trolley on wheels in front of her. She was typing into the laptop on top of the trolley, her fingers moving so fast they were nearly a blur. The vampire was dressed in blue coveralls this time, her hair covered with a paper cap, a mask draped around her neck. Contrary to the popular image of medical examiners, her coveralls were spotless and barely creased with wear.

"Give me a moment, honey," the vampire said, glancing up to acknowledge Max before turning back to the screen.

Max nodded, and stayed where she was by the door. She was reluctant, as always, to move further into the room. This was far from the worst place she had to visit in her job as Marshal, but the smells got in her clothes and hair and the chill seemed to seep into her bones. She also did not like being around the dead. She kept waiting for them to open their eyes and sit up.

"Alright. This is your first victim," Audhilde said, leaving the laptop and going to the farthest table. She peeled the sheet to the body's waist, exposing the pale flesh and cut marks.

Max moved across. She would have preferred photographs, but Audhilde would not have called if it wasn't important. So Max looked down at the victim, the pattern of the wounds clearer now that they had been cleaned. Audhilde would have the exact count and measurements. Perhaps in the report she had been working on.

"The killer did not finish," Audhilde said. "As you saw earlier, there are far more wounds on the other man. This one died quickly."

"What was the cause of death?"

"Heart failure. The young man had a heart defect. It probably went undetected in his life, but when he was under stress, it killed him," Audhilde said in a matter-of-fact voice.

And being in the hands of someone cutting into his flesh with a knife was most likely more stress than the man had ever had in his life.

"Has he been identified?" Max asked.

"Not yet. The detective is taking his photograph to the Sorcerer's Mistress tonight," Audhilde said, her nose wrinkling. "Such a ridiculous name for a tavern. She has taken a photograph of the other man, too. We will have answers by tomorrow."

Audhilde sounded quite confident of that. Max had only been into the bar once, which had been more than enough, and couldn't imagine any of the patrons willingly talking to a detective. Or, at least, not most detectives.

"Which detective?" Max asked.

"Didn't I say? Ruutti Passila. If there are any answers to be had, she will get them."

"She will," Max agreed. If Ruutti asked, then almost all the wannabe magicians in the bar would confess their entire life history to her. And probably ply the woman with over-priced drinks at the same time, too. "So, no name yet. Is there anything else of note about this man?"

"He was a magic user," Audhilde said, her nose wrinkling slightly. "Very low-level, even for patrons of the Sorcerer's Mistress."

"Oh? How can you tell?" Max asked, curious.

"There's a certain quality to a magician's blood. This one had the faintest trace of it. The other one had more," Audhilde said. Max tried not to think about how a vampire would know about the quality of a magician's blood, but her mind supplied the details anyway. It was difficult to imagine the warm, professional woman in front of her drinking blood, but she must do in order to survive. "There's nothing else of interest to this man," Audhilde said, pulling the sheet back over the body and moving to the next table. "This one has a little more to tell us."

Audhilde peeled the sheet back from the second body and Max recognised the victim she had seen earlier in the day. Like the first, he had been cleaned, the wounds now sterile, gaping holes in his flesh. There was a clearer pattern to the cuts. Max moved around the table to get a better look at them. It looked like a very primitive form of spellwork, and one she was not familiar with.

"His heart kept beating until it ran out of blood," Audhilde said. "So technically, his cause of death is similar to the first, which is heart failure."

"But it's not the same at all in practice, is it?" Max said softly, measuring the extent of the wounds. The man had cuts along the inside of his arms as well. Every one of them would have hurt. And he had lived through them all.

"No, it's not," the medical examiner agreed. "The killer was more confident with this one. He had sharpened his blade, too. The cuts are narrower, and shallower. Just enough to break the skin and draw the blood the killer needed," Audhilde said. There might be a faint trace of admiration in her words. Max chose to ignore that, focusing on what she was saying.

"But there's not a huge difference between the first and second," Max said. "Does that suggest that the killer had been practising beforehand?"

"I would say yes. But not on humans. We have not seen any other bodies with these sorts of markings. I have asked my colleagues," Audhilde said.

Max nodded, absorbing that information. "You said this one was also a magic user?"

"Yes. There was a stronger trace in his blood. Still quite mild," Audhilde said, sounding disappointed. "Not enough on its own to cause the damage to the road surface."

Max stayed where she was, eyes on the body, considering the information. "So, the killer was making specific cuts on this victim, then using his blood to paint the rest of the ritual on the road surface," she said slowly, piecing it together. "And the combination of the victim's blood and the ritual were enough to shatter the road?"

"That is what it looks like," Audhilde agreed. She was standing on the other side of the body, unusually serious. "And I would also guess that the ritual was not complete. Or defective somehow. I don't know of any rituals where the objective is to damage the ground."

Max shivered, the cold of the room seeping through her clothes. A ritual that had not been completed but had still been powerful enough to break the layers of hardened road surface. She thought about the possibilities that Lord Kolbyr had mentioned, none of them good. To get through the layers of the daylight world and into the world below would require a significant amount of power. Max set her jaw. The dark lord was not due to make another attempt at breaking free from the underworld for nearly another hundred years. And she had hoped to be far, far away when the Portents appeared again to herald the next attempt by Arkus to open the Gates and gain his entrance to the daylight world.

Chapter Ten

A VOICE MURMURED IN *the darkness, meant for her ears only, telling stories of pain and fire. Miscellandreax lay awake, huddled under the thin sheet and ancient wool blanket, pressing her fist into her mouth to hold in her whimper. The voice liked it when she cried, or whimpered. But if she made any sound, she might wake the others around her. The other inhabitants of the dormitory. No one else could hear the voice. She'd asked them, more than once. And no one believed her that someone could get into the room after dark and speak to her, keeping her awake for hours at a time.*

She was heavy-eyed and thick-headed when she was summoned from the classroom later that day. Trying not to listen to the night-time voice, she had forgotten what day it was. Her birthday, or so she had been told. And that meant a visit from him. A man dressed in black, who would ask boring questions about her lessons, how her schooling was progressing, and what she had learned since he had last visited. She didn't want to go and see him, but the teachers told her she should be grateful that someone was taking an interest in her welfare. They clearly had hopes that the man might offer her employment when she was old enough, so that she didn't need to be a burden on the orphanage any longer.

With the murmurs of the night voice in her ears, she had gone into the school office to find him there, as remote as ever. He never seemed pleased to be there, or to see her, so she had never been able to understand why he bothered to visit. One of the other orphans had speculated that he might be a relative. Perhaps even her father. She had asked him outright, once, if he was related to her. He had denied it, with a curl of his lip that suggested he was horrified at the thought. She had understood that expression well, even then.

This morning, as he turned to her, she saw something shift under his skin. Another face peered out and the night voice whispered to her. Better run, little girl. I will enjoy chasing you.

Max woke with a gasp, coated in sweat, heavy weights on either side of her. Cas and Pol. They had her pinned under the blankets, keeping her still. The nightmare faded. It hadn't been the worst she'd had. Very little of it was an imaginary product of her sleeping mind. Most of it - up until the very last part - had been memories stitched together. She drew a breath in, her heart slowing down and reminded herself that the memories couldn't hurt her.

The dogs eased back, letting her sit up. She scrubbed her hands across her face, trying to erase the memory of that quiet voice and the disdain on her visitor's face. After that one time, when she had asked Kitris if he was a relative and seen the depth of his disgust at the idea, she had never asked him again why he took such a close interest in her. Why the head of the Order had taken such a close interest in a girl in an orphanage with no particular skill in magic. She had not been sure she wanted the answer. Not then, and not now. When he had informed her that it was her duty to join the Order and then to oppose Arkus, she had believed him. Had trusted him.

It took a long, hot shower to shake off the nightmare and memories. By the time she was dressed, she was back in the here and now, memories pushed to the back of her mind where they lurked, ready to leap out again in any moment of weakness. But she had plenty of other things to distract her.

There had been no word from Ruutti overnight, or in the early morning. Which probably meant that she had decided she could solve the murders on her own without Max's help, Max thought sourly. The detective loved being the centre of attention.

It was frustrating, but if it was one human killing another then it was outside the Marshals' jurisdiction. And she had plenty of other work to be getting on with. Reports to write, for one thing. She would almost rather be back at the mortuary among the dead, but Cas and Pol would be happy to visit with Leonda while Max wrote up her reports. And focusing on something like that would keep her mind away from her past. She hoped.

She was most of the way to the Marshals' offices when the phone rang. It was Therese.

"You've been assigned to work on the wards today," the woman said, with no preamble.

"What?" Max asked, taking her foot off the accelerator, sure she had misheard.

"The Wild barrier where the breach happened," Therese said, speaking very slowly, as if Max was a small child. "You know where that is?"

Max drew a breath. Every Marshal knew where the breach had happened. It still didn't explain her assignment. "Yes, but-"

"They are expecting you now," Therese said, and hung up.

Leaving Max staring at the blank phone screen, wondering if she had imagined the whole thing. Working on the wards was part of a Marshal's duty, as the wards kept the worst of the Wild out of the city and stopped curious fools from the city from wandering into the Wild without permission. There was normally a strict rotation of Marshals, and Max wasn't due to take her shift until the following month. With a breach of the barrier, it made sense for Marshals to be pulled off their regular duties more often to work on the repairs. But she was not the best choice for it. She dialled the office.

"What part didn't you understand?" Therese asked.

"Why am I being assigned to this now?" Max asked, not bothering to hide her impatience. The woman was impossible to deal with.

"You're the only available Marshal and it needs done."

"I don't believe that," Max said, the words out before she could check them.

"What part?" Therese asked. The woman was unbelievably rude, but didn't bat an eyelid when people were rude back to her.

"That I am the only available Marshal," Max bit out.

"Oh. Well." For the first time that Max could remember, Therese sounded uncertain. "That's what I've been told."

Max narrowed her eyes at the phone, even though the dispatcher could not see her expression. "Did Faddei give the order?" she asked. As the head of the Marshals' service, Faddei was the only person who could give Max, or indeed any Marshal, a direct order and expect it to be obeyed.

"Yes," Therese said, with no hesitation.

Max leant back against the headrest and blew out a breath. She did not like Therese, and was sure the feeling was mutual, but the woman had never lied. Max could argue. She could contest it. She had argued about her orders before. More than once. But she had also learned when to pick her battles. And this one was not worth fighting. Even if it was going to leave her with another magic hangover.

Faddei knew his people well, and knew that she was one of the least powerful Marshals at his disposal. If he needed her to take an extra shift helping to work on the wards, then that meant he considered it necessary.

"Alright. I'll make my way there. But I don't expect to be called back to it until my assigned slot next month."

"Understood," Therese said, and hung up again.

Leaving Max to turn the pick-up around and head out of the city, trying to soothe her temper with the knowledge that Cas and Pol would love running around outside the Wild almost as much as they would have liked spending time with Leonda.

The city's road just ended abruptly, disappearing into the barest suggestion of a rough road that led out through tangled shrubs and small, stunted trees towards the looming mass of primordial forest that formed this part of the Wild.

To anyone with no magic sensitivity, it just looked like a stretch of untamed land full of vibrant plant life. It was tangled and disorganised and beautiful. Among the endless shades of green and different shaped leaves from the slender stalks of grasses to the wide, fat tree leaves swaying in the breeze, there were vivid red stalks and great, frothy white blooms bigger than Max's head that added a sweet scent to the air for anyone lucky enough to get close. It was a far cry from the more muted colours and sharp angles of the city, with its pavements and roadways and buildings. There were green spaces in the city, but they were carefully tended and nothing approached the untamed tangle of the Wild.

Even with magic sensitivity, Max could appreciate the beauty. The Wild was certainly far more pleasant to look at than the square concrete boxes that passed for houses in the poorer parts of the city. Or even the Marshals' own headquarters.

There was a buzz against her skin out here, away from the city's own protections. Magic slid along her fingers and arms, lifted her hair, tugging her forward. There was power in the air. So much power. Just at the end of her fingers.

She gripped the steering wheel with far more force than was needed, resisting the temptation. It got easier with practice. And she had seen what happened to people who gave themselves over to the lure of the Wild. Almost unimaginable amounts of power, yes, but also insanity. And while she might be frustrated with her own limitations in magic, she wasn't ready to exchange that for losing her mind.

There was what might be described as a clearing not that far ahead of her, filled with vehicles. Another battered-looking truck a bit like her own, and a pair of sleek vehicles that she did not recognise, but which hummed against her heightened senses with defensive warding.

She turned her pick-up to face back to the city and parked, letting Cas and Pol out. The dogs ran into the undergrowth with happy, huge bounds.

Leaving Max to make her way to the group of people on the other side of the vehicles. Another Marshal, Zoya Lipka, dressed in a similar fashion to Max with a leather jacket and dark, close-fitting trousers. Zoya raised a hand in greeting. There were two youngsters next to her that looked to be in their late teens, wearing plain long-sleeved tops and loose-fitting dark trousers, the dark colours highlighting their pale faces. They looked like they were going to be sick. A few paces away was a quartet of armed people with body armour over their casual clothing. Max checked in her stride as she realised that one of the armed people was Bryce.

Three times in a week. That was some awful bad luck, Max thought, almost turning tail and heading back to the city. But she had been assigned here, and keeping the wards active and intact was an important job, even if she didn't like it.

"There you are," one of the youngsters said, lifting his chin. "You are late. Another Marshal, I presume?"

"Marshal Ortis, yes," Max answered, brows lifting. "And you are?"

"Not important," the youngster said, turning away from her. "Come on. We haven't got all day."

"A moment," Max said, not moving from her spot. Even when she had been part of the Order, she had never taken her instructions from youngsters like this.

Zoya had folded her arms across her middle, not moving, either. The other Marshal was a muscular, compact woman with warm-toned brown skin and waist-length hair that went through remarkable transformations from time to time. Her hair was currently dyed a colour somewhere between blonde and strawberry, complementing her skin tone, and had been woven into long, narrow braids, held back from her face by a simple leather tie.

The youngster turned towards Max, power sliding under his skin. He was almost the same height as her, but hadn't filled out to his frame yet. He had the sort of pale skin that would never tan, and black hair swept back from an unremarkable face.

"You are here to assist us," the youngster said.

Max put her hands in her pockets, standing with her feet braced slightly apart. "I am a Marshal of the city. The maintenance of the wards is part of the Marshals' job. I don't answer to you. I am certainly not here to assist you. Whoever you are."

"I am Alexey T'Or Radrean," the youngster said, staring back at her with open hatred. "And you will obey me."

An apprentice. The Lady help them and save them from over-confident youngsters, Max thought. Apart from her own experience, she had yet to meet an apprentice who didn't think they were more capable than they actually were.

Then the name caught up with her. Radrean. She remembered him. All too well. The always-popular boy who had thought it would be funny to pick on the awkward orphan girl. First, he had made her his friend, had made her believe he had cared. And then he had taken it all away. The humiliation he had orchestrated for her still stung all these years later. And now apparently he was teaching his own apprentices. It was as chilling a thought as facing a full-grown Harridan.

"And where is your apprentice master?" she asked, hoping it sounded like a reasonable, casual question and didn't betray her real concern, that she might have to face her former tormentor. Or, rather, one of her former bullies.

"Not your concern," Alexey said, still glaring at her. He glanced across at the armed men. "Are you going to let her treat me like this?" he asked.

"We're here to keep you safe," Bryce answered, in clipped tones that suggested he had had a little too much of Alexey already. And the day was still young. "The Marshal hasn't threatened you or your sister in any way."

Max tried to keep her expression neutral as Alexey's face turned into a scowl. Clearly he had believed that he and his sister were in charge, not the warriors. If they had been full-fledged Guardians, he would have been right, as warriors took their orders from Guardians. But warriors did not take their orders from apprentices. The warriors would keep the apprentices safe while they carried out their assignment, but weren't required to obey them. It seemed that Alexey had not worked out that distinction. Then again, he had Radrean for an apprentice master, so it was no wonder he was arrogant.

"Alexey, stop being such a drip," the other youngster said. She was as tall as her brother. Twins, if Max had to guess. "Marshal Ortis, is it? I am Sandrine T'Or Radrean. I'm pleased to meet you."

"Miss," Max replied, inclining her head slightly.

"The correct term is apprentice," Sandrine said, but there was no malice in her tone. As if she was simply giving Max a piece of information that she thought Max didn't know. "I've never been this close to the Wild before. It's quite impressive."

"That it is," Max agreed slowly, keeping a close eye on both twins. She wondered just how many people they had drawn in with this routine. One arrogant and abrasive, one genial and compliant. She wondered if they ever switched roles, although it was difficult to imagine Alexey ever being compliant. Or genial. They were like the split parts of Radrean's own personality. On the one side, outwardly charming and easy-going. On the other side, the side that she had been unlucky enough to see, breathtakingly arrogant and sure enough of his own position and power to undertake some foul things.

She wondered, as she had done before, if the Order knew just how dangerous Radrean was. Swiftly followed by the more disturbing unanswered question; did they care?

"Do you have today's assignment?" Max asked Zoya, turning her shoulder to the two apprentices.

"We're to continue work repairing the barrier breach," the other Marshal answered promptly. She glanced aside to the two apprentices. "There was no mention of additional resources."

"We are not resources," Alexey announced, lifting his chin.

"You are here to assist us, though, aren't you?" Zoya asked, brows lifted. Max hid a smile. The other Marshal had managed to make it sound like a genuine query.

"That was our assignment," Sandrine said, her pinched expression suggesting that she didn't like it one bit and could think of far better things to be doing with her time.

"Their teachers felt that Apprentice Alexey and Apprentice Sandrine would benefit from some real-world experience," Bryce said, in a carefully neutral tone. Impossible to tell from his expression what he thought of it, but Max had no difficulty in interpreting his words. The two apprentices had made nuisances of themselves within the Order to the extent that their teachers had seized on the opportunity to send them outside the safety of the Order's walls.

For a moment, Max was tempted to tell the youngsters and the warriors that she and Zoya didn't need their help. The Marshals were not there to train troublesome apprentices. Maintaining the Wild wards was usually left to the Marshals, although the Order and the law enforcement magicians did help out occasionally when there had been a breach. Sending them away would only cause more problems, though, as the Order would doubtless see it as an insult. And the city needed the wards repaired as soon as possible. So Max swallowed her impulse and braced herself for a difficult day ahead.

"Let's get some more weapons and head in," Max suggested.

"Alright," Zoya said, and turned to her own battered vehicle.

"We have weapons," Bryce said in a mild voice.

Max glanced around at the four warriors and had to agree with him. All four were wearing body armour and carrying an army's worth of weaponry among them, from the heavy guns Bryce and one of the other men were carrying to the lighter pistols they all had at their hips or strapped to their thighs. And those were just the weapons she could see. They would all be carrying hidden ones, too.

"We have some specially adapted ammunition," Max said. Not disagreeing with Bryce, just making a point. She went to her own vehicle and opened the box in the back, taking out her Marshal-issued shotgun and checking it was loaded. The Marshals' weapons experts had taken a basic shotgun design and added an automatic loader with a capacity of twelve shots. The magazine in place was full. She picked up a bag and filled it with spare ammunition for good measure. The shotgun magazines were bulky and heavy to carry, but it was preferable to running out of ammunition later. She already had her pistol and the spare magazines tucked at her back. And the dogs, of course. That should be enough. She hoped.

She returned to the others to find Zoya similarly equipped, with Alexey openly impatient at the delay.

"Zoya, you've been here most recently. Do you want to lead the way?" Max asked.

"Sure," the other Marshal said, glancing around the warriors and the two apprentices before heading off towards the forest, her shotgun held ready in front of her.

Max let the others go in advance, bringing up the rear. She didn't expect any trouble, but no one went near the Wild without being prepared for it.

Cas and Pol came to join her, silent shadows to either side, their eyes gleaming. They would feel the pull of the Wild as well. Like her, they were used to resisting it. And their far sharper senses should alert the group to any danger long before it appeared.

They had barely gone twenty paces from the vehicles when Alexey stopped and left the group, heading for something in the tangled head-high shrubs. A sharp call from Bryce had the youngster glancing over his shoulder rather than returning to the group.

As the rearguard, Max had a perfect view of the discussion that followed.

"But there's something here," Alexey protested, not moving.

"There's a ton of stuff out here," Bryce said, sounding like he was trying to be patient. "We can't stop and stare at everything. Come on, there's work to do."

"But it looks like a wall. There was a building here," Alexey protested.

Max waited, shotgun pointed to the ground. At the head of the group, Zoya was standing with her back to them, tension gathering across her shoulders. They weren't into the Wild proper, not yet, but there might still be dangers here, such as predators who had slipped through the breach.

"Is there a problem?" Max called, trying to keep her voice neutral.

"There was a house here," Sandrine said, looking back at Max. "I didn't think anyone lived in the Wild."

"This wasn't always the Wild," Max answered. It was basic information that every child should know, and she couldn't help wondering what game the twins were playing, or if it was just their normal behaviour to be so difficult.

"What was here before?" Alexey asked. There was a demanding edge to his voice.

"I don't know," Max said. "But we've still got a fair distance to go."

"Get moving," Bryce said to Sandrine, and waved Alexey back to the group. "You need to stay with us."

"But we're not at the wards yet," Alexey protested, sounding surly, as he came back to the group.

The wall he had been standing next to, about the same height as him and covered in green plants, shivered slightly. Max lifted her shotgun to her shoulder, ready to fire. The wide, flat head of a snake poked out of the greenery, its unblinking gaze on Alexey's back as the youngster came back into Bryce's shadow. One of the other warriors raised their own weapon, pointing at the snake.

"Don't fire," Max said, keeping her voice calm. "It's just having a look at us."

"There was a snake there the whole time?" Alexey asked, voice rising. "Why didn't you tell me?" he asked, turning to Max.

"You were told to return to the group," Max answered, not taking her eyes off the snake. "Zoya, let's keep going."

"Copy that," Zoya said, and set off again.

Max walked backwards for a while, taking care where she put her feet, watching the snake. It lowered its head back onto the green-covered wall, disappearing into the leaves with barely a ripple. Max could still feel eyes watching her, though, as she turned to face forward and follow the others. This close to the Wild, there would always be eyes watching.

Chapter Eleven

The distance between the vehicles and the breach where the Marshals had been working was scattered with tall trees, the gaps between the trees choked with undergrowth and shrubs, many of the plants bearing thorns or sticky leaves that got caught in clothing and hair. Apart from the effort of making forward progress, the main hazard was the two youngsters who kept trying to stray from the path, or stop to look at this or that they spotted along the way. Neither of them seemed to have learned the lesson from Alexey's close encounter with the snake. Max left their antics up to Bryce and his team to deal with, and Zoya just kept walking, forcing the warriors and apprentices to keep going, too, or lose their guide.

At length, Zoya stopped at a point where the trees and undergrowth faded away to lush, knee-length grass that rippled like a river in a barely there breeze. The grass expanse was about a hundred feet wide, and on the other side of the grass river, an ancient forest rose into the sky. Max moved forward to stand beside her fellow Marshal.

The scene looked beautiful and serene to the untrained eye, but in the middle of the grass river, the wards rose, easily visible to anyone with magic sensitivity. The wards stretched to either side, a barrier between the supposedly civilised world and the Wild. The formulas that made up the spells should be sleek and straight, the curves and lines of them smooth and locked together. But the point ahead of them was fragmented, the tears in the guarding wards painful when Max tried to look at them. The Marshals had been working almost around the clock to repair the damage of the breach. They had managed an emergency repair, but there was a lot of work still to be done.

And something had been gnawing at the wards again, Max realised, as she engaged her magic sense. The curves and lines of the formulas that made up the Wild wards were frayed, bits of them torn and flailing in the slight breeze. The wards were holding, but only by the thinnest of margins.

She tensed, alert for any sign of danger. There were a few creatures that could chew through magic like that, and all of them were bad news.

"That wasn't there when I was here before. Day before yesterday," Zoya said, voice grim. "That thin patch. Do you see?" She was pointing in the daylight world. "We'd almost repaired the thing."

Caught in the world of magic and power, Max nodded. "It looks like an animal attack of some kind," she said.

"Animal?" Alexey's voice, sharp and unwelcome, broke through her concentration. "Don't be so ridiculous. What kind of animal eats magic?"

"A Harridan, for one," Max answered almost absently, still taking stock of the thinned-out wards. "We're going to need some more muscle for this," she said to Zoya.

"I'd kind of assumed that's why the kids are here," the other Marshal answered.

"Shame no one told them that they were here for our back-up," Max said, with sour humour.

"A Harridan? Harridans don't come this far south. They prefer warmer climates," Alexey said, utterly confident. Max spared a moment to be glad that he had learned something in his classes.

"I wish that were true, but I cleared out a Harridan nest in the city less than a week ago," Max said grimly, glancing at the warriors, making sure they were paying attention to the level of potential threat. She need not have worried. All of them were wearing serious, focused expressions, standing in a loose group and facing outwards so that they could keep an eye on their surroundings, weapons held ready.

"Time to see if these kids actually have the juice they claim," Zoya said, looking at the twins. "Do you know how to repair a ward?" she asked them.

"Oh, please," Alexey said, scorn dripping from his voice. "We've been working with wards since we were five."

"Yes, we can work on and repair wards," Sandrine said. She was wearing an abstracted expression, looking straight ahead. At the place where the wards were. "This is really complicated work," she said, the admiration in her voice the most unguarded emotion she had produced so far.

Alexey's lip curled and he turned to face the same direction as his sister, a frown furrowing his brow. Magic rose around him. Not the cool, disciplined magic that a Guardian would use, but the hot, impulsive magic of an untrained magician. His pride was stung and he was determined to prove himself, it seemed.

Before Max could say or do anything, he had unleashed his magic on the fragmented wards. She could see, somewhere in the mess he had produced, the codes for repair. But they were overwhelmed by too much power. Far too much power.

Rather than repairing the wards, the power scorched through the remaining barrier, tearing the ward down completely, leaving a gaping hole that grew wider as Alexey poured more power into it.

"Stop now!" Zoya shouted.

"Alexey, stop, you're making it worse!" Sandrine called, grabbing her brother's arm and shaking him.

That finally got through. Alexey dropped his magic, a dazed expression on his face. He stared at the spot where he had torn away the wards, a trail of blood beginning to leak from his nose. "That should have worked," he said, disbelieving. "You," he said, turning to Max. "You did something. You ruined it."

"Not me," Max said, lifting her shotgun to her shoulder and staring out into the Wild. Nothing. Yet. She dropped the bag of ammunition at her feet and opened it for quicker access to the extra rounds. "Zoya, do you want to shoot or repair?"

"Let me start the repairs. I've still got the patterns in my mind," Zoya said, moving to stand closer to Max as Max straightened so that they were shoulder to shoulder.

Max nodded, shotgun held ready. It was sensible. Zoya should be able to pick up the trailing fragments more quickly than Max.

"Cas, Pol, on guard," Max told her dogs. They came on alert at once, eyes fixed ahead, ears slightly lifted, watching the forest ahead of them. Their bodies rippled, shifting into their attack forms, with longer, tougher hair, their teeth and claws extending.

"What is it?" Sandrine asked.

Max ignored her, holding her position as Zoya's breathing slowed, the other Marshal dropping into the trance-like state that made magic-working easier.

"There's a hole in the ward," Bryce answered the twin, sounding grim.

"Yes, I can see that," Sandrine said, sounding like her brother for a moment.

"Why is the ward here?" Bryce asked, with what sounded like forced patience. Max had almost her entire concentration on the forest ahead of them.

"To keep the Wild contained," Sandrine said, impatience clear. "To keep all the bad things there. Oh. Wait. So if there's no ward, there's nothing to stop the things anymore?"

"That's right," Bryce said.

"I can fix it," Alexey said. Max could feel him gathering more magic.

"No," she said, with as much force as she could, not taking her eyes off the forest. "You've done enough damage. Stay out of our way."

"What are you afraid of?" Alexey asked, in a singsong voice that made Max's fingers itch with the urge to smack him. With her exit from the Order, she had thought her days dealing with over-confident, arrogant apprentices were behind her. And had not been sorry to lose that particular experience.

Before Max could answer, something moved in the forest ahead of them. A sinuous shadow that sent shivers across her skin.

"Zoya, we have company. Keep working," she said. She had her shotgun ready, extra ammunition in easy reach, and her dogs nearby. Cas and Pol took a slow, careful step forward, out to either side of her and Zoya.

"On it," the other Marshal answered, voice tense. She was staring into the magic with single-minded focus, and Max could feel Zoya's power gathered in the air, released in a long, steady stream, painstakingly picking up the frayed ends of the wards, coaxing them towards each other. A far cry from the hot flare that Alexey had used.

"What is that?" Sandrine asked, sounding fascinated.

"Stay where you are," Bryce snapped.

The curving shape in the trees grew closer, sliding through the forest without a sound. A pitch-dark head, longer than Max was tall, peered between leaves, yellow eyes with great, vertical slit pupils unblinking as the creature stared across the small clearing and at the people gathered there. A forked tongue, dusky pink, flicked out, tasting the air, and the thing hissed. The sibilant sound made Max's stomach churn. Harridan. Full-grown. And where there was one, there was often another.

The creature slid further around the tree, showing its stumpy forelegs and claws. They might look small on the creature, but Max knew that they were more than large enough to grab her, or any one of the people around her.

Her palms were sweating against the grip of the shotgun, the surface rough against her skin, the smell of gun oil coating her tongue and dry mouth. Cas and Pol had slid forward a few more paces, spreading to either side. Her hounds were expert hunters and knew exactly what the thing ahead of them was.

The Harridan, a female if Max had to guess, stayed in the trees for a moment more, turning her head this way and that, tongue flicking out. Tasting the air. Getting a good sniff of her prey. Even though the creature was holding its position, its hide was rippling in constant motion. Harridans were never still. The movement made Max's stomach churn as if she was on a ship in a storm, not sure which way was up.

Nearby, Max heard a whimpering sound. One of the twins, at a guess. She could only hope that fear would hold them still and compliant and not tempt them into trying something stupid.

The Harridan slunk forward a pace or two.

"What are you doing?" Alexey hissed. "Shoot it!"

"It's not threatening us just now," Max told him, words bitten off. "It's within the Wild, where it is allowed to be. It only becomes a problem if it tries to get through the ward or crosses it."

"It is beautiful," Sandrine said, sounding awed.

"You're gross," Alexey said.

Max kept her eyes on the Harridan, trying to ignore the bickering that followed. The creature was settled, seemingly quite content to hide among the trees and keep an eye on the group of people. It was not the first time a predator had simply sat and watched her, and it was just as uncomfortable as it had been before. It was hard to breathe through the thudding of her heart, the dryness in her mouth and the giant knot in her stomach.

Still, she held herself motionless, letting Zoya work on the wards, keeping the Harridan in the sights of her shotgun. By accident or by design, the creature was out of range. She found herself hoping that it stayed where it was, and let Zoya complete the initial repair on the wards. Once the wards were intact, they could use the youngsters' power, carefully managed, to make a full repair. Alexey had already demonstrated that he had magic to spare. Assuming the twins would cooperate, of course.

Just as she was beginning to hope against hope that the Harridan might just stay there and watch, a fast, smaller blur of darkness moved through the forest to one side of the waiting creature. Rather than pausing at the forest's edge, this one kept going, sinuous black body sliding across the ground through the trees and then across the grasses, moving almost impossibly fast.

Max was firing before her brain had time to catalogue the newcomer. Another Harridan. Smaller than the female. Male, she guessed. Perhaps the female's mate. And still heading for them despite the full load from the shotgun. She crouched, grabbed a fresh magazine of cartridges and reloaded with fingers that knew what they were doing, straightening up already firing again, hearing more gunfire around her as the warriors also opened fire.

The thing burst through the wards as if they were tissue paper, ramming into Zoya with a force that sent the other woman flying. It had gone straight for the one person working magic, ignoring everyone else, not even brushing Max in its attack. Max ducked and rolled out of the way, reloading her shotgun on the ground and firing again. Three full loads into the thing. Three dozen cartridges, and it was still going. Its once-smooth hide was peppered with holes from the warriors' weapons, along with the larger, gaping wounds from her shotgun shells.

Another reload. Another kick of the shotgun against her shoulder. She was still on the ground, firing up at the monster as it reared over her head.

A quiet, soft sound of pain. Zoya. She had taken a hard hit.

Screams. The twins. Terrified out of their minds.

Gunfire from the warriors, who had moved to protect the twins.

Silent shadows as her dogs leapt onto the creature's head.

"Stop firing!" Max yelled, reloading her shotgun and scrambling to her feet. Her dogs were in the way.

To her surprise, the warriors' guns fell silent and they all watched as Cas and Pol slid around the creature's neck, the shadow-hounds' teeth lengthening along with their claws as they tore into the Harridan's neck, seeking the main artery.

"Duck!" Max yelled, following her own advice and landing back on the ground, face down, one arm up over her head, as the hounds reached the artery and foul-smelling Harridan blood sprayed through the air.

The ground shook with the force of the monster landing, twitching as the last of its blood left it.

There were screams. The twins, she thought, lifting her head. Despite its death throes, the Harridan had died silently, her hounds making sure it was dead by biting into its nose and watching for any reaction before they left it, coming across to her, their eyes glowing and bloodied teeth bared in fearsome grins.

"Good boys," she said, her voice high and shaking, scrambling to her knees. She was covered in Harridan blood, the black, filthy substance all over the ground around her. She wiped her hands on her thighs, then petted her dogs. "Very good job," she told them.

They sat in front of her and tilted their heads, eyes fixed on her pockets. She could not help a soft laugh and reached for her pockets and the biscuits there.

Before she completed the move, they had turned again, back towards the forest, the pets she knew once more vanished into formidable predators.

The other Harridan. The female. Larger and more cunning.

The larger Harridan stalked towards them, with no more pretence at patience, her tongue flicking out. She had just seen her mate killed, and while Max did not believe that the creatures were capable of emotion, there was a bond between mated pairs that provoked fury when it was disrupted.

Max started firing again as the female Harridan crossed the empty space where the wards had been. The creature was now into Marshal territory.

The shotgun clicked, its magazine empty. Her fingers fumbled for another load of ammunition and found the bag empty. She spat a curse, dropping the shotgun next to Zoya's too-still body. She drew her gun and unloaded a full clip into the Harridan. It seemed to have no effect.

Around her, the warriors were also firing, a steady pounding of bullets that hit home. And still the Harridan kept moving.

"We've got a rocket launcher in the car," one of the warriors said, voice grim.

"We'll never make it back in time," Bryce said, equally grim.

"Rocket launcher?" Max said, tilting her head. "Can you cover me?" she shouted over the sound of gunfire.

"Yes," Bryce said briefly, shifting position slightly.

Max knelt on the ground and took a breath, trying to still her thumping pulse and shaking hands enough to focus. Just for a moment. Just for a little bit. It had been years since she had tried this. And she could only hope it would work.

She gathered her power and *reached*, putting her hand out in front of her, fingers spread. Magic swirled around her arm. It was working.

A solid surface, cold and unyielding, met her fingers. She pressed her hand to it. "Open," she ordered. The surface yielded. Her hand disappeared from view. She frowned, closing her eyes. Where had she put it? Where? "Rocket launcher case," she said, power in her words.

A hard plastic handle brushed her reaching hand and she closed her fingers around it, pulling it towards her. The swirl of magic widened to let the bulky, heavy case through into her presence. "Close," she ordered the Vault, whole body trembling with effort.

The long matte case lay on the ground beside her and she put her thumb to the electronic lock, opening it up. There was a rocket launcher in the case, along with ammunition.

"Good," Bryce said, suddenly next to her. "Cover fire," he called to the others, and picked the launcher up from the case, shouldering it. Max huddled on the ground, whole body trembling with the after effect of using magic, covering her ears as Bryce fired.

It took three strikes to bring the Harridan down, and Bryce was reloading for a fourth when Cas and Pol ran forward, seeing their opening, grabbing the Harridan by her neck and tearing out her artery the way they had done for her mate. Bryce spotted the dogs before Max had time to shout, holding steady while he watched her dogs make their second kill of the day.

Max ducked again as another spray of Harridan blood washed over them. Although as she knelt on the ground, trembling with exhaustion of the effort of reaching into her Vault, she wondered why she had bothered. She was filthy already.

In the shocking silence and stillness when the Harridan was finally dead, she heard a high-pitched whimper. She clamped her jaw shut, hoping she had not been making the sound, but it was coming from the twins who were huddled together on the ground not far away, both of them soaked in foul, black blood, and both of them visibly shaking.

Max made it to her feet, wobbling, and pulled a cleaning spell from one of her pockets, slapping the paper onto her sleeve, letting the magic course over her. She'd need more than one spell, and a good scrub under a long, hot shower, but the first cleaning took the worst of it off. She used more spells on her dogs, then fed them handfuls of treats from her pockets on her way across to Zoya.

The Marshal was lying on her side, eyes closed, smothered in Harridan blood. Max found one final cleaning spell and doused Zoya, kneeling beside her and putting a hand in front of her mouth and nose. She was breathing, at least. But there was blood seeping from the side of her head.

Max pulled her phone out and hoped that it had survived the fight. It had. She had no idea what the Marshals' research team did to the phones, but they seemed to survive most things.

"What?" Therese answered on the third ring.

"Zoya is injured. Unconscious and bleeding. We need a medical team here now. And more Marshals. There's been a full breach of the wards. Two Harridans. Both dead. We need clean up for that, too."

There was a short, charged silence, then Therese sighed. It was the most human sound Max had ever heard from her. "Alright. Medical team's on the way. The Marshals might be a bit longer, along with clean-up. Stay and monitor the breach until then."

"Fine," Max said, and hung up.

"How long?" Bryce asked, coming to crouch at Zoya's other side.

"Medical team will be here in minutes," Max said, looking down at the woman's too-still face. "Not sure about back-up. It might be a while."

"You need to take us back home," Alexey said. He was standing a few paces behind Bryce, spattered head to toe in black blood. Even through the blood, Max could tell he was furious. "This is not acceptable."

Bryce had his back to the boy, and Max saw his face tighten. Not happy with the youngster. Max didn't blame him, and wondered just how many similar demands Bryce had faced from apprentices over the years. The Order prized its magicians far more than its warriors.

"Are you injured?" Bryce asked, standing up and facing the youngster.

"What? No. But look at me. It's disgusting."

"Do you know cleaning spells?" Bryce asked.

"Cleaning? You expect me to do cleaning?" Alexey asked.

"If you hadn't broken the wards, the Harridan wouldn't have broken free. Marshal Lipka would not be injured, and we wouldn't all be covered in blood," Bryce said, voice tight. "If Marshal Ortis hadn't managed to pull through some extra weaponry, we would all be dead right now."

Before Max or Alexey could respond to that cool, clipped assessment, Bryce had turned to the rest of the warriors. They were equally blood-spattered, but all of them had their weapons ready, the ground around them littered with empty ammunition clips. "Gemma, get back to the vehicles. Load all the weapons and supplies into one and bring it as close to here as you can. Hop and Killan, eyes on the wards."

"Sir." The tallest member of the group, a pale-skinned woman with a shock of pink-tipped, spiky blonde hair, nodded, and turned back into the tangled undergrowth, disappearing from view in moments. Max had a feeling she would sprint the whole way and be back to the vehicles in moments. The other two warriors, both stocky men a head shorter than Max, simply nodded and moved a few paces apart, attention moving to the wards and the forest ahead of them.

"Keep watch," Max told her dogs. They moved away, silent as usual, spreading out to either side of the two warriors. Max turned back to Zoya. There was probably nothing she could do, and the medical team was on its way. But it felt wrong to leave her lying on her own.

The other Marshal's face moved, twitching into a grimace.

"Holy Lady, what is that smell?" Zoya asked, words slurred.

"Don't get up. Stay where you are. You've got a head injury. Help is on the way," Max said, putting a hand on Zoya's shoulder to keep her down. "It's Harridan blood."

Zoya made a sound of disgust. "Next time, you do the magic and I'll do the shooting."

"Deal," Max said, shaky with relief that Zoya seemed to be alright. She gently squeezed Zoya's shoulder, fingers trembling, eyes stinging.

Before she could say any more, a low rumbling sound announced Gemma's return with one of the Order vehicles, and a thumping sound overhead announced the arrival of the Marshals' medical team.

"You have a helicopter?" Bryce asked, seeming to be impressed.

"We have good medical cover," Max corrected him, watching as a pair of people in bright yellow jumpsuits descended on ropes from the helicopter overhead, bulky packs dangling at their feet.

She wasn't sure just what discussions had taken place between the head of the Marshals and the city's rulers, but it had resulted in a rapid-response emergency team with their own, dedicated helicopter that could be anywhere in the city within minutes. There was a lot of speculation among the Marshals as to how their head had managed to arrange that. From the little she knew of Faddei, Max thought he'd probably told the city rulers that the Marshals would go on strike if they didn't get their way on this. They were chronically under-resourced in other ways, and there were always too few Marshals, so it made a certain sense to keep the existing Marshals in as good health as possible.

The two medical professionals made their way across the grass, barely glancing at the two dead Harridans. Max stood up and took a step away from Zoya to give the medics space to work.

"Marshal Ortis," Max introduced herself. "This is Zoya Lipka. She took a swipe from the male Harridan. She was conscious and lucid a moment ago," she added.

"Alright," the shorter one said, putting down her pack and pulling off her helmet to reveal pale skin covered with freckles and short, curling brown hair. She pulled on gloves and knelt next to Zoya while the taller medic put his pack on the ground and opened it up.

Max moved away to give them more room and privacy to work. Something crunched under her foot and she looked down to find she'd stood on one of the ammunition cages for her shotgun. She cursed. Leonda was going to be annoyed at having to re-form that thing. Again.

But clean up would have to wait. There was still a gaping hole in the wards, and the noise and blood would most likely attract other predators before too long. A Marshal's work was never done.

Chapter Twelve

Even as Max re-loaded her gun, and checked how many full magazines she had left, the warriors around her were moving. They had brought their own rocket-launcher from their vehicle and were setting it up along with an enormous gun on a tripod. Max blinked.

"You're expecting a herd of Harridan?" she asked.

"We like to be prepared," Bryce said. He was still standing beside her, she realised. Still covered in foul blood. "That rocket launcher was a nice touch. It's an older model, but still effective."

"Thank you," Max said, not able to think of another suitable response. She turned to the forest ahead of them, looking at the wards, and sighed.

"The damage is bad?" Bryce asked. Like most of the Order's warriors, he probably didn't have magical sensitivity, and training in magic was reserved for the apprentices and Guardians.

"Yes. Worse than when we arrived. It's going to take a lot of energy to repair."

"Good thing we brought some batteries, then," Bryce said, surprising her with the sour humour, eyes travelling to where Alexey and Sandrine were standing close to the dead Harridan female. Too close, in Max's view, but they were not her responsibility. "Alexey. Sandrine. Come away from that and make yourselves useful."

The twins glanced at each other before turning away from the dead monster with evident reluctance and coming across to Bryce. They had managed to effect cleaning spells, Max saw, not a spot of blood or dirt on either of them. It had evidently not occurred to either of the twins that the warriors might like to be clean, too.

"What?" Alexey asked.

"We need to repair the wards. You will help Marshal Ortis with that," Bryce told them.

"You don't get to tell us what to do," Sandrine said, then her nose wrinkled. "But I suppose you're going to tell me that it's dangerous with the wards down?"

"That's right," Bryce said, the faintest gleam of something that might be approval in his eyes. Max shared the sentiment. It seemed that one of the twins, at least, was learning.

The twins stared at him for a moment with almost identical expressions of irritation. Max waited for Alexey to say something cutting, but he simply glanced at her, brows lifted in a silent question. She pressed her lips together to hide a smile. It seemed he was learning, too.

"What do you want us to do?" Sandrine asked.

If she hadn't just seen the girl's temper, Max might have believed the offer. It was said in a calm and reasonable tone.

"I'm going to make a bridge repair across the broken part of the ward. If I make the first lines, can you copy them and repair the hole?"

"Of course," Alexey said, sneering. "We don't need your bridge to start with."

"You will follow my lead," Max told him, voice clipped. "And release your power slowly, like I'm sure you've been taught, not all at once."

High spots of colour burned in his cheeks. Max ignored him, turning back to the wards, gathering her power. She didn't have much, not compared to Alexey, and after *reaching* into her Vault she was worn thin, but she had enough to start the repair work.

The formulas for the wards shivered in the air in front of her and she gently coaxed them back together, twisting the lines around each other.

"Gosh, you really are weak, aren't you?" Alexey said.

Max set her jaw, trying to ignore him. Her lack of magical power had been mentioned more than once by the other apprentices and her teachers at the Order, to the point where she had wondered, more than once, why she had not been dismissed. She didn't seem to possess the necessary magical power for an apprentice, and certainly hadn't had the necessary physical skills for a warrior.

Most of the Marshals were in awe of the formulas that made up the Wild wards. To Max, they just looked like a jumbled mess of nonsense. She had never been good at maths, and this was maths so complicated it made her head hurt.

Still, she just had to follow the lines that had been there before.

No sooner had she connected the lines, gossamer-thin threads bridging the gap in the wards, than the twins' power rose around her, spilling out in a steady, controlled stream. They did indeed have power to spare. If the Order had co-operated with the Marshals' service sooner, the wards could have been repaired as soon as the breach had happened two weeks before.

But Max knew that the Order did not co-operate with other groups easily. Alexey and Sandrine were only here because they had annoyed their teachers. And if Alexey hadn't tried to show off, the twins would just have spent a slightly uncomfortable day outside the safety of the Order, without being in mortal danger. After today, perhaps Kitris would realise that having the breach in the Wild wards was not good news, even for the Order, although Max did not hold out much hope. Kitris was as arrogant as the twins, although he hid it better.

By the time the twins had fully repaired the wards, sealing the breach as if it had never been there, the medics were loading Zoya onto a stretcher and the helicopter was descending from the air to collect her.

"Good work," Max told the twins, and headed over to Zoya and the medics. "How is she?"

The other Marshal was covered in a light blanket, oxygen mask on her face, eyes closed. She didn't look to be in pain. Perhaps the medics had knocked her out with something, or she had not woken up again.

"Fractured skull and a few other broken bones at least," the female medic said. "We're taking her to the central hospital for more scans. She'll be there for a few days at least."

Max's throat tightened for a moment. Zoya hadn't deserved this. Despite her forceful personality, her bones were just as fragile as any other human's. And Max had failed to protect her. She put her hand on the other woman's arm, gently. "Get well soon, hear me?" she told the other Marshal.

Zoya didn't react, and Max watched as the medics carried her away, carefully lifting her into the helicopter, the female medic strapping Zoya's stretcher securely into the vehicle while the man came back and collected their packs.

The helicopter lifted up into the air and was gone from view in moments, leaving behind shocking silence and the bloody mess of dead Harridans.

And she still had four warriors and two apprentices nearby. She turned to the warriors, who were maintaining their vigilance despite the restored wards.

"Thank you for your help," she said to them.

Hop and Killan inclined their heads slightly. Gemma, manning the enormous gun, glared at her.

"The wards are repaired," Max told Bryce. "I need to wait for the clean-up crew, but that's all."

"We'll head back, then," Bryce said. He hesitated, as if he wanted to say something more, then turned to the others and signalled them to move out.

The warriors had their rocket launcher and gun dismantled and packed away in moments. They took time to collect their empty magazines and the shell casings they could find while Alexey and Sandrine took their seats in the back of the vehicle, the twins not acknowledging Max at all.

Max could not help wondering what tale the twins would tell their fellow apprentices back in the safety of the Order buildings.

While the others were busy, Gemma approached Max, expression tight.

"I know who you are," the warrior said in a low voice, scowling. "I never understood what was so special about you. You've no right to be breathing, let alone wearing that badge."

Max stared back at her, mind empty of words. It was not the first time someone from the Order had spoken to her with open contempt, and doubtless would not be the last, if she couldn't manage to avoid them in the future. But it had been years since she had faced down that sort of open disgust. It did not matter, not one bit, what the Order or its warriors thought of her. Not one bit. Except that the sliver of hurt working its way through Max's chest told her that was a lie.

"Gemma, we're leaving now," Bryce said.

The woman glared at Max for a moment more, and Max tensed, sensing the potential for violence. She had learned a lot in the years since she had been in the Order, but she doubted she was any match for a fully trained warrior. The violence never came. Gemma turned on her heel, stalking across to the vehicle.

With the twins taking up the entire back seat of the vehicle, Bryce and Hop were on foot behind the vehicle, Killan in the driver's seat. Gemma took the front passenger seat. As the vehicle moved forward, Bryce glanced at Max with an expression she could not read, but didn't say anything, simply following the vehicle away through the undergrowth.

Cas and Pol came to lean against her as silence fell. After the unwanted excitement of the day, it was oddly peaceful to just stand for a moment with her dogs, even with the two dead Harridan and the air thick with the stench of Harridan blood.

She stroked Pol's silky soft ears and stroked Cas under his chin, in the spot he loved, as she took a long, deep breath, trying to set aside the vicious hate Gemma had shown, and all the unwanted, unsettled feelings that had risen up when dealing with the apprentices and being reminded of Radrean's existence. She didn't want the memories or feelings. She'd survived eight years on her own. She didn't need any of them. She could only hope it would be another eight years before she had to deal with the Order again.

Chapter Thirteen

After waiting by the wards for other Marshals to inspect the repairs, and for the division's clean-up crew to collect the Harridan remains, it was late afternoon by the time Max pulled into the Marshals' parking lot, Zoya's vehicle dragging behind her own making the turn more difficult. As she drew to a halt, one of the mechanics lifted his head from the open bonnet of another battered pick-up. She waved to him as she got out of her pick-up, going to the back to release Zoya's vehicle.

"Is that Zoya's truck? Is she ok?" the mechanic asked, coming across.

"She took a bad hit," Max said. "She's in central hospital. I think she's going to be alright, but it will take some time."

"That's a shame. She's a fine lady," the mechanic said. Despite the old-fashioned term, he was about the same age as Zoya, Max estimated. "Give me her keys. I'll make sure her truck is ready for her."

"Thank you," Max said, handing over the keys. Zoya had left them in the ignition, as most Marshals did when they were working near the Wild. Being able to jump into your vehicle and quickly get up to a speed to outrun predators, or even just have the protection of a metal box, had saved more than one Marshal over the years.

Max found a parking spot for her own pick-up, let Cas and Pol out and then hefted the sack of spent cartridges, empty magazines and ammunition cages over her shoulder, heading for the larger building. Leonda would protest at the state of everything while also appreciating that Max had brought the things back. With the limited resources available to the city, reusing and re-purposing as many things as possible was essential.

Max emptied the contents of her sack into a large metal tray on the table left outside the armoury for that purpose. The armoury door was open, showing mostly empty shelves, although it was clear that Leonda and Raymund and their teams had been working hard to fill the empty spaces. Max gathered replacements for the ammunition and cartridges she had used, as well as a handful of cleaning spells, leaving even more empty spaces on the shelves, the sack across her shoulder weighing considerably more when she left the room.

Next to the armoury, the workshop door was closed - a necessary safety precaution when the team was working. The toughened glass windows in the wall showed Max a room full of people working. Leonda must have called every one of her team in, and borrowed a few from Raymund, too. All the workers were wearing protective heavy aprons, elbow-length gloves and face shields as they worked with the various bits of machinery to fashion new bullets or repair the Marshals' weapons. At one end of the room, closer to the door, a pair of workers were filling magazines with swift, economic movements. Max watched for a moment, the process somehow soothing. Even working with rapid efficiency, the magazines still took far longer to fill than the mere seconds they took to empty when she used her gun. There was a trolley next to the two workers ready for the filled magazines, and a daunting stack of empty magazines and racks of new bullets to the other side, waiting for their attention.

Pol made a low sound beside her, alerting her to someone approaching. Not alarmed, just letting her know.

She turned and saw the familiar figure of the head Marshal moving slowly along the passage beside the workroom wall.

Faddei Lobanov looked like a heavyweight boxer, or someone that a nightclub owner would employ to throw out troublemakers. He was built of muscle, with broad shoulders and a bald head covered with apparently random tattoos. The appearance was deceiving, Max knew. He played up to his overall look, with the tattoos and casual clothing, but he was one of the most intelligent people she had ever met, and had a boundless thirst for knowledge.

Faddei had been one of the first Marshals in service to the city, and had taken more than his share of injuries. He had lost the lower part of one of his legs and three fingers on one hand, but had refused to retire, instead taking the position as the head of the service. His appointment had been before Max joined the service, and the stories she had been told of his confrontation with the city's rulers grew more far-fetched and lurid each year. Whatever the truth, every Marshal knew that Faddei understood the dangers they faced in a way that most of the city's rulers never would. Even if the Marshals might question his orders from time to time - being sent to deal with supernatural predators required a considerable amount of independent thinking, and none of the Marshals, not just Max, took orders all that well - he was deeply respected and trusted by every one of them.

"Therese told me about the Harridans," Faddei said, coming to stand beside Max, looking into the workroom with her. He was shorter than she was, his head barely reaching her shoulder. It always surprised her to realise that anew every time she was in his presence. He had a personality and aura far bigger than his physical form. "The breach is closed, yes?" He already knew that, as Max had called ahead when she was bringing Zoya's vehicle back. But he liked to hear confirmation now and then. A checking in with his people, he had said more than once.

"Yes. The apprentices were useful after all," Max said, not bothering to hide the sharp edge to her voice.

"I'll want a full report on what happened," he told her, not looking at her.

"If I ever get to my desk, I'll be happy to write one," Max said, wincing slightly as she realised her tone was sour and displeased, but not able to do anything about it. All the Marshals had been working hard, not just her. She didn't expect or want special treatment, no matter what her tone of voice implied.

"It's been a bad few weeks," he said in an even, patient tone.

Max kept quiet. It had been a bad few weeks. Zoya was not the only Marshal who had been injured. And he had more to say. He had not simply come to find her to ask her about the breach. So she waited.

"Were you recognised?" he asked, after a long silence during which the two workers nearest to them had filled another half dozen magazines with shiny newly made bullets.

"Yes," Max said.

Faddei was the only one of the Marshals who knew who and what she was, or had been. He had promised not to tell anyone else, and she trusted that promise.

"What do you want to do?" he asked her.

"I haven't had a chance to consider it," Max said honestly. "But at the moment, nothing. Kitris dismissed me from the Order so he can hardly complain that I'm working elsewhere."

"His loss and our gain," Faddei said, turning to look at her. There was a glint of humour in his dark eyes. "You are a good Marshal," he told her.

The praise was unexpected, and she had no idea what to say to it. It warmed her all the way through, reaching back down to the eager-to-please, hard-working student she had been as a girl. None of her teachers then had given her anything close to that amount of praise. She did not think she was any better, or any worse, than the other Marshals. She tried to do what was assigned to her and stay out of trouble.

It wasn't like Faddei to give out praise, and once the shock had settled, suspicion rose.

"Are you about to try to saddle me with a rookie to train?" she asked. They had gone through some spectacular arguments in her service as a Marshal. Even though she had made him promise she could work alone, and even knowing her background, and reasons for not wanting a partner or a trainee, Faddei still tried to request that she consider one from time to time. The last time, Max had threatened to quit. That had been two years ago, and he had not mentioned it since then.

"Not exactly," he said.

"What, then?" she asked, irritation spiking. He had survived being head of the Marshals for a long time by being good at politics, something which Max had little patience for.

"There's been another death in the city. Another human," he told her, turning to face her, a frown gathering on his face. "Detective Passila has requested your help."

"Has she, now?" Max folded her arms across her stomach, trying to quell the sick feeling that had started there.

"This one is like the second one. So she says."

"Humans killing other humans isn't our business," Max said bluntly, chills running over her skin. Dark magic blood rituals possibly connected to Arkus were not something she wanted to get involved in. Or so she told herself. Firmly. Some instinct was telling her that this series of killings would trace back into the city, and she didn't want anything to go there. She had left that all behind. Marshals worked on the fringes of civilisation, not in the middle of it. That suited her just fine.

She tried to squash the little voice in her mind, the little trail of guilt threading through her that reminded her of the two dead bodies she had seen. People killed to satisfy an unknown killer's agenda. And now, it seemed, the killer had struck again. It might not be her job to track down the killer, but her conscience was prompting her to act. There might be something she could do.

"Now that the breach is sealed, we can spare you," Faddei said.

Max glared at him. "You've already agreed, haven't you?"

"She said you'd seen the previous two crime scenes and bodies. It doesn't make sense to bring in someone else," he answered her, sounding perfectly reasonable. "I thought you'd want to help," he added.

Damn the man. He knew her far too well. Max was not feeling reasonable. Her temper spiked. "I don't like it."

"I know," he said, surprising her. "But I also had a call from Audhilde. She wants you to see the third body as well."

Max blinked, startled, her temper fading and the apprehension returning. Audhilde's word carried a great deal of authority across the entire city, despite her apparently lowly position as medical examiner.

"Alright," Max said, grudgingly. "I need to wash and fuel my truck, then I'll head out. Did Ruutti give you an address?"

Faddei held a slip of paper out to her. Max recognised Therese's handwriting, as blunt and no-nonsense as the woman herself.

Max turned on her heel, temper spiking again, and stalked away. Faddei did not follow. Wise man.

Chapter Fourteen

Both Ruutti and Audhilde were still at the scene when Max arrived, Audhilde in a slim-fitting, dark blue tunic-and-trousers outfit that had probably cost more than Max's house, Ruutti in her usual leather jacket and jeans. They were standing near each other, not talking or looking at each other. The crime scene techs around them were keeping their heads down, avoiding eye contact. Max could not help wondering what argument she had just missed.

"You asked for me?" Max came to a stop a few paces from them, and looked past them to the crime scene. It was still daylight, giving her a good view. There was no tent up over this one, and she could see the cracks in the concrete surface spreading out almost to where she had parked her pick-up.

The killer had chosen an old games court this time. A once-pristine and painted surface where youngsters had battled each other for the privilege of simply winning.

There were no children or indeed anyone else living in this area now, which was among the most run-down in the city. The few remaining buildings all looked vacant, the doors and windows blank spaces suggesting that there was nothing of value left inside to protect if even the window glass and doors had been taken.

The playing surface had been surrounded by tall, chain-link fences at some point. A few upright posts remained. Probably dug in too deep for the scavengers to take, Max guessed.

Roughly in the middle of the former games court was a dip in the ground and a too-still figure lying amid a series of symbols painted onto the surface. Even from this distance, Max could tell that the dead man had been cut like the others and the paint used had been his blood.

"Another one," Ruutti said, face and voice grim.

"What did you learn about the others?" Max asked in return.

Ruutti's nose wrinkled in distaste. "They had both been seen at various gatherings through the city and had been into the Sorcerer's Mistress more than once. As far as I can tell, they had never actually met."

"So apart from being magic users, and visiting the Sorcerer's Mistress, there's no connection so far?" Max asked.

"So far, yes," Ruutti said. "I've got people questioning friends and neighbours, so we'll see."

"What about the bar? Anything there that might give us more information?" Max asked. It was their only point of connection so far.

"Nothing that will help this investigation," Ruutti said. She was not looking at Max, or Audhilde, staring straight ahead. The odd phrasing caught Max's attention and her brows lifted. She had no reason to suspect the detective of lying, but there was an undertone to her voice that made Max uneasy. Ruutti shook her head without looking at Max. Not wanting to discuss it.

All the same, Max considered Ruutti's words and what she knew of the detective. Ruutti was one of the most competitive people she knew. If there had been anything in the Sorcerer's Mistress to help her find the killer's identity, Ruutti would have told Max.

Or so Max believed, based on what she knew of the detective.

"Do we know who this is?" Max asked, looking ahead.

"Not yet. Nothing on the body apart from the remains of his jeans," Ruutti said, and finally looked at Max. "What do you think?"

"I think there's a very dangerous killer with an agenda somewhere in the city," Max said. "And if you're sure there's no connection to the Sorcerer's Mistress-"

"I'm sure," Ruutti interrupted.

"-then we don't know quite what that agenda is, or how he is targeting his victims," Max finished.

"You think the killer is male?" Audhilde asked.

"Not necessarily," Max said, "but that's my instinct." She remembered the extent of the knife wounds on the second victim, the damage vivid under the lights of the mortuary. It had taken a certain sort of single-minded focus and ruthlessness to do that much harm and paint the ritual markings on the ground. And the killer had also had to get his victims to those spots, too.

"I agree," Ruutti said, surprising Max. "Although I can't say why for certain."

"It makes sense," Audhilde said. Her mouth lifted in a humourless smile when Max turned to her. "There's a certain coldness to this that I don't like. Whatever agenda the killer has, they are not ready to stop."

"I forgot to ask. Was there any clue as to how the killer had subdued his victims? I doubt they would have just lain there and let him cut into them," Max said.

"I haven't found anything yet," Audhilde said, her normally pleasant face in a tight expression. "We didn't find any of the usual toxins. We're running more tests," she added, "although there's not much of the second victim's blood left to test."

Max nodded, hearing the frustration in Audhilde's voice. She had no doubt that the medical examiner and her team would find whatever had been used to keep the victims still. In time. But in the meantime, the killer had struck again.

"What about evidence at the scenes?" Max asked. The crime scene techs looked as if they were working just as hard here as they had at the other sites.

"Nothing. Not even a damned eyelash out of place. The killer knows how to cover his tracks," Ruutti said, her own frustration clear.

With that line of enquiry closed, Max looked back at the body and the symbols around it. "Lord Kolbyr mentioned a few options as to what the ritual might be," she said. "I wonder if he would be able to narrow them down."

"You want to bring him to the crime scene?" Ruutti asked. "This is Lord Kolbyr we're talking about. He is hardly likely to-"

"I've called him," Audhilde said, cutting across whatever hasty words Ruutti was about to speak. "He's on his way, but he has requested that the site be cleared of people so he can get a better look at it."

Ruutti glared at the vampire, white bracketing the siren's mouth. Annoyed at having her authority upturned, Max guessed, but also frightened. Lord Kolbyr had made a powerful impression on the normally confident detective.

"Fine," Ruutti said at length, the word a snap in the air. "I'll clear out the techs."

She stalked away.

Max watched her go for a moment, then turned to Audhilde. "You called him?" she asked, keeping her tone mild.

"He asked to be kept informed," the vampire said, not looking at Max. The normally bright and lively vampire was unusually subdued. Max did not pretend to understand the workings of vampire society, but from the way Audhilde had spoken, it sounded almost as if she had had no choice but to obey Kolbyr's request. "And he is the most knowledgeable person to ask."

"Assuming he didn't do this himself," Max said, then shook her head. "Although this seems too public and too crude for him."

"You flatter me," Lord Kolbyr said from far too close behind Max.

She jumped, but managed not to cry out, and turned to find the ancient vampire standing a few paces away. He was dressed in black, his skin shockingly pale in the fading sunlight. He was also smiling, apparently in genuine amusement, which made Max's skin crawl.

"Lord Kolbyr. You've ventured out of your home twice in the space of a few days. You honour us," Max said, choosing her words with care. Legend had it that vampires could smell a lie. Max did not want to find out if that was true or not.

"It's not often that one gets to see rituals for Him in real life," Kolbyr said, still with that smile. "Ah. I see the siren has everyone cleared away. Shall we go?"

"I assumed you'd want to inspect the site alone?" Max asked, staying where she was as the vampire moved forward.

"Thoughtful of you, but it will be more efficient if you all come with me. We can talk as we study," Kolbyr said. "You, too, Hilda. You might learn something."

Max very carefully did not look at Audhilde as she followed Lord Kolbyr across the broken surface to the body. She did not want to get in the way of whatever was going on between the two of them, even if it was simply vampire politics.

"My duty to you is done," Audhilde said, words short and clipped. She was walking beside Max, though. "I am here for curiosity. Nothing more."

"Of course, dear Hilda, of course. It should be fascinating," Kolbyr said, not looking at anyone, his attention focused on the scene in front of him.

He stopped without warning and Max managed to avoid treading on his heels, taking a couple of steps back to maintain a distance from him. Not that the distance would do much good. If Kolbyr or Audhilde decided to attack, then the far side of the city was the only safe distance.

Still, they were both being extremely civilised, wearing their human faces and behaving with their best approximation of how a human might behave.

And Max could not avoid looking at the body any longer.

The dead man had short hair crafted into spikes, the hair too white to be natural, and sallow, pockmarked skin on his face. And Max recognised him.

"This one is another magic user," she said, catching the attention of both vampires and Ruutti, who had followed them.

"You know him?" Ruutti asked.

"He came into the Hunter's Tooth a few times," Max said. "Thought he'd be a big player, as he could do a few magic tricks."

Audhilde made a sound that on a less dignified person would have been a snort. "Human?" she asked.

"Oh, yes," Max said. She took a step sideways and forward, closer to the body. "He went by the name of Nico. Had a place in the Hive," she added for Ruutti's benefit, naming the tightly knit warren of buildings that butted against the Barrows. "One of the taller blocks, I think. Anyone in there is likely to know him."

"He wasn't quiet, then," Ruutti said.

"No," Max said slowly, "used to brag about stupid stuff. Like tangling with a nest of crow spiders. Saying he'd single-handedly defeated them with magic."

"So, a liar as well as an idiot," Audhilde summarised.

"Indeed," Kolbyr said. "But whoever and whatever he was, he had attracted the attention of one of His worshippers."

"This is definitely a ritual for Arkus?" Max asked.

"Yes. It's not quite right, though. And there is some variance from the last one. Here, for instance, the symbol is the other way around," Kolbyr said.

Max almost asked him if he was sure. After all, he had only seen the previous ritual markings on Ruutti's tablet screen. But this was Lord Kolbyr, who had made a point of studying the sort of dark magic that would send most sane and sensible people running for their lives, screaming. If he said the ritual was different, it was different.

"Is there any way of telling if it was an accidental error or a deliberate choice?" Max asked. Ritual magic had been one of the few classes she had understood during her training. Write the symbols down as shown in the spell, say the activating word, and then the magic should rise. Simple. A far cry from the complex, formula-based magic that the Order used. Max's brain had simply refused to process and understand the mathematics involved in those calculations.

"An excellent question," Kolbyr said. He started walking in a slow circle around the body, staying outside the perimeter of the bloody symbols. "The symbols the maker has reversed attempt to change the nature of the spell from a summoning to a listening."

"The original spell was a summoning?" Max asked, words sticky and unpleasant in her mouth.

"Oh, yes. Now I see it in the entirety, it's quite clear. The last one was trying to summon. This one is trying to listen," Kolbyr said. His eyes were bright. He appeared to be enjoying himself.

"So the last spell was trying to bring something from the underworld into the daylight world," Ruutti said, sounding as sick as Max felt. "But it didn't work, right?"

"That is correct," Kolbyr said. He looked across at the detective, the human façade slipping for a moment and his true age and nature showing. Vampires in their natural form were inhumanly beautiful to look at, so beautiful that they were terrifying. At least in Max's eyes. A lot of people found the beauty mesmerising. It was another weapon that vampires wielded to draw in prey.

Max managed to hold her ground and kept her hands still by her sides. Not reaching for her weapon. Kolbyr was not threatening them, she told herself. He was just excited, which was almost worse. She remembered what he had said earlier, that it was rare to get the chance to study a ritual in real life. He might be one of the foremost authorities on dark magic, but most people who used dark magic used the lower-level spells, and for very personal, selfish reasons. Asking for fame or beauty or money. This was altogether different. Whoever had worked this ritual had been trying to break the barriers between this world and the world below. And even though they had not succeeded, they had raised enough power to shatter the ground again.

So Kolbyr was getting a rare chance to see the after-effects of powerful dark magic.

Max looked around the ritual markings again. "I don't see Arkus' symbol," she said.

"No," Kolbyr said. He was almost dancing from foot to foot in excitement. "The magician wasn't trying to contact the dark lord Himself."

"That seems like it should be good news," Max said slowly, "but why do I get the feeling it isn't?"

"We cannot tell what the purpose of the communication was. I can speculate," Kolbyr said.

"Please do," Max invited.

"The previous spell. The one of summoning. It did not work. So I may speculate that the magician was trying to find out why."

"Hold up. Let me understand this. You're saying that a human magician in this world killed another human and performed a ritual to let him ask some creature in the underworld why his spell didn't work?" Ruutti asked, sounding incredulous at the idea.

"Yes. That is my speculation," Kolbyr said. "Elegant, isn't it?"

"No," Ruutti said, sounding absolutely sure of that.

"That means it's most likely that the killer doesn't have access to other dark magic users or experts in this world," Max said. "He's working alone."

"That would seem correct," Kolbyr said, looking down at the ritual markings with something akin to regret on his face.

"You want him to succeed in bringing something from the underworld?" Audhilde asked, her tone one of respectful enquiry. At least on the surface. Audhilde was at least as old as Kolbyr, and just as accustomed to hiding her true nature. It made her an expert at deceit.

"It would be interesting," Kolbyr said. It wasn't really an answer, Max knew. For someone who studied dark magic, it was a less than enthusiastic response. A bare moment's thought gave her a possible reason why one of the world's foremost experts in dark magic did not want a being from the netherworld summoned to this one.

Kolbyr was powerful, as were all vampires. A master predator in an expensive suit.

But there were things in the netherworld powerful enough to chew Kolbyr up as if the vampire was nothing more than a light snack.

Kolbyr would not want to die. Nor would he want to be a servant to anything that might crawl out of the deep.

Even worse, anything that could frighten a vampire of Kolbyr's age and power would be able to destroy almost everyone else with less effort.

"We need to find and stop this killer. Fast," Max said.

Even as Ruutti was agreeing with Max, Kolbyr was moving forward, picking his way between the symbols on the cracked ground.

"Where are you going?" Ruutti asked. "This is a crime scene."

"I want to see what the message was," Kolbyr said.

Ruutti and Max exchanged puzzled looks, then turned to Audhilde, who shrugged. "This isn't my field of expertise. But if you want to find out what he knows, you should follow him."

Max went after Kolbyr, picking her way just as carefully between the ritual markings until she reached the space around the body. The daylight was fading fast, but there was still enough light for her to avoid stepping on the symbols. There was a narrow strip of blank ground around the body and Kolbyr was standing by the dead man's head, the vampire holding one hand in the air above the man's mouth.

"What are you doing?" Max asked.

"Don't you want to know what the killer heard?" Kolbyr seemed confused.

"I don't understand," Max said slowly. "What do you mean?"

"It will be easier to show you," Kolbyr said. He spread his fingers wide and icy spiders crawled down Max's back as the vampire gathered his power, speaking a few words in a language she did not understand.

The dead man's face twitched.

Max had her gun in her hand before she was aware of moving, the muzzle pointed at the dead man.

"Wait," Kolbyr told her sternly.

She waited, gun ready. Logic told her that the dead man could not possibly have moved. But there was magic involved. So perhaps logic was wrong. She kept her gun where it was. Just in case.

The face twitched again. No, she had not imagined it. The rest of the body did not move, so Max stayed still, gun in hand. She was vaguely aware of Ruutti beside her, with her gun out as well.

"Give us the message," Kolbyr commanded, power in his voice.

An awful gurgling sound emerged from the dead man's half-open mouth, the noise chilling Max all the way through and making her finger twitch on the trigger. After a moment, she recognised the sound as something like laughter.

"Keep looking." The dark, hollow voice came from between the dead man's lips before his face and mouth moved into an awful semblance of a grin before the magic faded, releasing the corpse back into stillness and death, face still in that terrible grin.

"*Keep looking*?" Max repeated. "That's the message from the underworld? Was that it?"

Kolbyr laughed his dry laugh. Having just heard the sound of laughter running through a dead man, the vampire's laughter was less chilling than it had been, but every hair on Max's body stood up and it took all her willpower to keep her gun trained on the dead man and not point it at Kolbyr.

"How wonderfully cryptic. The underworld has a sense of humour at least," the vampire said, still with that dry laughter in his voice. "Do put your guns down, my dears. They won't work on me, and he's already dead."

Chapter Fifteen

Max put her gun away, slowly and reluctantly. Beside her, Ruutti did the same.

The casual assurance from the vampire that their weapons would not work on him was unsettling. In Max's experience, it was possible to kill anything if she used enough bullets. She had a moment's temptation to try unloading a clip into Kolbyr and see if it did, indeed, have no effect. But if she didn't kill him outright, she would then have an angry vampire to deal with, and no means of defending herself. And he was not threatening them. Far from it, he had dismissed them from his attention already, turning back to the ritual markings.

"Ah," the vampire said a few moments later.

Max exchanged glances with Ruutti, the siren rolling her eyes. Trust Ruutti to spot an attention-seeking behaviour. The siren probably knew every trick there was.

"What have you found?" Max asked. The vampire wanted an audience. She wanted information. It seemed a reasonable trade-off.

"Absolutely fascinating. Do you see here, this series of five symbols?" Kolbyr asked.

"Yes," Max said, taking a carefully measured step through the markings to get a better look at what Kolbyr was pointing to.

"Well, from the first pictures, I had assumed this was an amateur. But these symbols have been made with no hesitation whatsoever."

Max waited for the vampire to continue.

When he stayed silent, she heard movement behind her. Ruutti.

"Well?" the siren asked.

"What, my dear?"

"What is the significance of there being no hesitation?" Ruutti asked, in a voice so sweet it had a diamond-hard edge.

"I am glad you asked. It means that this practitioner of yours is very skilled indeed. Yes. Very skilled. These symbols have been made with one continuous movement. You can tell by the thin lines."

Almost against her will, Max found herself crouching down to get a better look. As she did so, she saw what Kolbyr meant. The symbols were complex patterns that did not mean anything to her, but they had been drawn freehand on the hard surface of the games court, using the dead man's blood. And there was not one blot or smudge that Max could see.

"He's skilled," Max said, voice flat.

"Yes."

"So the rituals that he has drawn - the summoning before, and the communication here - they were not accidents. He hadn't stumbled across them. He's been practising his craft somewhere."

"Quite so, Marshal," Kolbyr said, his voice full of a warmth that made Max very aware of the short distance between them.

"But he is working alone," Max said slowly as she stood up, remembering their earlier discussion. The killer had changed the ritual around Nico to seek answers, wanting to find out why his previous effort had failed. And had received a message from the dark lord's realm to *keep looking* in return. Looking for what?

"And we should expect more bodies," Audhilde said, startling Max. The petite vampire was standing near Ruutti, arms folded across her middle. "Because the killer has been told to keep looking, he will keep going until he succeeds."

"Or until he is stopped," Max said, not really wanting to think about what might happen if the killer succeeded in his original plan. A summoning of something from the underworld. Max was absolutely certain she did not want to find out what that something might be.

"There is one piece of good news," Kolbyr said.

"Really?" Ruutti asked. "Please, tell us."

"The ritual was one of summoning, not of opening," the vampire pointed out.

"That is good news," Ruutti said, her voice flat. "The last thing we need is for some idiot to try to open the Grey Gates."

Memories flooded into Max's brain, blinding her to the here and now for a long, awful moment. *Smoke and screams. The stench of charred flesh.*

When she came back to herself, Audhilde and Ruutti were staring at Kolbyr and Max wondered what she had missed.

"You don't agree?" Ruutti asked the vampire.

"That the Grey Gates should remain closed? Of course that is sensible," the vampire said.

There was a short, charged silence in which Max tried not to think about the Grey Gates and failed.

"There are a few things we're missing here, I think," she said at length, looking back at Nico's body. "Lord Kolbyr, you've said this killer is skilled at dark magic. He knows what he's doing as far as the rituals are concerned. If that's the case, I don't understand why the last one didn't work."

"That is an excellent observation," Kolbyr said, favouring Max with a smile that made her want to reach for her gun again. It might not do any good against the vampire, but it would make her feel better to have it ready. "I would speculate that something was missing. But I cannot tell what that might be."

"More bodies," Audhilde repeated, as grim as Max had ever seen her. "And we should warn all magic users in the city to be alert."

"That would start a panic," Ruutti said at once. "The chief will never agree to it."

"Then he will need to explain his reasoning to the families of the next victims," Audhilde said bluntly, "and when the families ask me how this happened to their kin, I will send them to the chief of detectives for him to explain."

"If we can find a connection between the three victims so far, we might be able to narrow down the possible targets," Max said, before Ruutti could speak and say anything hot-tempered or unwise to one of the most powerful vampires in the city.

"Fine," Ruutti said, voice a snap. "I'll start asking around about this one. Nico, you said?"

"That's right. Malik might know more. I can ask him," Max offered. A trip to the Hunter's Tooth would be out of her way, but it was never a hardship to visit Malik.

"Let me try and find Nico's neighbours first," Ruutti said. "I might have more questions for Malik, too." There was an edge to her tone that Max could not place. Not anger. Something else. For a moment, Max wondered if she should warn Malik that the detective seemed to be in a mood with him. The moment passed almost at once. Malik could more than deal with one angry woman.

Before Max needed to make a response, Kolbyr held a small rectangular piece of white card out to her.

"You will call me when you learn more," he told her.

She took the card, because if she didn't it would probably be an insult. It was a plain white card with a number printed on it.

"That is my personal number," he told her.

"I do not work for you," Max told him, holding the card in front of her as if it might bite. "And Detective Passila is in charge of the investigation."

Kolbyr's already thin lips almost disappeared as he pressed them together. Displeased.

"And I don't work for you, either," Ruutti said, with more bluntness than normal, "but I would be happy to keep you informed if we find any other rituals or things you might find interesting."

Max's brows lifted. It was not like Ruutti to willingly share information.

Ruutti held her hand out to Max, reaching for the card.

"No," Kolbyr said. "I will not deal with you," he said. "Only you," he said to Max.

"Fine," Max said, cutting through whatever protests Ruutti might have made. She tucked the card into a pocket, thinking hard. "If Detective Passila gives me any information about rituals of the dark lord in relation to this case, I will pass it on to you," she told Kolbyr. It was not wise to lie to vampires. It was even less wise to make promises to them. Vampires regarded a promise as a sacred contract, not to be broken.

Kolbyr's brows lifted, eyes gleaming, and his lips twitched up into a smile. "Oh my dear, how very clever of you. Such a narrow, little promise. Very well. I accept. And now, I must go or I will be late for afternoon tea," he said, and drifted away.

"Afternoon tea?" Ruutti hissed to Max. "Who does that?"

"It's an important ritual in many of the older households," Audhilde said, a gleam of her usual mischief on her face.

"Why do I think that there might not be any tea involved?" Max asked.

Audhilde laughed, back to her normal manner. "Because you are smarter than you look, my child. Now, I must arrange transport for this unfortunate soul. Good day to you both," she said, and moved away as well.

Leaving Max standing next to Ruutti and a dead body on the abandoned games court with the last of the daylight fast fading around them. She looked around and wondered why the killer had chosen this location. Or indeed either of the others.

"As you don't need me, I'm going to do some research of my own," Max told Ruutti.

"Oh?" the detective asked. "What could be so important?"

"Why did the killer choose these places in particular? And is there any significance to the orientation of the bodies? They were all pointing the same way," Max noted. "I'll let you know if I find anything helpful."

"You better," Ruutti called after her.

Chapter Sixteen

Max's plans to do some research were hampered by another call from Therese, summoning her to the aid of local law enforcement again. It was a common enough request, and one Max could not ignore.

Sometimes the call-outs resulted in discoveries of things like Harridan nests or crow spider dens, particularly this close to a breach of the Wild wards. And sometimes they turned out to be nothing. Following up reports of sightings of "something big and hairy with lots of teeth", Max and her dogs spent most of the night combing through a warren of inter-connected buildings, searching for the creature or creatures. The buildings had once been three-storey high residential buildings, designed around what might have been a nice central garden space. By the time Max was carrying out her search, the central garden had long since become choked with weeds, all the apartments robbed out of anything useful.

Whatever might have been in the buildings, it had long gone. Cas and Pol followed some kind of scent trail, but it eventually led out of the complex. From the way they were behaving, Max could tell that whatever they had scented was harmless. She found no evidence of a nest or a den. She did, however, end up covered in ancient cobwebs and foul-smelling mud courtesy of a fallen-in section of the roof.

After heading home for a much-needed shower and some equally necessary sleep, Max woke close to noon, startled to find that she had slept for a decent length of time without nightmares. It had been a long time since she had had uninterrupted sleep. She even managed to cook breakfast from the contents of her fridge.

Before she could get too comfortable, or think about what she might do that day, her phone rang. It was Therese again. There had been another sighting of "something big and hairy with lots of teeth" a block away from the property Max had searched the night before.

Not looking forward to the prospect of another search through an abandoned building, Max made sure she had some cleaning spells with her when she got into the pick-up and set off for the new address.

It was a single, large building, this time, that looked like it had been an office block rather than a residential property. It was in slightly better condition than the complex from the night before, and Max spared a moment to hope she wouldn't end up covered in foul-smelling mud again.

The local police who had been called to the scene included a number of familiar faces, and Max exchanged a few greetings as she headed past them, making her way to the building's front door. These police knew better than to approach anything supernatural, or to get in the way of a Marshal and her job.

Along with Cas and Pol, Max started at the bottom and worked her way up. The bottom two floors were empty of all life, and had been robbed out of almost everything apart from the pillars supporting the building's structure. After clearing the first two floors, Cas and Pol went on alert, staring up the next flight of stairs. A moment later, Max heard a soft sound. Something moving on the floor above. She raised her shotgun and the dogs went ahead up the stairs, slow and steady, their bellies close to the ground. They had definitely sensed something.

The next floor had a few internal walls still standing. Max caught a glimpse of a shadow moving around the corner of one of the walls. Cas surged ahead, Pol heading off to one side, ready to trap whatever-it-was in a pincer movement.

Cas made a low, snarling sound when he saw whatever it was, menacing enough to raise the hairs at the back of Max's neck.

There was a squeak of what sounded like pure fright, and Cas barked, taking a step forward. He was in full hunting mode, teeth bared, claws extended.

Another squeak and something moved at the other side of the wall, creeping around the corner. It stopped when it saw Max, her shotgun levelled.

The thing was just slightly shorter than Max, with long, tangled brown hair all over its body and long, white incisors at its open mouth.

When it saw Max, it put up its hands. Max blinked. That had never happened before. Supernatural creatures generally attacked or ran away. They didn't stand still and assume a human posture of surrender. And then she narrowed her eyes. The thing was shadowed in the lee of the wall it was standing next to, but its face looked painted rather than real, the mouth fixed in an open position. A costume?

"Don't shoot," it said in a young, human voice.

Max was tempted to fire just on principle. "Take that damned headpiece off," she said.

The thing moved, pulling off the fearsome-looking head to reveal a very young-looking human male, short blond hair sticking out in all directions. He looked genuinely frightened.

"We were just having fun," he said. "We didn't mean any harm."

"We?" Max asked.

Before she could react, Pol surged across the floor, darting behind another wall. There was a startled yelp, then Pol appeared again, dragging another long-haired creature by one of its legs. Pol dragged the other creature across next to the unmasked human, then let it go, shaking his head as if trying to rid his mouth of a foul taste as he took a few steps back.

The second creature got to its feet.

"Mask off," Max said, her shotgun still pointed at the pair.

The second one pulled off its head piece to reveal another young blond male. They were both wide-eyed, gazes travelling between Max and her gun, and the dogs settled to either side of them.

"We didn't mean any harm," the second one said, voice too high and fast.

"Was that you last night as well? In the building three doors down?" Max demanded.

They giggled, which was answer enough.

She really wanted to shoot them. "Are there any more of you?" she demanded.

They exchanged a glance.

"Tell me before I send my dogs through the building," Max ordered.

"No. It's just us," the first one said, sounding surly. "We thought it would be fun."

"Fun? Do you know how much trouble you've caused? The police have been called out twice, and I spent hours searching that place last night, when I could have been doing actual work."

"Hours?" the second one said, grinning. "We had no idea."

"Get moving," Max said, using her gun to point to the stairs. "The police outside will have something to say to you."

"Oh, come on. It was just a laugh," the second said.

"And I'm sure the police will be highly entertained," Max said, waiting for them to move ahead of her into the stairwell.

"Do you have to point that gun at us?" the first one asked.

"Yes," Max said. "Just be grateful I haven't shot you yet. Get moving. Downstairs. Go."

As the pair descended the first flight of stairs down, giggling, a shadow moved overhead in the stairwell. Max paused, lifting her shotgun up, Cas and Pol moving to stand on either side of her, their focus on the upper floors.

"I thought you said there wasn't anyone else involved," Max said to the pair.

"There wasn't," the second one said.

"Then what is on the floors above us?" Max asked.

"I don't know. We hadn't got that far before you showed up," the first one said, sounding sulky again.

"Get out. Go outside of the building and report to the police there. The officer in charge is Sergeant Randall. Tell her that I'm clearing the building. Do not even think about running away. My dogs have your scent and they will find you," Max promised. The threat was probably unnecessary. Ellie Randall might hold the relatively low rank of Sergeant, but she was a formidable woman and would not let the pair of idiots escape without consequences.

The pair looked at Cas and Pol. Neither hound moved from their focus on the upper floors. Whatever was there was a lot more dangerous than a pair of idiot humans.

"Get going," Max instructed, when the pair of humans simply stood there. She turned her gun on them again. "Or I can shoot you?" There was a strong command given to all Marshals to try not to shoot or otherwise harm humans in the course of their work. But the shotgun was loaded with tranquilliser rounds, and she had a feeling that Faddei might forgive her some minor injuries in this case. The Marshals' resources were stretched thin as it was - the last thing they needed to be doing was chasing down idiots in costumes.

Something in what she said must have made an impression as the youngsters turned and began making their way down the stairs.

Max turned her attention back to the upper levels. Just in time to see another shadow cross one of the upper landings. On the top floor, two floors up, she thought. She waved Cas and Pol ahead of her. The dogs knew what to do without being told.

They took a moment to explore the next floor, just in case, while Max kept watch, but quickly came back to the stairwell and headed up. Max followed. She had a pair of spare magazines for the shotgun tucked into a loop next to her thigh holster, but spared a moment to wish she had brought more. It was impossible to have too many bullets, in her experience.

As soon as she set foot on the top level of the building, she knew something was very wrong. The feeling of powerful, dark magic crawled over her skin, the seven-pointed badge tucked into the front of her jacket warming enough that she could feel it against her chest, reacting to dangerous magic. The light around her faded to something closer to twilight.

Cas made a low, dark sound, and both dogs came back to Max's sides without being asked. Whatever was there had alarmed them enough that they wanted to stay close together. And her dogs were among the bravest creatures she had ever come across. Apprehension slid across her skin as she moved forward.

She stepped through the empty doorway to one side of the stairwell. The floor was mostly open, like the one where she had found the boys, with a few partial internal walls still standing and a number of structural pillars breaking up the space. There were a few bits of abandoned furniture here and there. The ugly beige floor tiles were mostly intact, with some large, dark stains on the ground that Max decided she didn't want to think about too much.

But what caught and held her attention were the markings on the floor, close to one of the outer edges. The daylight spilling in through the floor-to-ceiling windows was more than enough light for her to see a circle painted on the floor, with symbols inside it. At the centre of the circle was a small brazier, still burning, with a pot on top of it. A magician's spell circle. But this one was formed of dark magic.

Movement to one side of the circle drew her attention and she snapped her attention away from the circle. There was a partition wall there, and something next to the wall, surrounded by its own layer of darkness.

"Marshal's service," Max announced, hoping her voice sounded confident and firm and not high-pitched with adrenaline and tension. "Show yourself."

"Marshal, is it?" a voice said. It was soft, carrying more than a hint of smoke. The promise of searing heat and screams. "Little Miscellandreax. It's been too long."

Max's mouth went dry and her finger tightened on the trigger, but she managed not to fire. Only just. The temptation was strong. She knew that voice. It had spoken to her out of the dark, bringing nightmares to her childhood before she had known that monsters were real. As she had grown, she had realised that it was not normal to have a voice whispering to her while she lay huddled under her blankets on the thin, hard orphanage bed. No one else seemed to have an imaginary demon who spoke to them only at night, when everyone else was sleeping. The priestesses at the orphanage had dismissed her tales as attention-seeking nonsense, and a make-believe tale to justify Max's sluggishness in the mornings. She had been forbidden from speaking of it again. With threats of unspecified, awful punishment hanging over her head, she had ignored the voice as best she could and tried to stay awake through her lessons. And then she had been moved to the Order's training quarters, and the voice had never bothered her again. Until now.

She was no longer a child, and she now had extensive experience of monsters. The thing before her was not something out of her imagination, but was as real as she was, standing here in the daylight world. And if she needed any more proof of that, she only needed to look at the shadow-hounds beside her, who were absolutely focused on the whatever-it-was that was lurking in the darkness in front of them.

"Have we met?" Max asked. And her voice was still too high, but she didn't care about that now. Not now, faced with a nightmare made real.

"We have never been formally introduced," the voice said. The creature took a step forward, further into the light. The shadows around it moved, suggesting a far larger creature, but the shape that stepped away from the wall was human. It looked like a wealthy, ageing human man, complete with greying hair at his temples and the sort of deep, unnatural tan favoured by a lot of high-profile corporate types. The suit he was wearing looked custom-made, fitting his tall, slender form beautifully. The whole disguise was effective until she caught sight of his eyes, which were formed of smoke and held the promise of pain.

If she had been magic-blind, she would only have noticed his eyes. As it was, she could sense the foulness seeping through his immaculate tailoring even from across the room. Not just a creature of the dark, but a higher-order demon from the underworld here in the daylight world, wearing a human suit.

For an awful, stomach-churning moment, she wondered if she had been responsible for setting this thing loose in the world. If she had been too late in closing the Grey Gates, and some horrors had slipped through. Then she remembered the voice whispering in the dark in her childhood. The demon had been here for years before she had been sent to close the Gates. Perhaps even since the last time the Portents had shown and the Grey Gates had risen.

"Who are you?" Max demanded, keeping her gun levelled at him. The temptation to pull the trigger was strong. But he hadn't openly threatened her. Not yet.

"You would not be able to pronounce my true name. But you may call me Queran," he said, and inclined his head. "May I call you Max? That is the name you use now, yes?"

"You may call me Marshal," Max said through gritted teeth. "What are you doing here?" she asked. She couldn't risk taking her eyes off him to look at the spell circle.

"Just a little housekeeping," he said, waving a hand towards the circle.

"What does that mean?" Max asked.

"You really have grown to be a fine young woman," the demon said, baring his teeth in the parody of a smile. Queran. "Although I heard that the Order dismissed you. Such a shame. Didn't they appreciate your talents?"

"I'm asking the questions," Max said, grip tightening on the shotgun, skin crawling at a demon offering her compliments. The Order had not appreciated her any more than the orphanage had. She had been a mediocre student at the orphanage, too worn out from disrupted sleep to be effective, and a less than mediocre apprentice at the Order, consistently failing to meet her teachers' standards. It should have been a relief when Kitris dismissed her.

"I am shocked they couldn't see your potential," the demon said, smiling again. "You were one of my better projects," he told her.

"What in hells does that mean?" Max demanded.

"Oh, my dear, you are so young. Still quite unformed," Queran said. "Such a pity. Well, this has been delightful, but I really must be going. I've left a little gift for you. A bit slap-dash, as I didn't have much time to prepare. I didn't expect visitors, you see, but I do hope you like it."

"Stay where you are," Max ordered.

Queran ignored her, turning away and heading for one of the windows. Max fired.

The shotgun cartridge flew through the air, coming to a stop a few feet away from the demon. He turned and lifted a dark brow, shaking his head slightly.

"Dear me, you do have a lot to learn, don't you? I look forward to talking with you again soon, Miscellandreax."

Max pulled her handgun and fired again, hoping live ammunition might get through where the tranquilliser rounds had failed. The bullets got fractionally closer to the demon, but still stopped short of hitting him.

The demon didn't even turn around this time, instead stepping onto the window ledge and then disappearing from view.

Max ran across the floor, careful to skirt around the spell circle, and arrived at the empty window in time to see Queran on the ground far below, twitching his jacket back into place before he strode away, apparently unharmed from the long fall.

Before she could do anything reckless, a cold nose followed by a warm, familiar body pressed into the front of her legs. Pol. She glanced down, startled, realising she was almost at the very edge of the building. She gave in to the pressure from Pol's weight and moved back, Cas joining him so that she was surrounded by her dogs, unable to follow Queran even if she had wanted to. Their warmth and weight kept her still and safe. Running after a demon was not a sensible thing to do.

Max shoved her gun back in its holster. She still had the shotgun in her other hand, but if it hadn't hurt the demon in these close quarters, it wouldn't do anything at a distance. So she tucked the weapon under her arm and patted her dogs instead, mind spinning with what she had just learned.

The night visitor from her childhood was perfectly real. Not something she had made up. Queran was a higher-order demon, and seemed to be taking a close interest in her. That thought alone made her go cold. As powerful as Queran was, he existed at the whim of the dark lord Himself. It was never a good idea to attract the attention of His followers, let alone a demon from His court.

Before her thoughts could spiral down too far, spitting and hissing sounds from across the floor drew her attention, Cas and Pol moving away, coming on alert.

The spell circle. With the conversation with Queran still fresh in her mind, she had all but forgotten the dark magic the demon had left.

She raised her shotgun again as she turned to face the spell circle. The brazier at the centre of it was still burning. The pot had bubbled over, though, its lid falling to the ground, and what looked like molten metal spilling out and down the sides of the pot. As the spill hit the ground, and the markings on the floor, hissing filled the air and the metal rose again, beginning to mould into a form. She could not tell what it was supposed to be. Not yet. But anything formed of dark magic would not be good.

"What in the Lady's Name is *that*?" a familiar voice asked.

Startled, Max turned her shotgun to the stairwell, jerking it away as she recognised the tall, solid form of Sergeant Ellie Randall. The human policewoman was in uniform, her own shotgun held in front of her.

"Some kind of dark magic," Max said. "Is the rest of the building clear?"

"Yes. I heard the shots and saw that man walking away. Wanted to make sure you were ok," Ellie said. Her words were meant for Max, but her attention, and shotgun, were directed to the spell circle.

"That's not protocol," Max said automatically.

"You're welcome," Ellie said in a dry tone. Max felt heat rising to her face.

"Sorry. I mean, thank you for your concern. But please don't do that again. Wait for other Marshals."

"I can take care of myself," Ellie said, not backing down. Ellie was one of the few human women who could match Max's height, and was also a master in various martial arts. Max had seen her tackling armed suspects and taking them down single-handed while male colleagues stood around, worried by the weapons. She could more than take care of herself, in Max's estimation.

"I know you can. But we're trained for this sort of thing," Max said, moving across the floor, skirting around the circle again, and joining Ellie at the door to the stairwell. "Head out. I'll follow," she said.

Ellie shot Max a sideways glance, one brow lifting in open scepticism.

"Go," Max prompted.

Ellie took a step back into the stairwell.

Cas and Pol growled, the sound raising the hairs on the back of Max's neck again.

The whatever-it-was in the spell circle had grown and looked almost fully formed. It had four legs, a tail and a hound-shaped head.

Max's mouth was dry as she faced the thing. Queran had been cooking up a dark magic shadow-hound in his spell pot. Too late, she remembered he had referred to a little gift. Hastily prepared, he had said. She wondered if he had known how awful it would be for her to face a shadow-hound, or if he had simply picked a familiar shape to use.

It was difficult to kill shadow-hounds at the best of times, but one formed entirely of magic would not be taken down by any conventional means. Not even the many bullets that Max had about her person. She would need to use magic.

"Cas, Pol, guard it," she told them. Even if the thing was formed of magic, she couldn't ask her hounds to kill one of their own. She shoved her shotgun into a loop on her trouser leg and held her hands out together in front of her, palms up, the sides touching.

As she drew a slow, deep breath, searching for the calm she needed to work magic, she heard Orshiasa's voice in her mind. Her apprentice-master had been patient with her in the beginning, and there were a few lessons she had managed to learn before he gave up hope on her. This was one. *Imagine gathering light to you. The Lady's light is powerful against creatures of the dark. Gather the light and hold it in your hands.*

The tiniest of sparks formed on Max's palms. She drew another breath, feeling sweat breaking out all across her body, her legs trembling with the effort of holding herself up. She ignored that, focusing on the spell, the framework of lines and curves she had been taught, drawing in more of the Lady's light until the spark in her hands grew and grew and grew until it was as large as her head.

By then, the dark magic shadow-hound was nearly fully formed and was standing at the edge of the spell circle. It was the same size and shape as her hounds in their attack forms, and her eyes and senses battled for a moment, not wanting to fight the familiar shape. But she knew she could not trust her eyes. Not completely. This was not a living, breathing creature but a magical construct, and it was staring at her as if she were its prey, its smoke-grey lips peeled back to reveal icy fangs, its smoke-grey eyes filled with hate.

"Come and get me," Max invited.

The shadow-hound leapt, soaring out of the circle, its movements almost too fast to track.

A shotgun blasted just behind Max's head, deafening her. Both barrels. The shells soared through the magic hound, striking against one of the window supports. The hound glanced over its shoulder and Ellie cursed even as she reloaded her gun.

Max had no time to spare for the human woman, instead turning her hands and throwing the ball of light at the hound.

The light set fire to the hound's long, insubstantial fur. It howled, fury and pain combined, and whirled, heading straight for her.

Max took an involuntary step back, almost falling as her legs did not want to support her weight. The magic in her hands was almost down to a mere spark again. She had no time to call down more or think.

The hound barrelled into her, sending her backwards, off her feet, its hot, fetid breath washing over her face. It felt real. She could feel the fur brushing her exposed skin, feel the great weight of it pinning her down. It wasn't real, though. It had been called into being by a demon, and left here for her. A *gift*, Queran had said. How like a demon to leave a gift that wanted to kill her.

Acting on instinct, Max pushed up, shoving her hand with the tiny spark of light into the hound's mouth. She then grabbed hold of the hound's muzzle with both hands, holding it closed with as much strength as she could muster.

The magic creature writhed, trying to twist away. Max held on grimly, dragged across the floor as the hound tried to escape her. Smoke frothed out of the creature's nose, its fur catching on fire from inside.

The dark magic hound exploded, sending bits of insubstantial smoke scattering across the floor, and throwing Max backwards into one of the support pillars.

Max slid to the floor, trying to catch her breath. Being thrown across a room was nothing new. It hurt, though. It really hurt. Her heart ached with the memory of the long fur against her skin. It felt like she had just killed a shadow-hound. As if she had just destroyed one of Cas and Pol's brothers or sisters. Even though she knew, absolutely *knew*, that was not the case. She struggled to hold that knowledge to her, eyes streaming, lungs burning as she fought to breathe. There was no air for a long, long moment.

Dark shadows moved in front of her. Cas and Pol, standing guard. Making sure she had a tiny bit of space and time to breathe. Just breathe.

Her hounds were calm, settled, their eyes soft. They were real. She held onto that. They were real, flesh and blood and magic. They were alive and standing beside her. She had not betrayed them.

Air rushed back into her lungs, bringing fresh pain with it. She rolled to her side, taking huge, gasping, painful breaths.

"Are you alright?" Ellie asked. She was still standing by the stairwell, shotgun still ready. "Is that thing gone now?"

"Gone, yes," Max managed to say. It took an enormous effort to get her feet under her and to stand up, using the pillar for support. The world spun in a nauseating spiral and she rested her head against the pillar until the spinning stopped. "I'll heal," she added.

"What can I do?" Ellie asked.

"Give me a moment," Max said. She put a hand on Cas' shoulder, as he was nearest, and made her way, slowly, across the room to the spell circle. The pot was empty, the brazier fire dying. All the same, Max took a pouch of salt from her pocket and sprinkled some over the edge of the circle, tossing the rest onto the fire. That done, she turned and made her way back across the floor to Ellie, still using Cas for support. Her hound moved at her pace and was steady and firm. "You'll need one of the department magicians to clear the floor," Max said, her voice harsh and rasping in her ears. "It's safe," she added, "but it still needs to be cleaned."

"Will do," Ellie said. She had lowered her shotgun. She tilted her head at Max, her dark eyes assessing. "Does this happen a lot in your line of work?"

"Being thrown across a room by a ghost dog?" Max asked, trying to laugh and coughing instead. "More than I would like."

"Were those kids involved?" Ellie asked.

"I doubt it. They seemed to just be playing a stupid prank," Max said. "Did you arrest them?" she asked as she moved towards the stairs.

"I sure did. They told me that their father sits on the city council," Ellie said, her lip curling. She kept pace with Max as they started down the stairs. "I sent them off to be processed in the station, but I suspect by the time I get there, they'll be out."

"If you let me have their names and details, I'll pass that on to Faddei," Max said. The head Marshal would be equally unimpressed by their family line.

"Oh, now, there's an idea. The last pair of idiots who pressed a false report got to spend a few days with that gorgeous scientist clearing out the animal pens, didn't they?" Ellie said, eyes gleaming.

Max had to pause to process the phrase *gorgeous scientist*. "Do you mean Raymund? You think he's attractive?" she asked, startled.

"Oh, Max, that man is a brain on legs," Ellie said, with a sigh worthy of a teenager in her first crush.

Max choked on a laugh. On the surface, she could not imagine a more unlikely pairing. But then, Ellie was a powerful, formidably intelligent woman in her own right, and Raymund possessed a quiet sort of strength. Perhaps it wasn't such a strange combination.

"Have you ever actually spoken to him?" Max asked, trying to distract herself from the pain shooting through her body as she slowly made her way down the stairs.

"Once or twice. I'm not convinced he noticed I was there," Ellie said.

Ellie was trying to keep Max distracted, too, Max realised, a lump forming in her throat swiftly followed by wondering just how awful she really looked. There were sharp points of pain all the way up her back from where she had hit the pillar. It was possible she had broken some bones, although she hadn't heard anything crack that badly. Sighing, Max fumbled in one of her pockets and found a painkiller patch, applying it to the bare skin of her neck. The healing magic eased off the worst of the physical hurt, at least, keeping her upright as she and Ellie made their way out of the building, Cas and Pol at their heels, into the grey day.

As they were leaving the building, Max's phone rang. Therese. Max wondered, not for the first time, if the woman had some kind of magical tracker on Marshals. She always seemed to call just as one job was finishing.

"What?" Max said. Ellie's brows lifted at her rude tone.

"There's a shipment of anti-venom injectors at the clinic for us. You need to pick them up and bring them to the armoury," Therese said, and hung up.

Leaving Max staring at the phone, wondering just what she had done to deserve such an ordinary assignment. Still, it would be nice to simply sit and drive for a little bit and not get into another fight.

Chapter Seventeen

By the time Max had collected the box of anti-venom injectors from the clinic and transported them to the Marshals' compound, darkness had fallen. The painkiller she had used earlier had long since worn off, and she had discarded the patch in one of the clinic's medical waste bins. She was stiff and sore as she got out of her pick-up to deliver the injectors to the armoury.

At least she had stopped for some food on the way across the city, the dogs staring at her with single-minded focus as she ate her meal. Apparently, they had not been impressed with getting dog food when there was human food so close to them.

She found Faddei outside the armoury, talking to Leonda. Cas and Pol made a beeline for Leonda, apparently ecstatic to see her, their tails wagging furiously.

"You look awful," Leonda said to Max, even as she bent to pat the dogs clamouring for her attention. "What happened?"

"I ran into a demon and a dark magic shadow-hound," Max said.

Leonda blinked, straightening up and taking the box of injectors from Max's hands. "That doesn't sound like a normal day," she said, and glanced at Faddei. Leonda had never been out into the field, but she had a good sense of what the Marshals dealt with. She needed to, in order to do her job.

"I'd like to hear more about that," Faddei said. He eyed Max up and down. "There's coffee and some pastries in the staff room," he said.

"Alright," Max said. "Leonda, can Cas and Pol visit with you for a while?"

"As long as you like," Leonda said at once, smiling. "I'm going to be here most of the night."

"Thank you," Max said, and walked with Faddei out of the building and two buildings further down. As she moved, she became aware of the various bruises around her body. It was going to be a few days before she fully healed. Assuming she was given the chance. The Marshals seemed to have been unusually busy the past few weeks, particularly after the breach of the Wild wards.

What Faddei described as the staff room was an all-purpose, large room which had a few comfortable seats, including some sofas which Marshals occasionally used to sleep on, and a haphazard collection of desks for the rare occasions that the Marshals actually got time to work on the reports that Faddei and Therese liked them to file. There was also a large set of shelves on one side of the room. None of the Marshals had an assigned desk, but they all had assigned shelves for their personal effects.

The room was empty of people, but filled with the smell of fresh brewed coffee.

Faddei waved Max to one of the comfortable chairs and went over to the coffee machine, bringing back two cups and a paper bag, which he handed to Max. She opened the bag, somehow not surprised to find one of her favourite pastries inside. Faddei was an observant boss, and had probably memorised the food and drink preferences of everyone in the Marshals' service. It didn't make up for the extra long hours, but it definitely helped. She set the pastry aside for the moment, curling her hands around the mug and letting the warmth seep into her. She sat back in the chair with some care, easing her back up against the cushions.

"A demon?" Faddei prompted. He was concerned, Max saw. As well he should be. The Marshals were equipped to deal with supernatural creatures of all shapes and sizes, but a demon was something else entirely.

Max stared into her coffee for a moment, wondering how much to tell him. How much would be safe? Faddei knew more about her and her background than anyone else in the service. She trusted him. Mostly.

"Whatever it is, I'll listen," he said softly. He had sat at an angle from her, so they weren't face to face. She turned slightly and assessed him. He looked tired, too. He might not go into the field any longer, with the injuries he'd suffered, but he would have been working just as hard as everyone else. And had the added stress of the city politics to deal with.

Max set her coffee to one side and ran her hands through her hair, scrubbing her face.

"The demon said I could call him Queran," she began, linking her hands together in her lap and staring at them instead of Faddei. "I've met him before. When I was a child. He used to whisper to me at night."

"Sounds unpleasant," Faddei said. His voice was calm.

The acceptance of what she was saying loosened some tight knot in Max's chest she hadn't been aware of carrying until then. She was being believed.

"I never actually saw him before today. And he disappeared when I moved into the Order. Until now. I think he was waiting for me today," she said slowly, the truth of that settling on her shoulders. "But I don't know why."

"We'll figure it out," Faddei said, still with that infinite reserve of calm.

"Well. Anyway. Today he had made a spell circle with a brazier and a pot in the middle of it. When he left, the pot boiled over and a shadow-hound emerged. Not a real one. I mean, not a flesh-and-blood one. A dark magic one."

"You destroyed it?" Faddei asked.

"Yes," she said, not looking at him. She picked up her coffee, ducking her head towards it, hoping it would hide the tears gathered in her eyes. She had killed a shadow-hound. One that was trying to kill her, yes, but it still hurt.

"That must have been difficult," Faddei commented. She glanced across and saw nothing but concern on this face. "Do we need to send clean up?"

"Ellie Randall was there. I told her to get one of the city magicians to clean the area," Max said. "The circle was dead when I left it," she added. It had fulfilled its purpose.

Her eyes were still stinging, a spark of anger warming her as she wondered if Queran had truly meant to kill her, and why. As she had told Faddei, she had not heard him whispering to her since she joined the Order. But the demon had remembered her. Had recognised her. And he had spent a lot of time tormenting her in her childhood. The anger was smothered by ice as she wondered just what she had done to deserve the attention of one of Arkus' demons.

"I'll check in with them later," Faddei nodded. "You've no idea why the demon was there?" he asked. It was almost a statement, rather than a question. He wasn't accusing her of anything, just seeking confirmation.

"No, no idea." Max clamped her jaw shut, then let out some of the words bottled up in her mind. "I've no idea why he picked me when I was a child, or why he tried to kill me today." Or even if that had been his intent, she added in her mind. A stronger magician, or one with more training in combating dark magic, probably would have been able to counter the spell before the shadow-hound had got loose.

"Make sure you have salt on you at all times," Faddei said, perfectly serious. It was a standard ingredient for Marshals to carry. It wouldn't stop a demon, but it should cancel out a lot of dark magic. "And let me know immediately if you sense him again. I know you won't want to call on them, but demons are more the Order's business than ours."

"I know," Max said, not looking at him. He knew her well enough to understand that inviting the Order into her life was the last thing she wanted. Even if it was the proper thing to do. She glared at the surface of her coffee, wondering what the chances were of never seeing Queran again.

"I will let the Order know we have a demon in the city," Faddei said. "No more than that."

"Thank you," Max said around a lump in her throat. Faddei would protect her identity, as he would any one of the Marshals, she was sure, and that certainty made her eyes sting.

"The Marshals' service is just as necessary to the smooth running of this city as the Order," Faddei pointed out, in a mild tone that made Max smile. Every Marshal knew that, among all the other things that were true in the world, Faddei would fight for them.

"Oh, before I forget, the call out from last night, and the one today, was a hoax. Two idiots in costumes. Ellie has them in custody, but she thinks that they'll be released soon. Their father is on the council," Max said, hearing the bitterness in her voice.

"They had got the police and a Marshal out to investigate twice?" Faddei asked. He still sounded mild, but Max could hear the edge to his tone. If there was one thing guaranteed to set fire to his temper, it was someone wasting Marshal resources and time.

"Yes," Max said. "Ellie is going to send me the details." She hesitated, and glanced at her boss. "I thought you might like the information."

Faddei's mouth curved up in a small, hard smile. "I would, indeed. Send the information on when you get it. I'll make sure it's dealt with."

Max nodded and finally managed a sip of her coffee, brows rising. "How much healing did you put in this?" she asked. For all his tough appearance, Faddei had a gift for gentle healing magic. The drink he had given her was laced with it.

"A little," Faddei admitted. "You looked like you were about to fall over," he added.

Even that one sip had made her feel better. She thanked him and drank most of the rest of the mug, then turned her attention to the pastry while Faddei asked her questions about her encounter with the demon. He didn't ask too much about the hound, which she was silently grateful for. Queran was the real threat, after all.

By the time Faddei was done with his questions and Max had finished her drink and snack, she was feeling almost back to normal and somehow lighter. She had shared a childhood secret and had been believed, not dismissed.

Faddei had told her to take the rest of the day off, which had made her laugh as it was already into the evening. But as she put her mug into the dishwasher, she remembered that she had research to do. With her body almost healed, and fuelled with caffeine, it seemed a good time for that.

The Marshals' library took up the entirety of one of the mid-sized buildings in the Marshals' complex. In defiance of his warrior-like appearance, Faddei had made it a core principle of his leadership that the Marshals should have access to as much information as was available and that might be useful to them. So the very ordinary-looking concrete building housed floor-to-ceiling racks of books, folios, scrolls, and included maps of the city. Not content with amassing as much printed or written material as possible, the resources included shelves of outdated video tapes and more modern electronic storage, as well as network access to the city's databases.

From what she knew of Faddei, Max suspected that this was as much to fuel Faddei's love of knowledge as to support the Marshals. Faddei loved learning, and wasn't too particular about what it was. There were manuals on treating wounds in combat alongside texts describing the various orders of demons that might exist in the underworld and even a few works of fiction that featured supernatural creatures, or things from the world below.

Whatever the reason behind it, when she needed to do research, the Marshals' library was the obvious place to start. If there was an answer to the questions she had about the city and the alignment of the bodies, Max was confident she would find it within the library. Or, at the very least, find clues to where she might look next.

Happy in the knowledge that Cas and Pol were being spoiled in Leonda's presence, knowing that would please all of them, Max took her Marshal-provided laptop, a large notebook and pens and headed for the library.

There was no one else around when she went in and settled herself at one of the large tables, beginning to pull information from the shelves and racks around her.

Several hours later, Max straightened in her chair and stretched, hearing and feeling her joints crack. She had been sitting too long. She got up to stretch more fully, wrinkling her nose as she looked at the mess she had created.

The large desk was covered with books and print-outs. The notebook pages were covered with her scruffy handwriting. She had set her ammunition belt, gun and one of her knives on the desk as well, tired of them poking into her as she studied. The laptop was somewhere underneath the mountain of papers, but as usual, she had preferred to write her notes out rather than type them.

Her head was spinning with newly acquired information from historic maps of the city to possible reasons for the alignment of the bodies to the information on summoning spells she had been able to find. All the information was too new to have settled into her mind, and she didn't know what to make of it. Not yet. And there was a foul taste in her mouth from some of the things she had read about summoning spells and the sacrifices used to complete the spells. The knife cuts that the killer was using were far from the worst thing he could be doing to his victims, and Max wished she could erase some of the other options from her mind.

Seeking distraction, she looked around. The large room was dark and deserted, with only the reading lights around and above her desk on. In the shadows beyond her pool of light, she could sense the height and depth of the building. She took a moment to be grateful for Faddei's thirst for knowledge, and his and Therese's efficient gathering and cataloguing of information about the city, including as much of the history of the land as they could find. What Max hadn't been able to find in the library, she'd been able to access through the laptop and the city's current records of layout and ownership.

It hadn't taken her long, looking through the city records, to come up with a possible explanation as to why the killer had chosen the places he had. But it had taken her a lot longer to accept that it might be a real reason.

Among the records in the library was an old set of maps that purported to trace the ley lines that ran across the city. The supposed lines of power that ran across the world, having some mystic significance that Max didn't understand. Someone had mapped them onto the city. Or, rather, the city as it had been, when the Wild had been many miles away and the core of the city had been surrounded by farms and industry. Max had managed to overlay the current city map, and the murder sites, over the old map. Each of the sites was on an intersection of ley lines.

Modern magicians ridiculed the idea that there could be untapped power beneath the earth. But older magicians had taken it seriously, as demonstrated by the fact that they had gone to the trouble of mapping them, using methods that had seemed to Max to be more based in superstition than actual magic.

Whatever the truth, it seemed too much coincidence that the killer had somehow chosen sites which all matched up with the supposed intersections of ley lines in the city. At the crossroads of a side street. At the games court. Outside one of the Lady's temples.

Even with the evidence in front of her eyes, Max still struggled to accept it. She remembered one of her early teachers laughing at the notion of ley lines. The Order had adopted similar teaching - ley lines were the magical equivalent of a witch's pointy hat. Nothing more than fanciful day dreaming by people who didn't understand magic.

And yet, each of the murder sites matched perfectly with a supposed intersection of ley lines, and she hadn't come up with any other connection between the sites. So now she was left frowning into middle-distance, trying to work out if she needed to change a lifetime of thinking and consider the possibility of ley lines.

"Are you finished, Marshal?"

The voice came out of the darkness and Max jumped, reaching for her gun before her brain caught up with the words and she recognised the speaker. She left the gun alone and turned towards the voice.

"Librarian. You startled me," she said.

"I am sorry," the voice said, sounding sincere. A small, human-shaped figure detached itself from the shadows, coming into the pool of light. "I thought you knew I was here."

"I should have remembered," Max said, ducking away from the Librarian's gaze. She should, indeed, have remembered. The Librarian was always present, in one way or another, even if it wasn't seen. Max had no idea what, exactly, the creature was or what kind of bargain Faddei had made with it to keep it here, tending to the Marshals' repository of knowledge. The Librarian might wear a human shape, but Max was sure its natural form was something much more deadly. Just now it was a pale cream colour from head to toe, its face a deeper shade of cream, as if it was wearing a sports bodysuit with only its face uncovered. And even then, describing it as a face was not strictly accurate. There were features, yes, but the Librarian's face was more like a blank shop mannequin. "And yes, I think I am finished," Max said, remembering the question.

"Then I will put everything away," the Librarian said.

"A moment, please," Max said, before the Librarian could move. On one of her first visits to the library, she had learned that the Librarian was very literal. If the creature said it was going to put everything away, it meant exactly what it had said, and Max would find her gun, ammunition and knife included in the library's collection of oddities. And once something was part of the library, the Librarian did not give it up easily. "Let me collect my belongings first," she told the Librarian.

"Of course, Marshal," the Librarian said. It took a step back and waited, with apparently endless patience, while Max sorted through the mess on the table, gathering her possessions along with her notebook, pens, the print-outs she had made, and the laptop. That done, she took another look through everything to make sure she hadn't accidentally left something behind.

"I have collected my belongings," she told the Librarian. It was best to be clear and careful with the creature. "You may put away what is on the table surface."

"Very good, Marshal." The creature moved forward to the table and picked up the nearest book, barely glancing at the spine before heading into the shadows to shelve it again.

"Thank you, Librarian. Good night," Max called.

"Good night to you, Marshal," the Librarian said.

Chapter Eighteen

Max headed back to the Marshals' office to drop off her laptop, notebook and papers, finding a stack of slips of paper on her assigned shelf. Telephone messages, in Therese's distinctive handwriting.

Max's brows lifted as she flicked through the messages. It seemed that Ruutti wanted to speak with her.

Max pulled her phone out, finding over a dozen missed calls from the detective and the voicemail icon blinking, which suggested that the detective had left a verbal message, too. The magic around the library stopped all phone signals, so she had had a stretch of uninterrupted time to study.

With a sigh, she leaned against the wall and dialled the detective's number. It was past midnight, but she thought that the detective would still be awake. Her call was answered on the second ring.

"Finally. I've been calling for hours. Why didn't you answer?" Ruutti's voice demanded.

"I've been busy," Max answered. "What do you want?"

"There's been another killing," Ruutti said. Something in her voice caught Max's attention. The detective was worried.

"Where?" Max asked.

Ruutti gave an address that made Max straighten away from the wall, grabbing the notebook and print-outs from her shelf. The address was closer to the heart of the city than the previous killings, which was bad enough. Worse, it was on the same street as one of the Lady's temples, and Max could only imagine the attention that would be getting.

"I'll be there as soon as I can," Max said, already on her way out the door.

Ruutti hung up without another word.

Cas and Pol came to Max's call, bounding out into the night and into the pick-up as if expecting to go on a grand adventure. Max gave each of them a pat, then settled behind the wheel, the notebook and papers on the passenger seat.

She drove as fast as the pick-up would allow, away from the Marshals' compound and towards the city.

With the address being close to one of the temples, she was not surprised to encounter a checkpoint about a block away from the address she had been given. The city police had set up flimsy wooden barricades designed to let only one car at a time go through, providing the police approved it, of course. Never mind that the barricades wouldn't stop anything really determined to get through.

Max pulled to a stop as requested by the police and rolled down her window, pulling her badge out to show to the young policeman approaching her driver's side.

"Marshals don't have jurisdiction in the city," the young man told her.

"Really?" Max said, blinking. "That's new. When did that happen?"

"Stop being a pompous ass, rookie," a familiar, deeper voice said from a few paces away. "Let the Marshal pass."

"Thanks, Ellie," Max called.

"Any time, Max," the tall woman said, waving.

Max pulled away, and in the rear-view mirror saw the rookie turning on his superior officer, shoulders squared. She shook her head. The rookie had no idea who he was dealing with.

Then she turned the next corner and forgot all about petty, power-hungry youngsters as the night sky was lit by what looked like an entire army's worth of red and blue lights. Closer to the ground, the spinning colours mingled with distorted shadows as people walked past vehicle headlights. It looked like most of the city police division was there, along with the white-suited crime scene techs. Max saw the familiar figure of Audhilde in the midst of the techs.

Max found a spot for her pick-up and left Cas and Pol in the back, the pair of hounds keeping an eye on things as she walked towards the chaos. She made sure her Marshal's badge was visible, the seven-pointed star catching the light as she walked.

There was a young female officer standing beside the nearest police vehicle, looking pale and shaken. Max recognised her from the night of the Harridan nest, and wondered if the square-jawed Sergeant Williams was present, too. The new female officer was seeing far more of the Marshals than she had likely ever expected. The rookie took in the Marshal's badge and swallowed, seeming to pale in the uncertain light. Max kept walking.

Ruutti was easy to find. She was in an isolated space, standing with a pair of men. The younger one, with close-cropped red hair, was someone Max had only seen from a distance before. He was dressed in a similar way to Ruutti, with jeans, t-shirt and a leather jacket. He towered over the petite woman and had the sort of physical bulk that came from working out at a gym. Evan Yarwood, the chief of detectives, and Ruutti's ultimate boss. Max didn't know much about him apart from that he was the youngest person to ever make the rank of chief. The other man was wearing a poorly fitting suit, despite it being the middle of the night. Probably some local council member, but Max did not think she had seen him before.

Beyond the glare of the lights, the Lady's temple rose into the night, the temple grounds stretching to either side, the faintest scent of green life carrying through the night. The temple itself looked serene despite the chaos not far away. The front had the usual six plain stone columns, rising at least three stories above the street. Between the columns, Max caught a glimpse of watchers. The Lady's priests and priestesses, no doubt wondering when the garish lights would be gone and they could get back to their devotions.

It would be a while, though. The city would not want to risk the Lady's wrath by doing a poor job of investigating a killing in front of one of Her Houses.

"There you are," Ruutti said, sounding almost relieved.

From the detective, that was very close to being a warm welcome and unexpected enough to make Max blink. Then she saw the rigid postures of the two men next to Ruutti and made a quick calculation. The men were not happy with the detective's progress, and doubtless Ruutti was glad to have someone else to share the blame.

"What do we have?" Max asked, ignoring the men.

"Come, I'll show you," Ruutti said, and took a step away from the men.

"We're not finished, detective," the older man said. Max disliked him at once. He was barely taller than Ruutti, plump around the middle, with a soft, pale face and a large, damp mouth. He had thinning hair that looked as if he had dyed it himself and then combed it over his head to try to hide what Max imagined was a growing bald spot on his crown. From her higher viewpoint, she could have told him that the attempted disguise was not working.

"Sir," Ruutti said, with forced patience, "the sooner we can get to work, the sooner we can put a stop to this."

The man glared at her, clearly not used to being spoken back to. Interestingly, he didn't appeal to the chief of detectives for support. The chief had a tight expression, but was letting the older man speak. There was some kind of power play going on between the two that Max wanted no part of. Then the shorter man turned to Max. "Who are you?"

"Marshal Ortis. Who are you?" Max demanded, in the same tone the man had used.

"What? You don't recognise me?" the man asked.

"Should I?" Max asked.

"David Prosser. I am the councilman for this district. I expect this to be dealt with swiftly and discreetly," he spluttered. Councilman. Max had guessed right. The position explained the bad suit and the entitled attitude. And why the chief of detectives was letting him run his mouth. Technically, the chief reported to the council.

"I can't help you with the discreet part," Max said, glancing at the circus of vehicles and people around them, "but I will work as fast as I can. Detective?"

"Yes," Ruutti said.

This time, when they stalked away, heading for Audhilde, no one called them back. Even though they were walking towards a body, Max was relieved to be away from the petty politics between the two men.

Audhilde was waiting for them, a serious expression on her face.

"The killer didn't get a chance to do the ritual this time," she told them. "If I had to guess, I would say that the victim died of an asthma attack. Doubtless brought on by stress," she added. "And it's a woman this time," she added.

"Show me," Max requested.

Audhilde led Max and Ruutti the short distance to where a cloth-covered form lay on the ground. She nodded to a nearby tech, who carefully lifted the cover away.

There was a young woman lying on the road surface, her eyes staring up into the night sky, face frozen with her mouth open, the faint traces of tears on her cheeks. She had died lying on her back, her arms out to either side, legs straight. She was wearing jeans and a sleeveless t-shirt. There was a series of cut marks on one of her arms, but she was otherwise untouched.

The woman had vivid pink hair, spiralling around her head, and a tattoo sleeve of ancient runic writing on her uninjured arm.

"Jessica Walsh," Max said, crouching down by the injured arm, a sick feeling gathering in her stomach.

"You know her?" Ruutti demanded.

"I've come across her before," Max said, not looking up from the body. "I wouldn't say I knew her. She came into the Hunter's Tooth a few times." When Max had still been with Malik, and spending more time in the bar. Jessica's hair had been orange then, but the tattoo sleeve was unmistakable and now that Max looked at her more closely, Max recognised her face as well. "She was a mid-level magician. Liked to play for a crowd," she said. Young, arrogant and hot-headed, from what Max remembered.

"Walsh," Audhilde said slowly. "As in Connor Declan Walsh?" she asked, naming one of the most powerful men in the city. One of the men who, like Lord Kolbyr, owned an entire city block. Walsh was human through and through, his power coming from vast wealth and a large family all loyal to their house.

"The same. Her uncle, I think," Max said, glancing up.

"You have got to be kidding me," Ruutti said, sounding disgusted.

"Do they know?" Max asked Ruutti, tilting her head towards the chief of detectives and councilman, who were still standing together.

"No," Ruutti said, with absolute confidence. "If they did, the entire city council would be here. They're here because of the temple," she added.

"We'll need to tell them," Audhilde said, words clipped. "They will need to find a way of managing Walsh."

Max let the discussion wash over her head. There was no managing someone like Walsh, she knew. And Audhilde knew as well. Once the head of one of the most powerful families in the city found out that one of his kin had been killed and the police didn't have any concrete leads, he would send out his own people to get answers. And he wouldn't care who got hurt in the quest for information. Finding out that she was the fourth victim would only enrage him further.

It would get ugly, Max knew. The city police might think they had a grip on human affairs and control of the city's streets. But it was an illusion. There were far too many arrogant and powerful people in too tight a space. People who had lost vast tracts of land, but not their fortunes, when the Wild had expanded a decade before. Tensions simmered under the surface all the time, bubbling up now and then. It was all politics and power-plays, and Max was glad she didn't have to deal with it. Patrolling the Wild, and dealing with the creatures that occasionally broke through, were simple and direct tasks. And she rarely had to cross the invisible line that separated the inner city from the outer districts.

Old man Walsh would want to know why his niece had been targeted. And, looking down at Jessica's frozen face, Max's stomach turned again. There was a reason why Max remembered the girl. She had breezed into the Hunter's Tooth, over-confident and seeking a court of admirers among the misfits and non-humans that often settled in the bar. When she had not got what she wanted, she had started dropping unsubtle hints that they should be grateful to her. That she had saved the world. When that didn't get her very far - as the patrons were used to boastful humans - she had outright said that she had been the one to close the Grey Gates, locking the dark lord away in His realm for ever more.

Talk of the dark lord, Portents and the Grey Gates might not be common in the mostly human city, but magicians liked to gossip as much as anyone else, and almost everyone with any magical ability had their own ideas about what had happened eight years before, and what had stopped Arkus from rising.

No one in the Hunter's Tooth had believed Jessica's boasting. Disappointed with the lack of reaction, she had left.

But if Jessica had told a group of strangers in an out-of-the-way bar that she had closed the Grey Gates, Max could easily imagine the girl might have repeated the lie elsewhere. And that might have attracted the wrong attention. Someone might have believed her.

Max's mouth was dry, her skin crawling. The last victim, Nico, had been a boastful one, too. She could easily imagine him dropping hints that he had somehow been involved in saving the world. No one with any real magical ability would believe him. He had been far too weak a magician, and a coward. At the first cut of a knife, he would have confessed the lie.

But she couldn't ignore that common point between Jessica and Nico. Both of them prone to boasting, and most likely both claiming connections to the underworld that they didn't have. Max's breath caught, heart rate picking up. Was that it? Was that what the killer was looking for?

Max remembered the message from the underworld - *keep looking*. Keep looking for the missing ingredient to the summoning spell? The spell that was designed to break through the barriers between realms and pull something up from the underworld.

A chill crept over Max's skin. If Jessica had been chosen because the killer thought that she had been into the underworld, had that been the reason for choosing the others, too? The killer was seeking a way to access the dark lord's realm, and Max could all too easily see how the killer would believe that the blood or power of someone who had been to the underworld was key to his - or her - plans. That person's blood and power would still, after all these years, carry a trace of the underworld in it. Just enough to add extra power to a summoning spell. Just enough to break through the Grey Gates and bring forth whatever the killer was trying to reach.

There was just one problem. None of the people the killer had targeted so far had ever been close to the underworld, let alone closed the Grey Gates eight years ago.

The person who had done that, and whose blood the killer was looking for, was Max. Her fingers and palms itched again with the phantom trace of searing heat, the metal firm under her hands as she pushed the Gates closed. She swallowed, trying to push the memories away. She didn't want to remember.

Not that anyone would believe her. Kitris certainly hadn't, when she had returned to his office, still healing from the wounds she had received, her scalp still bare from the fires that had burned away her hair. He had expected her to die, she remembered. And she had realised, a hole opening up inside her, that he had wanted her to die. She had been the sacrifice. Something he was more than willing to discard. The price of closing the Grey Gates. And as she had been standing in his office, he had not believed her when she had told him that the Gates were closed. That she had closed them.

But she had. She remembered standing in the entrance to the underworld, battered by invisible winds, skin scorched by the sparks that filled the air, her fingers closing around the molten metal of the first set of Grey Gates, using every part of her strength and will to push the gates closed, to seal the breach into the world below. Her mouth had been open in a silent scream, her voice long since gone, every part of her in blinding agony.

The Grey Gates had closed. She had left bits of her skin and blood behind when she had taken her hands away. Job done. The task that had been required of her completed.

At a far, far higher cost than her younger self had ever imagined possible. The entire team of warriors that Kitris had sent with her had died. And she had seen things in the underworld that she had no name for but which still dragged her from sleep to this day, bathed in sweat.

With all the horror and memories still so fresh, she had not been able to understand Kitris at first. Then when his absolute rejection of her had sunk in, that he had not believed her, and that he was dismissing her completely, she had been too numb for it to properly hurt. Not then.

"Max?"

Ruutti's voice cut through memories, and Max realised she was still crouched beside the body of Jessica Walsh, in the middle of the street outside one of the Lady's temples, in full view of dozens of people.

"Are you alright?" Audhilde asked. The vampire had crouched down beside Max, and was holding out a square of white cloth. Max stared at it for a while, her vision blurred, and then realised she was crying. She took the handkerchief and wiped her face, swallowing the hard lump in her throat.

"Sorry," she said, her voice harsh. "Bad memories," she said, straightening to her feet, hoping that neither Ruutti nor Audhilde would ask for more. They likely had bad memories of their own.

"We're sure this is the same killer?" Ruutti was asking Audhilde as Max drew a deep breath. It sounded like a question the detective had already asked more than once.

"I am," Audhilde said, her tone leaving no room for argument.

Ruutti cursed under her breath. "So, we have four victims so far. That we know of, anyway. All of them low- or mid-level magicians."

"Have you been able to find any connection between the others?" Max asked, voice harsh.

Ruutti sent her a frowning glance. "The only thing I've been able to find is that they all liked to pretend they were more powerful than they really were," she said slowly. "At least, that was true of the others. I need to make enquiries about this one."

"Same," Max said, skin prickling. "She liked attention." She tilted her head, remembering Jessica in the Hunter's Tooth. If the girl was looking for low-level wannabes, the next obvious place to try was the Sorcerer's Mistress. Max sighed. "Looks like we'll need to go back to the Sorcerer's Mistress," she said. "It's the sort of place that Jessica would go."

"I'll do that," Ruutti said.

Her tone was sharp enough that both Max and Audhilde looked at her.

"I've been there once already," Ruutti said, taking a notebook out of her pocket, avoiding their eyes as she made a note. "It makes sense for me to go again."

It sounded perfectly reasonable. And Max did not believe a word of it. Glancing at Audhilde, she saw that the vampire didn't believe her, either. It was almost impossible to lie to a vampire. Their sharper senses could pick up changes in breathing and heart rates that occurred when most people lied.

"When will you go?" Max asked, voice mild, as if accepting Ruutti's suggestion.

"As soon as I can," Ruutti said, face tightening as she looked back over the scene. "It's too late tonight anyway, and I'm needed elsewhere early evening," she said, scowling. Wherever she was needed, it was not somewhere she wanted to go. "I might get there later in the evening," she added.

Max nodded, keeping her face neutral, mind working. That gave Max a very narrow window of opportunity to get to the bar in the early evening, if she wanted, before Ruutti had a chance to visit again. There was no point in going during the day, not to somewhere like the Sorcerer's Mistress. And, given Ruutti's odd reaction and the fact that at least two of their victims had been seen in the Sorcerer's Mistress, Max thought that she needed to see the place for herself.

She didn't fool Audhilde one bit, though. The vampire sent her a wink, unseen by Ruutti, approving the plan that Max was barely forming in her own mind.

"You said she had an asthma attack, most likely," Max said, turning to Audhilde. "But she looks very still and stiff for someone having breathing difficulties."

"I've always said you were a clever one," Audhilde said, a smile showing. "Yes. She looks almost peaceful, doesn't she? But from my first exam, I'm confident that she suffocated. I'm speculating, but I'm guessing that she couldn't move for some reason. We still haven't isolated the toxin, whatever it is, from the other victims' blood. Perhaps with her having more blood left in her, and knowing now that we're looking for a paralytic, we'll have more luck here."

Max nodded, her eyes stinging again as she thought about Jessica Walsh lying there, unable to move while her lungs failed her. It seemed a terrible way to die.

"What do you need me to do?" Max asked, trying to distract herself from the girl.

"Unless you've got any ideas where we should start looking for the killer or how to find him, I don't think there's anything else to do just now. I'll need to tell her relatives. Councilman Prosser will probably want to be there," Ruutti said, face tightening again. She seemed to have as high an opinion of the council member as Max did. "We can regroup when I've visited the bar again. And Audhilde has finished the autopsy."

"I will do that at first light," Audhilde promised, looking down at the girl.

Max followed the vampire's gaze, a weight settling in her chest. First light wasn't that far away. By the time the body had been moved back to Audhilde's mortuary, it would probably be time for her to start. And Ruutti would be busy for the day. Not least, telling the head of the Walsh Family that one of its members was dead.

Which gave Max some time away from the detective's sharp eyes. She should tell Ruutti and Audhilde what she suspected about how Jessica had been chosen, and what she had learned in her research. But then they would want to know how she had come by her ideas. And she did not want to share that. Not now, not ever.

And the research she had done was too ill-formed in her mind just now. She wanted to revisit previous crime scenes and see if she could verify what she had learned.

And after that, always assuming that Therese didn't have any more assignments for her, she also had enquiries of her own to make. Tracking down anyone else who had boasted about visiting the underworld. The Sorcerer's Mistress seemed a good place to start with that.

Chapter Nineteen

It felt wrong to be walking away from the crime scene and the unfinished business of Jessica Walsh's death. But not wrong enough for Max to turn around and share her suspicions with the detective.

A foul taste bloomed in her mouth, memories threatening to rise and take over.

Without really thinking about it, she found herself heading for the temple and its wide, shallow steps. It had been years since she had been inside one of the Lady's temples. But today she felt unclean with the memory of the dark magic shadow-hound's death, her encounter with the demon, and Jessica's body still on the ground behind her. The Lady's Houses had always been places of refuge, full of a quiet serenity that she had craved as a child and had missed since she had been dismissed from the Order.

There were a few priests and priestesses gathered behind the pillars, their grey, floor-length robes blending with the shadows. They were keeping an eye on the crime scene without being too obvious about it, perhaps not wanting to be caught staring like ordinary people. They looked Max over but didn't stop her as she made her way between the large columns of pale stone and towards the dark entrance to the temple itself.

Max paused on the threshold, holding herself back from the invisible line that separated the outside and inside of the temple. From here she could smell the honey that was mixed into the temple's candles, the sweet smell pulling more memories to the surface, her throat closing with a hard, painful lump that took her by surprise. In the years since she had been into one of the Lady's Houses, she had forgotten so much. The push and the pull of the temple space rose up and threatened to smother her. Temples were supposed to be places of peace, worship and reflection. The possibility of some peace, of some quiet and distance from the memories she carried made Max want to step forward. At the same time, her mind echoed with the bitter disappointment of the priests and priestesses who had raised her and had continuously pointed out her failings. *Stupid girl. How many times have I told you? Do you even listen? No, not like that. Will you ever learn? Ungrateful child.*

Max blinked, not surprised to find more tears on her face. It had been a long time since she had cried at all, and now twice in a short space of time. She blotted the tears away with Audhilde's handkerchief and tried to distract herself by looking around the temple, trying to be a dispassionate observer as if seeing it for the first time.

The temple was filled with soft light from the candles set here and there around the space, apparently at random. Even from here, Max could feel the gentle warmth and quiet. The ceiling high overhead was painted with an impossibly perfect sunny sky with stars winking here and there in the subdued light. The floor was bare, made of plain flagstones. Max knew that if she set foot on the stone, her footsteps would be swallowed up in the vast space. The open expanse of the floor was scattered, seemingly at random, with chairs and stools and large cushions. The temples welcomed all worshippers, and made sure that everyone could settle comfortably in the space.

At the far end of the temple was a long, low slab of brilliant white stone that gleamed in the poor light, with a vast golden sphere hovering in the air above it.

As a child, the Lady's altar had been a source of absolute fascination for Max. After she had been apprenticed to the Order and started her training, she had realised just how much skill and dedication went into crafting and maintaining the spells that kept the stone glowing and the golden sphere perfect and suspended in the air.

Before then, as a child, she had simply known that the Lady's temples were a place of peace and wonder. A place where she had the sense that she might be worth something, might be accepted.

Tonight, Max froze at the sight of the golden sphere and the reminder of the magic built into the temple. There had been whispers among the Order that the Lady's temples had magic that could detect ill intent or darkness in a person and if someone unworthy tried to enter the temple, they would be struck down by the Lady's wrath. Max was almost certain that was not true. Even as a child, she had known that not everyone in the temple's service was good and pure. But she was quite certain that Kitris had told her to her face that she was dismissed not just from the Order but also from the temples, and she was also sure that there were spells that could block access to specific people. So it was possible that the temples were barred to her. She had never tested it before.

And now, on the threshold of the temple, she found that she could not move forward. Could not cross the invisible line that would bring her within the Lady's house. Despite the draw of the space and the possibility of peace, she couldn't move. She didn't want to find out that she had truly been barred.

"All are welcome here, daughter."

She turned, still outside the temple, to find one of the priests had approached her. He was one of the oldest humans she had ever seen, mere wisps of white hair across his head, shoulders bowed with age, but he had a bright gaze and a gentle smile as he looked at her.

"You seemed hesitant," he added as she stayed silent. "You should not be. All are welcome in our Lady's House."

"I am not sure that I am," Max answered. Words rose up in her throat, jammed in her mouth. She kept her lips sealed shut against the temptation to speak. Against the temptation to tell him that she carried the stain of the underworld within her. That she had never felt truly clean since she had come back to this world. That she had been denied access to the Lady's house for years. Ever since the head of the Order had called her a liar and thrown her out into the world.

"Who told you that?" the priest asked, frowning. "No one should be kept away from our Lady's grace and Her light."

"You are very kind, Honoured," Max said, putting the first two fingers of her right hand to her heart in a gesture she had learned along with walking. "The temple is beautiful. But I should not delay."

The priest looked like he wanted to say more, but Max turned on her heel, heading for the side steps down from the temple floor, eyes stinging. It had been a mistake to come here. She had resisted the temptation of the Lady's temples for years now. The small altar in her garden was a poor substitute, but it provided her with some peace. She had thought it was enough until she had stood on that threshold.

And lingering in the temple, giving in to her selfish desire for a moment of calm, would not help find the person who had abducted and killed Jessica Walsh, and who even now was probably hunting for his next victim. Enough people had died already.

Chapter Twenty

The first light of dawn was rising over the city as Max left the temple, heading for her pick-up. It was too early to be asking questions of anyone, and she felt too restless to go home and try to get some sleep. But there were other things she could do. She settled into the driver's seat and looked at the pile of notes and print-outs on the passenger seat. Ley lines. She almost snorted in disbelief. Hours of research, and the best idea she had about why the murder sites had been chosen was that they were all on intersections of ley lines.

Her disbelief faded as she realised that it didn't matter what was real. It only mattered what the killer believed to be true. So she had a possible reason why the killer had chosen the spots he had. Still, she wanted to check for herself.

Glancing in the rear-view mirror showed her Cas and Pol keeping an eye on what was happening around them. The mortuary van was there, a stretcher with black-wrapped cargo being wheeled towards it. Ruutti was back talking to Chief Yarwood and Councilman Prosser. From the body language, Max guessed that the detective was giving them the bad news about who the victim was.

Before any of them could think to stop her and ask her questions, Max turned the engine on and drove away, heading across the city. Time to see if her research was right or not.

She arrived at the quiet residential area where the second victim had been found when it was still early enough that almost no one was awake. She gathered the print-outs and notes she had made and let Cas and Pol out of the pick-up. The pair of them frolicked about in the early morning like puppies, drawing a laugh from her which felt clean and welcome after so much darkness.

The spot where the second victim had died was empty now. The crime scene techs had left and the body and the white tent had been removed, leaving just the shattered road surface. It wouldn't be long before that was repaired, she guessed. None of the local residents would want to have the reminder of the death so visible.

She shuffled through her papers until she found the prints she was looking for. One of the old maps, with the ley lines drawn, and a map of the current city. She frowned, looking from the paper to the ground, realising for the first time that the body had not been in the precise centre of the road, but off to one side. It had been impossible to tell that with the tent set up. The site of death had not been an accident, or a random choice. And, as far as she could tell by comparing the old and new maps side by side, the point where the body had been placed matched perfectly with the ley line intersection on the old map.

Max scowled at the ground. She needed to check at least one of the other death sites to be sure, but she had an explanation as to how the killer had chosen his sites. And how he would choose his next location.

Sifting through the papers again, she came to a larger print which showed more of the city. There weren't that many ley lines, perhaps a dozen, but they did seem to intersect a lot. Assuming that the killer wouldn't go back to a previous site, that still left a large number of places he might go next.

Disheartened, Max turned to go back to the pick-up and move to the next closest site. As she walked back along the road, she saw a person standing along the service road. From the distance, it looked like a man wearing dark clothing. He was standing next to one of the tall garden walls of the houses, almost blending into shadow. As if he didn't want to be seen. It was an odd hour for anyone to be out and about. She paused, attention sharpening, Cas and Pol stopping with her. She had the impression of a medium-height male, trying not to draw attention to himself. She couldn't make out any details of his face, but she didn't think the body height or shape matched any of the residents she and Ruutti had interviewed.

She was about to go towards him, to ask what his business was, when he turned and strolled away. The unhurried pace looked relaxed. Possibly just a local curious as to what she and her giant dogs were doing here so early in the morning. Possibly. And as a Marshal, she didn't have any authority to stop and question a human who might simply be minding his own business.

Frowning, she went back to her pick-up. The day had barely started and she was already imagining things.

The next murder site she went to, on the games court, also lined up with the maps. It was still early enough in the morning, and the scene was far enough from the main city, that there was no one else around. She settled cross-legged on the ground where the body had been, trying not to think too much about the fact that Nico had died here.

With Cas and Pol keeping watch, she slowed her breathing, stilling her body so that she could open her senses in a way she hadn't dared to do in the more built-up area she had just been in. Here, there were no other people close by to crowd her mind.

In a stark contrast to her more structured magic use, which always seemed sluggish and difficult, the world around her sharpened at once, her senses heightened. She could hear Cas and Pol's steady breathing, smell their fur. The faint, familiar scent of her dogs was home and safety and warmth, relaxing her body and mind. She heard the quiet click of their claws on the ground as they paced around her.

Beneath those surface sounds and scents was a deeper current, a thick, warm thread running through the ground underneath her. It reminded her of an electricity cable, except that there were none here. She had checked the city schematics. This was older, far older. More ancient than anything she had ever come across. It wasn't alive in any sense she understood. It simply was. And as she traced its length, running in a straight line up to her and away from her, she became aware of another current, deeper than the first, which crossed the original line just under where she was sitting.

Max opened her eyes and cursed. Lines of power. Ancient trails which were part of the fabric of the world itself. Ley lines. They were real. All her teachers had been wrong, and the long-dead people who had so carefully prepared the map she had found had been right.

When she tried to get to her feet after exploring the ley lines, she almost fell over, all at once weak and exhausted. Cas and Pol came to her side, and she used them as extra support to help her get up, the hounds patient and steady under her hands.

On her feet, the world spun around her, and she remembered that she hadn't actually slept for more than a full day. Perhaps a nap would be in order before she went to the Sorcerer's Mistress in the early evening.

She managed to get herself, her dogs and her pick-up home without causing any accidents, which she counted as a success. Walking towards the house, she saw that the Lady's altar in her garden had been disturbed. There was water splashed all over the bench. Doubtless a bird had decided to take a bath. Sighing, Max cleared off the surface of the bench, washed out the metal bowl and refilled it with clear water, setting it down in the middle of the bench with a reflexive, murmured prayer to the Lady.

Whether it was tending to the altar, or the prayer, or sheer exhaustion, Max fell into her bed and slept dreamlessly for hours, waking in the late afternoon to an unexpected feeling of calm, and two dogs lying next to her.

As soon as they realised she was awake, Cas and Pol leapt off the bed, standing in the bedroom doorway, ears lifted, tails wagging.

Max groaned as she sat up, rubbing her hands across her face. "Yes, alright, I'll feed you. Give me a minute to wake up."

They gave her exactly a minute before coming closer, tails still wagging. She glanced at the time. By some miracle, there had been no calls from Therese summoning her to another incident. She had managed some sleep, and still had time to feed the dogs, get some food for herself, and get to the Sorcerer's Mistress in the early evening, before Ruutti would be finished with whatever business she had.

With the new knowledge of ley lines coursing through her, Max got ready to leave. There were more answers out there, and she was determined to find them.

Chapter Twenty-One

She arrived at the street outside the Sorcerer's Mistress about an hour after dark. Late enough that the bar would be open. Too early for Ruutti to have made it there. Or so Max hoped.

Max left her pick-up parked on the street, the Marshal's tag clearly visible on her windscreen and Cas and Pol on watch in the back to prevent any over-enthusiastic city workers from trying to tow it away. The battered, filthy vehicle looked as out of place as she felt among the sleek, polished vehicles around them.

The Sorcerer's Mistress was in a basement under one of the many anonymous residential buildings in this part of the city - large blocks of tenement flats that housed some of the city's workers. Max had often wondered if being crowded together in the buildings made them feel safer. There were far larger, and cheaper, flats and houses to rent in the outer districts of the city and good transport links from almost all the districts into the city centre. Most people still wanted to be in the city itself, though - there was always the risk, however small, that something from the Wild would appear in the districts.

The street itself didn't seem to have changed since her single previous visit, although the bar had improved its soundproofing, whether magical or engineered, as Max could barely hear anything as she went down the shallow, wide steps to the blood-red front door.

Opening the front door revealed a large antechamber decked out in blood-red fabric along with a pair of large, glass-fronted display cases that made Max's brows lift. The cases were new since her last visit, when the room had simply been draped with fabric. There were interior lights in each of the cabinets, highlighting their contents. There was an honest-to-goodness wizard's staff in one, and an ancient pointy hat that might have been worn by a witch in the other. None of the witches

Max had ever met would be seen dead in a hat like that. And although some magicians would use a staff, the one on display here was carved with symbols that seemed to have been drawn at random with no purpose or design.

But then, most of the bar's patrons wouldn't know that the items were fake. This was not a place for genuinely powerful magicians. This was a place for city dwellers to feel like they were close to the darker edge that lurked within the city, all the while knowing they were perfectly safe and could go back into their sheltered, boring lives whenever they wanted. Along with the thrill-seekers, the bar was also known as a haunt for wannabe magicians to gather and exchange tall tales while sipping over-priced drinks.

There were two people standing at the door on the other side of the antechamber, both of them dressed in deep red shirts and black trousers. Whoever had done the interior design for the place had extended the colours to the staff as well, Max noted. They were both wearing frowns as they looked at her.

"No weapons," one of them said.

"I'm a Marshal," Max said, pulling out her badge. "I'm entitled to carry my weapons everywhere in the city." It was another concession that Faddei had wrung out of the city council, along with the excellent medical care for his people.

"You don't have jurisdiction here," the other said.

"Oh, really?" Max asked, remembering the young police officer saying something similar the day before. She wondered what announcement she had missed.

"We don't like your kind," the first speaker said. Max took note that neither of them had explained her lack of jurisdiction, and made a mental note to tell Faddei next time she saw him. The head Marshal would definitely want to know that the city folk were trying to hinder the Marshals.

"I hear that a lot," Max said, keeping her voice easy and friendly. "But I'm here on official business, and the sooner you let me in, the sooner I'll be away. Or I can come back later with a warrant and more law enforcement. Your choice."

The two exchanged glances, and the second one shrugged. "Fine." He pressed a button by his side and the doors between the pair opened, letting a wash of noise and scent and heat waft out and coil around Max.

Her brows lifted, recognising some of the scents that spilled out. "You are burning rosemary and sage incense? Does the landlord know you're doing that?" she asked.

"Nothing to do with us," the second doorman said.

Max believed him. Neither of them looked as if they had a clue as to the significance of that incense. But she would bet money that someone on the bar's payroll knew precisely what they were doing. No one used that particular combination of scents in a public space if they felt they had a choice. It was toxic to a number of supernatural creatures, and had often unpredictable effects on other non-humans. And the smell wasn't all that pleasant for humans, either. Rosemary by itself was fine, but combined with the sage, it began to smell more like wet socks than something wholesome.

Wondering just what had scared the staff enough to burn incense, Max went through the doors and into the bar.

After the smell, the first thing she noticed was the noise. A babble of conversation. But no music. That was unusual in Max's experience. Most city bars tended to have music playing, some of them even having live bands from time to time. Not here, not tonight. Just lots of people talking.

The black-and-red theme had been continued all the way through the place, from the shining black bar to the red covers on the chairs. The whole effect made the place seem smaller, the walls pressing in around her as she made her way across to the bar. There were slivers of mirror here and there on the walls and partitions - enough to reflect some light back into the room, but none of the fragments were big enough to be of use as an actual mirror.

The bar-room occupied almost the entire basement area of the building, and had been split into different levels, artfully arranged so that there were booths with the illusion of privacy as well as more open tables.

Despite it being a mid-week night, the place was busier than she had expected. Not full, by any means, but with many of the seats and tables occupied. The patrons all looked human to Max's eyes, most of them dressed in a variety of black clothing. Almost all of them were in groups, huddled together around their drinks. They were keeping an eye on Max as she made her way across the room to the ebony stretch of the bar. If they spent their time within the city limits, it might be the first time that some of them had seen a Marshal.

Max made her own study of the crowd in a much less obvious way. The patrons were a curious lot. Of course, bars did tend to draw in an odd selection of people at the best of times. There were groups of youngsters, some of whom she thought were probably too young to be in the place to start with. Outnumbering the youngsters were the older patrons, many of them in small groups, untouched drinks on the tables in front of them. A few of the older patrons had a restless, hard edge to them. The sort of people Max might see in ones and twos at the Hunter's Tooth, gradually relaxing under Malik's influence or getting into fights outside one of the run-down bars in the Barrows. Not the sort of people she would expect to find in an overpriced place like this.

There were two bartenders on duty, both dressed in deep red t-shirts and jeans. The nearest came across to Max. A human woman, her pale blonde curls held back from her face with a patterned scarf.

"Good evening, Marshal," she said, voice easy and pleasant. "What can I get for you?"

Max narrowed her eyes at the woman. The friendly greeting was not what she had expected, particularly after the hostility of the doormen. The easy tone was also at odds with the tension she could see in the woman's shoulders.

"Some information, please," Max said, taking a seat on the nearest bar stool.

A flicker of something crossed the woman's face. Too fast for Max to properly register the set of emotions, but enough to realise that she had unsettled the other woman.

"Of course. We're always happy to help law enforcement," the woman said. Her eyes flickered past Max to a particular point in the crowd. The glance was so quick that if Max hadn't been looking for it, she might have missed it.

"Do you know a girl by the name of Jessica?" Max asked. "Pink hair, pale skin."

"Jess, sure. She comes in here now and then." The bartender took another, more relaxed look around the room. "She's not here just now, though."

"What about last night, or the night before?" Max asked.

"Don't know, sorry. I was off those nights," the woman said. It was a perfectly reasonable statement, but the tension in her throat and jaw suggested something other than a normal pair of nights off.

It also meant that this bartender would not have been working when Ruutti had visited the bar. Max was quite sure that the detective would have spotted this woman's odd behaviour fairly quickly, and would have mentioned it if anyone in the bar had been burning incense when she had been here. At least, she hoped the detective would have mentioned those things. But Ruutti definitely had her own agenda.

"So, when was the last time you saw Jessica?" Max asked. She was no trained investigator, but she had spent enough time around law enforcement to know some of the basic questions to ask.

The woman's face flickered again, with an expression almost too fast for Max to track. But she thought she recognised fear. Her interest sharpened. She could not imagine why a bartender would be frightened to be asked about one of her patrons. Even if the patron was a member of the Walsh family.

"At the weekend, I think. We were really busy, so I can't be sure," the woman said, picking up a towel and turning her attention to wiping down one of the surfaces behind the bar that, to Max's eyes, looked spotless.

"Did you see who she was with? Or do you know who she normally hangs around with?" Max asked.

Another change of expression on the woman's face. That was definitely fear.

Max stayed quiet and still, wondering what was going on. The smell of incense which had first wafted out to her in the entranceway seemed all at once to get stronger. The change was powerful enough that the bartender noticed, her nose wrinkling in reaction.

"I can't help you," the woman said, not looking at Max.

And that was a lie. The friendly, cooperative manner had gone along with the woman's smile. Her hands shook as she folded the towel she had been using.

"Alright," Max said. There was no point in scaring the woman further. "Is there someone else I can talk to? Who was working last night?"

The woman was about to answer when movement behind Max drew her attention. She looked past Max's shoulder and lost what little remained of her colour.

Max's brows lifted and she glanced over her shoulder, turning around completely when she saw who was coming towards her. There were three men. Two of them looked like bodyguards. They had close-cropped dark hair and were wearing unrelieved black, both of them armed, their square jaws similar enough that they were probably related.

The third man was altogether different, and altogether more dangerous. He moved across the floor with absolute assurance, confident of his place in this particular setting. He wore a beautifully fitting dark suit with a matching shirt. Not black, Max thought. More like a deep navy. It set off his tanned skin, striking bone structure and carefully arranged, tousled blond hair.

The third man stopped a few paces away from Max and eyed her up and down. Max stayed where she was, settled on the bar stool, her seven-pointed Marshal's badge gleaming in the faint light. There was magic somewhere around. Not the bodyguards. Most likely the blond man.

He seemed to be waiting for her to speak, so she stayed silent, tilting her head as she looked him up and down as thoroughly as he was inspecting her. As far as she could tell, he wasn't armed, and she didn't think there was room in his slim-fitting suit for a wizard's wand. It didn't mean he was not dangerous, and the two bodyguards standing on either side of him were most definitely armed.

When the silence had dragged on a bit, the man frowned.

"You were asking about Jess," the man said, his voice clipped.

The noise in the room had dimmed. The other patrons were all trying to pretend not to watch the little drama being played out, whilst all of them were watching for all they were worth. Max just hoped that no one was stupid enough to try to record it on their phones. She had a feeling that the man in front of her would not like that at all.

"I was," Max agreed. "Do you know her?"

"I make a point of trying to get to know all the patrons here," the man said.

"And why is that?" Max asked.

The man's brows lifted in apparently genuine surprise, then returned to a frown. Not happy. Not happy at all. "This is my bar."

"Oh, really?" Max said, exaggerating her surprise. "The whole thing? You own it?"

"I do. I'm Grayson Forster," he told her.

A chill ran over Max's skin. The family name would be familiar to anyone who lived in the city. Another one of the powerful families who controlled everything. As powerful and influential in their own way as the Walsh clan.

And known for producing hot-headed magic users, too.

She hadn't heard about this particular member of the Forster clan before, but from the way he carried himself and the fact that he claimed to own this entire bar, she guessed he was high up in the clan. Possibly one of the matriarch's sons. The lady Forster had at least three sons, from what Max could remember.

Max forced herself to keep still, to remain calm. Not to react. It could not be a coincidence, though, that Jessica Walsh had visited the bar owned by one of the other powerful families. Max could not help wondering if that had been another bit of rebellion from the girl. She could not imagine that Connor Declan Walsh would be happy with his niece spending time in one of his rivals' establishments.

"Did you know Jessica well?" Max asked.

"Not really. She and I, er, moved in different circles," Grayson Forster said, his tone clearly meant to imply that his circles were far more elevated than Jessica's.

"Oh, really?" Max asked. "What do you mean by that?"

She had annoyed him again. Good.

"She would barely qualify as a witch," Grayson said, the words bitten out.

"Is that right?" Max asked. "Sounds like you did know her fairly well."

"What do you want?" he asked, a snap in his voice.

"I need to find Jessica's friends, or the people she spent time with," Max said.

"She didn't have friends. She was not selective about who she spent time with," Grayson said, voice dripping with disapproval. "Why do you need to know?"

"Jessica Walsh died last night," Max said, keeping an eye on the man, and also the two bodyguards.

He seemed genuinely surprised. And then relieved. An odd combination. So he had not been involved in Jessica's death. Which made sense, as he seemed very concerned with his status here. But it did make her wonder - if he was not worried about Jessica's death, then what was he worried about?

"I'm sorry to hear that," he said, with an absence of sincerity. "I am sure she will be missed."

Max made a non-committal noise.

"Did some creature kill her? Is that why the Marshals are involved?" he asked.

It was a perfectly logical and reasonable question, except that Max thought there was nothing reasonable about this man. She remembered the fear shown by the bartender, who had initially appeared bubbly and confident.

"Enquiries are ongoing," Max said, in her most neutral tone.

One of the bodyguards slightly shifted his weight, apparently bored with the conversation.

They were not in the least bothered about the fact that Jessica had been in the bar. Nor were they bothered about her death. Something else, then. Max remembered how Jessica had liked to talk, and wondered what Grayson Forster thought that the girl might have said. Max glanced around the room. She wanted to ask if Jessica had been boastful, but with almost every pair of eyes on her, and everyone listening, she held the questions in. She might need to come back, which was annoying, or see if she could get answers from the Walsh clan.

For tonight, Max could leave, her enquiries done for now. But Ruutti's odd attitude towards the bar had bothered her. And the Forster clan member in front of her was definitely bothered about something. Plus, the smell in the air was making her nose itch.

"So, tell me, why are you burning incense in the bar?" Max asked.

Grayson Forster went completely still, face freezing into a mask, eyes burning with suppressed emotion. Anger, mostly.

"That is not your concern," he snapped.

"Oh, I think it is. Rosemary and sage? It stinks," Max said candidly. "Not something a successful business owner would want to have in his bar if he had any other choice. But it does have some specific uses. It might be used to keep a creature sedated, for example," she said. An educated guess.

He twitched slightly, a tiny movement that he controlled as quickly as possible, then he glared at her. "I think we're finished here. Gentlemen, would you escort the Marshal to the door?" He flicked a hand to his bodyguard.

"Stay where you are," Max said, before the two men could move. They glanced at their employer and then back at her, clearly torn in trying to decide who worried them the most. She ignored them for the moment. They wouldn't act without Grayson's approval. "So, you have something in the bar that you shouldn't have. And you're keeping it quiet with rosemary and sage. What could it be, I wonder?"

"We're done here," Grayson said, voice flat. But Max had been watching his bodyguards, and they had both glanced in one particular direction.

She got off the bar stool, discovering that she was about the same height as Grayson. She met his eyes. He tried to look down his nose at her.

"We're done when I say we are," she said. "Supernatural creatures are a Marshal's concern. What are you keeping behind that wall?" she asked, tilting her head in the direction the bodyguards had looked.

His face tightened again, lines of anger appearing around his mouth. "Get off my property," he said. She wondered if that tone usually worked, and suspected that it did. The police who operated within the city would know exactly who he was and what his family was capable of. Max didn't care. There was not much he or his family could do to her that worried her.

"No," Max answered, and moved past him, heading for the wall, apprehension coiling in her stomach. She was in a relatively tight space, with innocent bystanders and the possibility of a creature nearby. She considered calling for back-up, but could not imagine Faddei being willing to send more Marshals onto Forster property without absolute proof there was something there. So, for now, she was on her own.

As she moved towards the wall, the scent of incense grew stronger, almost overpowering everything else. There were a few supernatural creatures that were more docile under the influence of sage, but it wasn't a particularly good method of keeping them sedated. They tended to build up a tolerance over time. And even the most docile supernatural creature could still do some serious damage in the middle of the city.

She felt rather than heard movement behind her and turned to find Grayson's pair of bodyguards trying to rush her. They were moving fast, attention focused on her. She sidestepped the pair of them, so they rushed headlong into the wall. The collision tripped a hidden latch and a panel of the wall moved, a crack appearing amid the crimson. Max had no time to look inside as the bodyguards were back on their feet, turning to attack her, faces twisted into almost identical expressions of fury.

She ducked under the first wild swing of a fist and grabbed a nearby chair, using it as a shield against the next attack, turning so that her back was against the solid wall. She threw the chair at the pair of bodyguards who were too close together as they surged forward again, then drew her main gun and the small weapon she kept tucked at her back, pointing the weapons at each of the bodyguards.

She heard a loud crack and felt the vibration of a collision through the wall at her back. There was definitely something behind that wall.

"It's a crime to try and impede a Marshal in the execution of their duty," she told the bodyguards, voice flat.

They weren't paying attention to her, or her weapons. Instead, their gaze had gone past her to the sliver of open door. The gap was dark, even darker than the bar, and a trace of that incense along with more primitive scents coiled out of the opening. Earth. Old blood. The faint scent of animal waste. Not things that should be in a city bar.

Then the sound of someone - no, something - breathing. A long sigh of air from a deep chest. Not a sound any human could make.

Max turned her head a fraction, keeping her weapons pointed forwards.

There was a shape moving in the darkness. Large and slow, it was shuffling forward to the open doorway, towards the light and the bar full of people.

Max couldn't see what it was, but the bodyguards started backing away. Grayson was still standing by the bar, looking furious. The bartender, and the other patrons that Max could see, looked terrified. All conversation had stopped.

A low rumbling sound vibrated the wall at Max's back. She lowered her weapons, turning her head just as a huge, three-toed, clawed foot shoved the door open. The owner of the foot came forward. A creature on all fours, its shoulders as high as her head. Trails of smoke billowed from its nostrils, curling around the two long, twisting horns that sprouted from its forehead. Its yellow eyes, its pupils vertical slits, looked around, and it opened its lipless mouth to show rows of jagged, yellowing teeth.

"A Keliotrope? Are you kidding me?" Max asked, astonished. She spared a glance at Grayson, still standing by the bar. They were incredibly rare in this part of the world, preferring a far warmer climate. She shoved her back-up weapon into its holster. The smaller gun would be useless against the creature's thick hide. Her main gun would not be effective, either, but it was better than nothing. She held her gun ready, muzzle pointing at the ground, and slowly backed away from the creature.

The Keliotrope, the only one Max had ever seen alive, turned as if mesmerised to follow her movement. A thin, dark tongue flickered out between those awful teeth, tasting the air. It lowered its head and moved forward on all four clawed feet, its body twice as long as it was tall, a thick tail the same length as its body sliding along the ground behind it.

"Do you have a tranquilliser?" Max asked Grayson as she kept slowly backing up. If what she remembered was correct, then slow and careful movements should not provoke the creature. It had poor eyesight, and was also hampered by the low lighting in the bar and the heavy dose of incense that still hung in the air.

"Not within reach," Grayson told her.

"You have got to be kidding me," Max said again. "You have a Keliotrope on the property and no tranquilliser?" The sheer stupidity of it was almost unbelievable. Except that this man had thought it was a good idea to have a Keliotrope next to his bar and a room full of people.

"Everything was fine until you arrived," he snapped at her.

"I am not the idiot who decided to bring a master predator into the heart of the city and try and keep it calm with incense," she snapped back at him. "Incense, for the love of the Lady. What kind of idiot are you?"

Grayson didn't answer.

As the creature moved forwards, most of the bar patrons managed to remember the lessons drilled into them from childhood. *If you find yourself anywhere near a predator, stay still and let the people with guns deal with it.* It was good advice and also stopped too many civilians from getting shot while the people with guns tried to deal with the predator. From the whimpering Max could hear, most of the gathered people were absolutely terrified. She did not blame them.

The stillness and silence held until one of the nearest patrons, a young woman dressed in a skin-tight, black mini-dress, screamed and ran, heading for the door.

"Stay still!" Max yelled.

It was too late. The Keliotrope whipped around, far faster than anything that large should be able to move, and followed the screaming woman. It grabbed hold of her with one claw and opened its mouth, teeth gleaming.

Max shot it. Three rounds, tightly spaced, into its side, the crack of her gun loud in the confined space. The bullets didn't penetrate the creature's tough hide, bouncing off and rattling across the floor.

She had got the creature's attention, though. It dropped the screaming and now bleeding woman, whipping around to face the new threat.

Max kept her gun raised, continuing to back away slowly. The creature turned its head this way and that, trying to work out who had shot it.

The rest of the patrons were staying as still as they could. There was more whimpering, though, and little sounds of pain from the woman on the floor. No one moved to help her. Max could only hope that she survived long enough for the emergency teams to get her.

First things first. Max needed to get the creature away from the innocent people around, and then deal with it. Somehow.

"Have your men open the doors to the street and get out of the way," Max told Grayson.

"What?" he said.

"Just do it."

"Do you have any idea how much that creature cost me?" he demanded.

"It could kill everyone in this bar, including you, and you're worried about cost?" Max spat back at him. "Get the damned doors open before I decide to shoot you instead."

She heard muttering behind her which suggested Grayson was doing as she asked. She kept backing away, moving in an arc that kept her ahead of the Keliotrope but out of its path to the doors.

A waft of cool air, full of the scent of damp tarmac and car fumes, drifted into the bar. The Keliotrope paused, one foot mid-air, tongue flickering out again. It turned away from Max, heading for the open doors, picking up pace.

Everyone in the bar managed to stay still as the creature left.

Max followed it at a run, arriving at street level just in time to see it climb over one of the sleek vehicles that had been parked outside the bar, leaving great gouge marks from its claws and dents from its weight. The car alarm blared, protesting but useless.

"Cas, Pol, guard it!" she yelled. Her dogs leapt out of the pick-up in one smooth, co-ordinated move and headed for the Keliotrope. Max pulled out her phone and dialled a pre-set number.

"What?" Therese answered.

"There's a Keliotrope on the loose outside the Sorcerer's Mistress. I need back-up and containment. And send a medical team. There's a civilian injured," Max said. She didn't wait for Therese's reply, ending the call and running for her pick-up.

Cas and Pol were standing in front of the Keliotrope, shifted into their attack forms, making themselves look as big and menacing as possible, their long hair raised, low growls threading the air. They sounded deadly enough that the hairs on the back of Max's neck lifted as she holstered her handgun and scrabbled in the back of the pick-up for a heavier weapon. Something that might actually penetrate the Keliotrope's hide.

She pulled out the shotgun and the only magazine of armour-piercing shells that she could find, her fingers moving quickly, steady despite her racing heart and dry mouth. She stuffed a pair of magazines of more conventional shells into the loop of her thigh holster.

By the time she was better armed, the Keliotrope was approaching her dogs. All three animals were in the middle of the street, all of them tinted orange by the street lights, locked in a near-silent stand-off.

Cas and Pol were smart enough to retreat from the Keliotrope, keeping its attention on them as Max made her way around the cars on one side of the road, looking for a weak spot on the Keliotrope where she might get a clear shot. She couldn't see anything. And as tough as her dogs were, their fangs would make no impact on the Keliotrope's hide.

The creature was getting annoyed at having her dogs in front of it. More smoke billowed out of its mouth and it lowered its head, horns sweeping down. One of those horns could easily rip into her dogs. Or a passer-by. The creature needed to be stopped.

"Hey, ugly!" Max yelled.

The Keliotrope paused, one foot off the ground, tongue flicking out again.

She knelt on the tarmac between a pair of cars, trying to see if she could get an angle on its under-side where the hide might be thinner. In the poor lighting, the creature's under-side didn't look different, but she fired at it anyway.

The armour-piercing shell slammed into the Keliotrope's hide and bounced back, rattling onto the road surface. Max spat a curse.

The Keliotrope turned towards her, its tail lashing out, sweeping Cas off his feet. Her dog righted himself in the air, landing on all four paws, as sure-footed as a cat, fangs bared. The creature whipped its tail around again, slamming into another pair of cars. More alarms blared into the night.

Max had no more attention to spare for her dogs as the Keliotrope was moving towards her, its tongue flickering out to taste the air. It lifted its head and she saw a lighter patch of hide under its chin.

She fired. The armour-piercing shell landed and bit into the creature's skin. It roared, its head snapping back. Max fired again, emptying the magazine into its neck.

Around her, she was vaguely aware of bright lights and more bodies arriving. She kept her attention on the creature as she reloaded the gun with conventional ammunition. There was a hole to aim for now, a gaping wound in the creature's neck.

The Keliotrope took a few rapid steps forward, steps uneven.

Max held her ground, weapon ready. Waiting.

"What are you doing? Shoot it!"

She wasn't sure who the hysterical speaker was. Perhaps one of the residents of the buildings around her. A low voice that she recognised spoke in return. Faddei was here. The Marshals could move quickly when they needed to.

Footsteps behind her made her tense.

"It's Vanko," a deep, accented voice said. "Faddei thought you might need back-up." Max risked a glance across as her fellow Marshal knelt nearby, his own weapon set at his shoulder. He and Faddei were distant cousins, she thought. They had the same overall build, and the same quick minds hidden beneath their muscles. "Tranq rounds?"

"Yes. I used a mag full of armour-piercing shells. Most of them hit home," she told him, turning her attention back to the creature that was wobbling on its feet.

"Then this big lad should be ready for a nap right about now," Vanko said, sounding cheerful. "Where did you find it?" he asked.

"In the Sorcerer's Mistress. The owner had been keeping it sedated with incense."

"Is he dead?" Vanko asked, in the same cheerful tone.

"Alive last I saw him," Max answered, tensing as the creature took another step forward.

The Keliotrope shook its head, more smoke emerging from its nostrils, the wound on its neck bleeding sluggishly, then its front legs crumpled, followed by its back legs, sending it to the ground with a thump that shook the street and set off a few more car alarms.

"Finally," Max said, breathing a sigh of relief.

"Here," Vanko said. When she turned, he was holding out what looked like a giant syringe full of amber liquid. "Just to be sure it's asleep. I'll cover you," he added.

Which meant she would need to get close enough to the creature to inject it. Her mouth went dry. Getting so close to a creature that might not be completely asleep was dangerous, and something the Marshals only did when necessary. Max took a quick look around. They were on a city street, with people hanging out of their windows in the buildings around them, and still more people gathered on the street, despite the local law enforcement's attempts to keep them back. A predator like the Keliotrope could do significant damage if left unchecked. Someone had to make sure that it was asleep. And she didn't have any more armour-piercing cartridges, so it made sense for her to carry the syringe.

Max left her weapon on the ground next to the empty magazine and took the syringe, standing up slowly and making her way towards the Keliotrope with some caution. Its eyes were open, tongue flicking out again as she approached, a long, dark sound emerging from its throat. She carefully avoided the horns, skirting around the head. It was lying partially on its side, one of its forelegs stretched out, revealing slightly paler skin at the joint. There. The syringe should get through that.

Get in with steady, slow movements, be firm, and then get out as fast as you can. The advice from Raymund rang through her head. The Marshal's scientist was responsible for training all new Marshals how to properly administer sedatives. It was a class he taught on a regular basis. New Marshals were often scornful at the idea they might have to get that close to one of the predators they hunted. More than one of the newbies had suggested that their job was to shoot, and it was the scientists' job to collect. After their first field experience, the same newbies often went back to the class, sitting alongside the more experienced Marshals as Raymund demonstrated the technique, patiently answering questions that had been asked at least a dozen times before. Max tried to take the class at least once a year, but it had been a very long time since she had had to use the syringe in the field.

Max kept her movements as slow and smooth as she could, hoping that the Keliotrope could not hear her thumping heart or smell her fear. When she was close enough - far too close to the predator - she jammed the syringe into the creature's armpit with as much force as she could, shoving the plunger home.

As she pulled the syringe out and darted away, the Keliotrope roared, writhing on the ground, its long tail sweeping around, catching Max's legs and sending her backwards through the air.

She landed with a thump on the roof of one of the sleek vehicles that lined the street, the breath knocked out of her, still holding the empty syringe. The car alarm blared, adding to the cacophony.

The Keliotrope roared again and Max forced herself up, breath coming in shallow, pained gasps. The healing dose Faddei had given her the day before had helped, but the hard landing had woken up the sore patches along her spine, and shoved the ammunition and spare gun she carried against the small of her back. She would have a row of bruises for days.

The creature was trying to get to its feet, and failing, its movements growing more and more sluggish as Max made her way back to Vanko's side, collecting her weapon.

"It might need another dose," she said.

"Give it time," the older Marshal suggested. He had not moved from his position, still ready with his own shotgun. "You okay? That looked like a hard hit."

"Winded. Bruised," Max said, eyes on the creature as its struggles to get up slowed, tail sliding across the road surface, its eyes gleaming with impotent fury as the drugs finally did their job. It slumped forward, head landing on the road with a thump Max felt all the way from her boots to her teeth, small trails of smoke still rising from its nostrils as its eyes closed. Finally asleep. Breathing out a sigh of relief, Max glanced at Vanko. "Is the containment team here?"

"Of course," Faddei's voice answered from a few paces behind her and Vanko. The leader of the Marshals chuckled. "When Raymund heard there was a Keliotrope, he ran for the vehicles."

"Raymund ran?" Max asked, sparing a glance over her shoulder to see Faddei's grin. The scientist was dedicated and careful. She had seen him walking briskly once or twice, but never running. The man himself was standing behind Faddei along with his team, all of them wearing dark cover-alls and all of them almost twitching with apparent eagerness to move forward and see their prize. It was likely that none of them had seen a Keliotrope in the flesh before, either.

"Indeed," Faddei answered. "Let's give them some room to work."

It wasn't really a suggestion. Max took another look at the Keliotrope before she moved aside, letting the scientists move forward.

Their excited babble rose up in the street, and she realised just how quiet it had become. The car alarms had been silenced. There were still people hanging out of the windows of the buildings around them, and more people gathered on the street, but no one had been talking much. It was possible they were in shock. Creatures were very rare in this part of the city. But Max would still have expected a murmur from the crowd.

She turned slowly, assessing the scene, ignoring the excited scientists, and saw Grayson Forster and his bodyguards standing at the top of the steps that led down to the Sorcerer's Mistress. Grayson's face was set in a tight mask of fury. And apart from his bodyguards, no one was standing near him. She remembered her first impression of him as dangerous. It seemed that she was not alone in that feeling.

"Faddei, the Keliotrope came from a room inside the Sorcerer's Mistress," Max said. "I didn't get a chance to look inside."

"Indeed?" Faddei asked, moving to stand beside her, also looking at Grayson Forster standing outside his bar. "You think there might be more to find?" he asked, sounding thoughtful.

"The room was well concealed, and the owner was, er, not pleased when it was discovered," Max said.

"That's Grayson Forster, isn't it?" Faddei asked.

They were speaking in low tones, and standing far enough away from Grayson that he should not be able to hear them. Still, the man was glaring at them.

"It is," Max confirmed. "You know him?"

"Only by reputation," Faddei answered. He held out his hand and Max realised she was still holding the syringe. Faddei took it from her and waved one of the scientists over to take it from him. He then beckoned Vanko over. "Gather the others. We're going into the bar," Faddei told Vanko. "You too, Max," he added.

Max opened her mouth to protest. It was instinctive. Faddei knew perfectly well that she did not like working with others around her. And he knew the reasons why. Nine highly trained warriors of the Order had been sent with her to the Grey Gates, and had died awful, agonizing deaths around her. Their faces and screams came back to her in nightmares at least once a week. She did not want to watch anyone else die around her.

But her boss had given an order, and had made up his mind. She snapped her mouth shut, checking her weapons instead.

The other Marshal just nodded and turned away to the vehicles gathered further along the street. Max saw another pair of figures bearing Marshals' badges, who came forward at Vanko's whistle. Pavla and Yevhen Bilak. The only married pair of Marshals, they always worked together. The other Marshals were carrying shotguns, too, extra ammunition tucked in their thigh holsters in the same way as Max had stored hers.

"Lead the way," Faddei said.

Chapter Twenty-Two

Grayson Forster did not want to let the Marshals into the bar. He stood at the top of the steps, his bodyguards flanking him, and glared at Max as she and the others approached. Max kept her shotgun pointing at the ground, not wanting to give his bodyguards any reason to get aggressive.

"This is private property," Grayson said, words snapping into the night air. "You have no authority here."

"You had a Keliotrope in your storage room," Max said. "We want to make sure you don't have anything else in there that doesn't belong."

Grayson glared at her, a muscle jumping in his jaw.

"Son, I suggest you stand aside. One way or the other, we are going to search the place," Faddei said.

Grayson glared at Faddei, then slowly took a step to the side, his bodyguards following. It seemed that the younger man knew precisely who Faddei was. Max wondered just what kind of reputation the head Marshal had to make the Forster stand back so easily. "You can be sure the council will hear about this," Grayson said.

"I look forward to that meeting," Faddei said, sounding sincere. He waved the other Marshals ahead.

With Faddei watching their backs, Max led the others down the stairs and through the red-draped room to the main doors of the bar.

"Is that an actual pointy hat?" Vanko asked as they went through the entrance. "Have you ever seen a witch wearing one?"

"No," Pavla, the other female Marshal said, laughter in her voice. "And I'm pretty sure that was a nursery rhyme carved on the wizard's staff."

Max didn't reply, focusing on the room ahead of her and trying to ignore the prickle of unease at having other people gathered around her as she walked into potential danger. The smell of incense had almost faded, with the doors having been opened. The bar's lights were still dimmed, but there was enough light to see. To her shock, she spotted a few people still in the bar. There was a pool of blood and scattered medical swabs where the injured woman had been. Max assumed that the medical team had taken her to hospital.

"Everyone out!" Max lowered her gun to hold up the seven-pointed star, the metal gleaming in the light. "Out, now!" she added, when no one moved.

"Or you can stay here and get eaten," Vanko added. "Your choice."

That got the humans moving, finally. They rushed for the door.

"I'll do a sweep in here. Make sure everyone is out," Faddei said. "The rest of you, keep going."

Even though his injuries had taken him off active service, the head Marshal could more than look after himself, so Max swallowed her instinctive urge to go with him and make sure that the bar was empty, instead heading for the far wall and the partly open door.

The interior of the room was as dark as it had been before. She nudged the door further open with her boot, gun ready. She could not see anything. Muttering a curse, she reached back to her ammunition belt, drawing out the small, powerful pen-light that sat next to her back-up gun. She clipped the torch to the holder on the top of the shotgun, setting the beam as wide as possible.

Moments later, the light from her torch was joined by three other light sources as the other Marshals set up their own torches. That done, Max led them on into the room.

The smell of incense was so strong that her eyes started watering and she stopped for a moment to let her eyes adjust.

The room they were looking at was simply a dark, open space. There was another pair of doors opposite the one they had come through, these doors wide open, hanging sideways as if something large and angry had broken through. Something like the Keliotrope.

Max took a step forward and heard a crunch under her boot. She swept her weapon down, aiming the light at the floor, and saw scattered remnants of what looked like glass jars. Doubtless they were the source of the incense that was almost visible in the air.

"Incense," Pavla muttered. "Idiots."

Max silently agreed, and led her group on to the next set of doors.

There was another dark space beyond the second set of doors, a warm draft of air carrying a mix of unpleasant scents. Animal waste. Rotting meat. Blood. And more incense.

They moved forward in a loose, co-ordinated group, without needing to speak. This was not the first time any of them had gone into the dark to flush out an unknown predator.

The beams from their torches showed a large, unlit passageway with a packed earth floor and walls formed of ancient brick, the mortar crumbling in places. Max tried not to think about the buildings overhead. There was no reason to think that the ceiling would cave in. Not now.

Their torches lit up a small space around them, but there was plenty of darkness ahead.

"Can anyone send a light ahead?" Max asked. She could, but it would take valuable energy and concentration she could not spare being the person in the lead.

She felt the stirring of magic behind her. She didn't know the other Marshals well enough to know who it was, but a moment later a faint mist spread through the group carrying a shimmer with it. The mist moved ahead of Max, coating the walls and ceiling, amplifying the torch light enough that Max could see further ahead. They would have much more warning of anything approaching them.

"Thank you," Max said and began moving forward again, keeping her pace slow and steady. The ground looked solid, but that was no guarantee it would hold, or that there weren't hidden traps.

After what seemed an eternity, but was probably only a few minutes, she saw another pair of doors ahead. Like the entrance to this tunnel, they were knocked aside as if something large had barrelled through them. Beyond the doors was more pitch dark. The smells were stronger here, too.

"Hold up a moment. We'll make some more light," Yevhen said.

Max stopped, keeping her weapon trained on the dark opening ahead as more magic rose behind her, a brush against her senses, and another cloud of mist drifted ahead of her, going through the doors and spreading out so that she could see that the doorway was empty.

"Thank you," she said to the pair, then started moving again, with the same caution as before.

They made it through the doors with no difficulty, and then Max's foot struck against a solid object. Unfamiliar magic trailed up her leg. She stopped at once, aiming her torch down.

There was a heavy band of metal sunk into the earthen floor, the gleam of it stretching to either side. From the way it curved away into the dark, she would bet a month's wages that it formed a circle. And there was powerful magic set into the ring. Max shook her leg, trying to cast off the trace of magic. It was fading too slowly for her liking.

"A spell ring?" Vanko asked, sounding as if he did not believe his own senses.

Max did not blame him. Spell rings were usually crafted by powerful magicians in their own workshops, as a place of safety to practice spells. Or containment to allow a spell to come to maturity, she added, remembering the gift that Queran had left her. Even that spell ring had been a tightly confined space. Most magicians only made their containment circle large enough for them and a small worktable. Not something of this great size, embedded into the earth far underground.

"There's another one," Pavla said, a light shining ahead of Max.

Max moved her light, too, and saw that Pavla was right. There was another heavy band of metal embedded into the ground several paces ahead, its curve a little more pronounced. She raised her torch, wondering what the rings were protecting, and had to blink to make sure her eyes were not deceiving her.

"Is that an amphitheatre?" she asked, disbelief in every word.

"It looks like it," Vanko said, matching her tone. "Pav, Yev, are you seeing this?"

"We are," Yevhen agreed, voice grim.

Ahead of them was a large circle of what looked like giant steps carved into the earth, the steps going down to a bottom that Max could not see from here. But she had seen a similar design in ancient theatres above ground. The giant steps were, in fact, seats, with shallower sets of steps cut at intervals for people to make their way up and down the structure. She could not imagine what it was doing here, under a residential building, at the end of a corridor leading from the Sorcerer's Mistress.

Max swept her torch slowly from side to side. The air around them was heavy, dead on her shoulders. The magic of the spell rings was probably keeping any sound from the amphitheatre contained.

Her light bounced off something metallic on the ground next to the nearest set of steps. Next to the gleaming object, there was a heap on the ground.

Stepping carefully over the spell ring, not wanting more unfamiliar magic crawling over her, she moved forward, the others with her.

As they drew closer, the metallic object turned out to be a dart gun, and the lump on the ground was a person. He appeared to be a human male, lying partly on his back, blood pooling on the ground around him. Not long dead, Max guessed. The man's t-shirt was saturated with blood, almost his entire torso cut open, his sightless eyes staring up at the ceiling overhead.

"The Keliotrope didn't do this," Vanko noted, crouching beside the body for a closer look. "The cuts are too thin. This looks more like fangs or razor claws."

"So, there might be something else on the loose in here," Pavla concluded. She and Yevhen had stopped a few paces from the body, keeping watch on their surroundings.

"Yes," Vanko nodded, getting to his feet. He aimed his torch ahead, into the theatre, and his brows lifted.

Max took a step forward, following his gaze.

There were about ten rows of seats leading down to a deep pit at the bottom. From her vantage point, Max could see a pair of metal gates in the side of the pit, darkness behind them.

There was another crumpled heap in the bottom of the pit. Another dead person, Max suspected.

"I'll wager it's a gladiator pit," Pavla said, voice flat.

"Gladiators?" Vanko echoed, disbelief back in his voice. But he wasn't questioning Pavla, not really. Max understood the question. She was having difficulty believing her own eyes, too.

As she swept her light around the part of the pit she could see, and then up the rows of seats, she saw indistinct movement at the edge of the light. She must have made a sound, as the others trained their weapons ahead, too. With the concentration of torches, Max could make out a group of people huddled together on one of the middle tiers of the seats.

With the distance, and poor light, Max couldn't be sure, but she thought they seemed frightened. She didn't think any of them were injured, but the shadows made it difficult to tell.

Before she could move towards the people, soft sounds behind them made them all turn, weapons lifted. Faddei stopped at the edge of the light, lifting a hand in a peaceful gesture against their weapons. He was a little out of breath, the seven-point star at his chest gleaming in response to the spell circles.

"Damned idiots," he said. "There was a group hiding under one of the tables. I almost shot them."

Max lifted a brow. There would be more to that story than just stubborn youngsters hiding. Faddei did not lose his temper easily. She squashed her curiosity for now.

The head Marshal had seen the dead man, brows lifting as he ran his torch over the body, assessing the injuries. "That wasn't the Keliotrope," he commented.

"No," Vanko agreed. "And there are more people over there."

Faddei spat a curse that made Max suppress an inappropriate grin. Her boss had a colourful way of expressing himself. "Let's get these idiots out of here, then we can search properly," Faddei suggested, moving ahead into the dark.

Max took a few running steps to catch up with him to take the lead again, heading around the top edge of the amphitheatre. As they walked, Max kept her light moving and spotted another pair of metal gates leading into the pit below them.

"Those gates are open," she commented to the group.

"I see it," Pavla agreed. "Yev and I will keep back watch," she said.

It made Max's skin crawl to think of what might have killed the dead man, and now be in the dark with them. At the same time, she could not help wondering exactly where the Keliotrope had come from. She couldn't see any ladders or steps up from the pit, and the great monster had not looked like it was good at climbing.

So how had it got out of the pit, if it had been in the pit? And if it hadn't been in the pit, where had it been?

When they reached the level above the huddled people, Max stopped, staring down. There were more people than she had thought. At least twenty. As the Marshals' lights landed on them, a few put up their hands, as if waving the light away.

"Stop it. Do you want it to find us again?" one man called up.

"Turn the light out," another woman pleaded.

"What is it?" Max asked, not moving her light. These people were not here by chance. They all looked well dressed and there were no obvious restraints that she could see. They had come here to see whatever illegal activity was supposed to happen in the pit below them.

"A Strump," one of the quieter members of the group said. He straightened a bit, peering into their lights. "Who are you?"

"A Strump?" Max repeated, not sure she could believe that. The giant, winged predators were usually found in colder climates, and preferred the high mountains. They only came to this part of the world during particularly hard winters. She had only ever seen one before, flying above the Wild, looking for other supernatural creatures to pick up for its next meal.

"We're Marshals," Faddei said, before anyone in the group could answer. "Come on, move. We'll get you out of here."

"The others got away," the woman said, her voice high and shaking. "Left us to die."

"Well, you're not dead," Faddei said in a matter-of-fact tone. "Get up and move."

"But the Strump-" one of the group objected, drowned out by the others moving, coming up the narrow steps cut into the earth as if their lives depended on it.

As the people moved, Max sensed rather than saw movement overhead. She swept her weapon and light up just as one of the darker patches above them detached from the ceiling and swooped down.

The creature that flew down had a wingspan to match the Keliotrope's length from tip to tail, its mottled, dense feathers blending with the shadows as it flew.

There was a beak that would be enough to give most people nightmares and yellow eyes that seemed to bore into Max as the creature descended.

She fired. Unlike the Keliotrope, the Strump didn't have an armoured hide. The cartridge slammed home, sending the creature off course. It shrieked in displeasure, the sound grating through Max's skull.

"Hold it off, and I'll get these people out," Faddei said.

"Right," Max said, kneeling on the ground to make herself as small a target as possible. She felt movement around her and risked a quick glance, finding that Vanko, Pavla and Yevhen were all kneeling with her, all of them facing in different directions.

"Did you see where it went?" Pavla asked.

"No. Max hit it, though," Vanko said.

Max didn't answer, keeping her focus ahead of her. She happened to be facing the direction that Faddei was moving, taking the crowd of people back through the tunnel that led to the Sorcerer's Mistress. The people were mostly moving quickly, huddled together, but one paused, looking back at the kneeling Marshals. In the poor light, she could not be sure, but she did not think he looked frightened. Rather, he seemed fascinated by what he was leaving behind.

A chill worked over Max's skin. These people had been here to witness something terrible in the pit. And while most of them had been rightly terrified by the Strump on the loose, there was one exception.

Before she could call out to Faddei, the Strump swept down from the ceiling again, heading for the group of people. She fired, making sure she was aiming high over the people's heads. The creature screamed, changing direction, heading for her instead. She kept firing and heard the flat reports of the other Marshals' weapons around her.

It took all four of them to bring the creature down, the Strump falling to the ground with an impact that rattled Max's teeth, the creature's momentum carrying it forward, sliding across the earth, past the two spell circles, heading for Max.

Too late, she realised it was not going to stop in time. She scrambled, trying to get to her feet and move, the bruises she had from hitting the car earlier slowing her down.

The Strump's outstretched wing, with razor claws along its edge, caught her leg as she tried to flee, sending her toppling forwards, down into the amphitheatre. She rolled forward on instinct and bounced off two of the great, hard-edged steps before coming to a stop, the breath knocked out of her, hot and jagged pain along her leg telling her that the creature's claws had torn through her toughened trousers and into her skin.

There was no time to be injured. She had kept hold of her weapon. It was one of the first things she had learned as a Marshal. Always keep the weapons. The torch had somehow survived the fall, still attached to the top of her shotgun. She ejected the empty magazine and slammed home her last full magazine, bringing the shotgun up, looking for the Strump, letting out an involuntary cry as she saw the creature's open beak far too close to her face, its fetid breath washing over her.

She scrambled sideways on the ground, ignoring the agony in her leg for the moment, shotgun at her shoulder, trained on the creature. It didn't move. Its eyes tracked her movement, expression full of hate. But the creature itself stayed where it was, splayed across the deep steps of the arena.

Max managed to get her feet under her, pulse thumping in her ears, and bit off another cry as she tried to put weight on her leg.

She swept her torch across the creature, making sure it really was down for the moment. They had all been using tranquilliser rounds, and even wounded from the cartridge strikes and the fall, the Strump wouldn't stay down forever. Still, it was out of commission for the moment.

Not far away, she heard a groan. She turned to find Vanko on one of the top steps of the arena, his shotgun beside him. He was sitting up, grimacing as he did so.

"Blasted creature," he said, looking at Max. "It got you?"

"Leg," Max said, trying to take another step forward and almost falling again. She muttered a curse she'd heard Faddei use more than once.

"Sit down. I've got some field dressing," Vanko said, getting to his feet and descending the steps towards her. "Pav. Yev. You still with us?" he called as he joined Max.

"Yes," Yevhen said. He appeared at the top of the arena, next to the fallen Strump, Pavla beside him. "This thing is huge. How in hells did they get a mature adult here?"

"That's a good question," Max said, thinking back to the bar and the tunnel they had come through. There was no way that the Strump would have fitted through the bar's front doors, and no possible way that even Grayson Forster could have smuggled a full-grown Strump into a city bar without being noticed. Almost grateful for the distraction giving her something else to think about other than her injuries, she lowered herself onto one of the seats, trying not to cry out in pain.

"I don't see anything else," Pavla said, eyes travelling over Max. "Can you walk?" It was a calm, professional question. Pavla, and the others, needed to know if Max was capable of working with them.

"Give me a minute," Max said. Vanko had pulled a field dressing from one of his pockets and she had to bite back another cry as he slapped it onto her leg over the ragged tear in her trousers, tying it around her leg. The white surface of the bandage stained quickly with her blood and he added another layer. The dressings were designed as an emergency measure to help a Marshal survive and get to safety. Max had used them before and knew that it would sting like nothing else when it was taken off, but it should help her keep moving for now.

"Try that," he suggested.

She stood up and put her weight on the leg. Red hot agony coursed through her. But her leg held. She nodded once, eyes watering.

"I can still shoot. Someone else better take the lead," she suggested, shuffling her way to the nearest set of shallow steps. Before she could start making her way upward, Pavla and Yevhen came down.

"We can't see any other movement on this level," Pavla said. "We need to go down."

"And there's an open gate," Yevhen pointed out as the pair moved past Vanko and Max.

"Alright," Max said. It wasn't the craziest idea she'd ever heard. She made her way, slowly and painfully, after the other three, pausing for a moment to get a painkilling tab out of her pockets, slapping it against her neck. A heartbeat or two later and relief washed over her, the pain dulling to a more manageable level. It wouldn't last for long, but for now she was functional. "I only have one magazine left," she told the others.

"Same," Vanko said, and grimaced. "We should have brought more."

"Just be careful with your shots," Yevhen suggested, practical as always. He and Pavla had arrived at the edge of the pit, and Max was somehow not surprised to see another spell ring embedded into the rim of the pit.

"That's quite a drop," Pavla said, leaning over the side. "There's another open gate here."

Pavla had been right about the drop, Max realised. Now that she was at the edge, the pit was about the height of three humans, from its base to the metal ring they were standing beside. She trained her light on the crumpled heap in the pit. Another dead human, a pool of blood around him and another dart gun lying on the ground beside him.

"We'll go first," Vanko said, glancing at Max. "We can catch you."

Max grimaced, not liking the idea, but she didn't have any other option. There was no way she could manage a drop and roll into the pit. "Alright," she said.

Max kept watch while the others tossed their shotguns down first, the torches making crazy patterns on the walls as their owners dropped into the pit, all of them rolling in smooth movements, coming back to their feet without a hitch. Pavla went over to the crumpled man on the ground and came away quickly, shaking her head. As dead as he looked, then.

"It smells like a butcher's shop down here," Vanko complained. He came to the side of the pit and held up his hands. "Come on, Max."

Max dropped her shotgun as well and lowered herself over the side, clinging on to the metal spell ring as long as she could, until she was stretched out down the side of the pit before letting go, sliding down the wall, the packed earth scraping along her clothes and getting into her nose and hair as she fell.

Hands took hold of her before she reached the ground, one of them clamping down on the wound in her leg, making her bite off a cry, but she was set on the ground with minimum fuss. Vanko was right. It did smell like a butcher's shop. A shoddy butcher's shop that didn't care about hygiene. The place stank of old blood and rotting meat, making her eyes sting.

Vanko handed her the shotgun and frowned at her. She wondered what she looked like and brushed some dirt off her front, trying to stand straighter. She didn't want the others trying to protect her. They needed to look after themselves.

"I'll manage," she told him, breathless from the white-hot pain coursing through her.

Slightly to her surprise and relief, the others took her at her word and moved towards the nearest set of open gates. Max followed them as best she could. The field dressing had hardened, as it was supposed to, making her leg stiff. The slide down the pit wall had woken the pain up again, despite the painkiller, and she had to bite her lip more than once to hold in a cry.

The gates were half the height of the pit walls, made of heavy metal welded into a grate pattern, the gaps small enough that not even a crow spider would be able to get through.

The pair of gates that they went through had been flung open with some force, one of the gates buckled as if from a heavy weight. Max frowned, wondering if the Keliotrope could have done that. She wasn't sure. The creature was huge and powerful, but the gates were heavy and seemed designed to contain something like a Keliotrope. Which meant there might be another creature on the loose. Just what they needed.

Through the gates they found themselves in another tunnel, this one as high and wide as the one that had led from the Sorcerer's Mistress. On the other side of the tunnel here, though, were more metal bars. Cages.

Movement in the nearest cage drew all their attention, and the Marshals trained their torches on it.

A small, furred creature sat in the middle of the cage, staring back at them with glowing green eyes. It had large, triangular shaped ears that twitched as it looked back at them, its black-and-tan striped fur rippling as it breathed.

"That's a shadow-fox, isn't it?" Yevhen asked. "I thought they were extinct."

"It looks like one," Vanko agreed. He swept his torch over the cage. "Looks secure, at least."

Max turned her light to the next cage and saw a pair of giant fangs gleaming through the bars. She took an involuntary step back, finger on the trigger, relaxing a fraction when she realised that the creature seemed secure.

A shout from outside the tunnel drew their attention. Pavla went to the gate to answer, and moments later, Faddei joined them. He was carrying extra ammunition and a shotgun of his own, handing out extra shotgun magazines as he scowled at the cage.

"I've sent for more containment for the Strump," he said, still frowning, "but we're going to need more, aren't we? What else is here?"

"We've just got here," Pavla told him.

"What the hells is going on?" Faddei asked, a hard edge to his voice.

"Supernatural fights," Vanko said, in an equally hard voice.

"This has been here a while," Max said, and heard the others murmur agreement. "There is no possible way that the local police didn't know something was going on here," Max said, remembering Ruutti's odd reaction to the mention of the Sorcerer's Mistress.

The small pen light on her shotgun didn't provide a strong enough light to reach far along the tunnel, but all she could see were more cages.

She wanted to be sick. It was one thing for her and the other Marshals to hunt down and contain creatures that had escaped from the Wild and were a danger to the city's population. As with all the other Marshals, she did her best to tranquillise and contain the threat. Raymund and his team would relocate as many creatures as possible back into the Wild. Killing was a last resort.

But this was something altogether different. Creatures taken from their own habitats. Brought here and thrown into a pit as entertainment for the crowd. And in the process, no doubt, making Grayson Forster very wealthy.

She remembered the quiet, wary people on the street above and thought that most of the bar's neighbours probably knew that something was going on under their feet. Something connected with the bar. She wondered just how many of the bar's patrons also knew. The wannabe magicians, and those who wanted a taste of the dark side of the city. This was probably too dark for a lot of them. Or so she hoped.

"Yes," Faddei said, voice dark, agreeing with her.

"It's likely that the Strump killed the two men outside," Pavla said, "but we need to make sure there isn't anything else on the loose."

"Yes," Faddei agreed. He glanced across at Max. "The containment team should be here soon. They're going to need someone to watch their backs. I saw a ladder just inside the gate," he added, before Max could say anything more.

Effectively dismissing her without saying the words. Even though it was the sensible thing to do, it still stung. Faddei would be a more than adequate replacement for her. So Max just nodded and made her way back out to the pit itself. There was, indeed, a ladder tucked away against the wall. An extending one that should reach to the top of the pit.

She tried to ignore her stinging eyes as she dragged the ladder out of the gate and to the side of the pit, struggling to get it set up and secure enough that she could get out. Faddei was just being practical. With the leg wound she had, she would only slow them down. And they could not afford to be distracted by her injury. She did not want to be responsible for anyone else getting hurt. Not ever again.

Chapter Twenty-Three

By the time she reached the top of the ladder, the painkiller she had taken had worn off. Each step was accompanied by a fresh jolt of white-hot pain and she was short-tempered and hissing curses as she limped her way up the steps to the top of the arena. By the time she reached the ground level, the double layer of bandage Vanko had put on her leg was soaked through with blood and she was light-headed, vision wavering.

The Strump was still where they had left it, its eyes closed. That didn't mean it was completely asleep, she knew. But it was a little bit of good news, at least.

The magic that Yevhen and Pavla had created was still active, the faint mist giving the smallest hint of light, serving mainly to remind her of how big and how dark the space was. Her torch didn't reach very far. She tried not to think about what else might be out there in the shadows, waiting for her to drop her guard.

Max searched in her pockets for more painkiller, her fingers shaking. Marshals were only supposed to use one patch in the field, but she wasn't going to be any use to anyone if she passed out from pain.

Before she could find another dose, a faint noise in the dark caught her attention. She straightened, shotgun ready at her shoulder. It hadn't sounded like a creature. More like footsteps. But two-legged things could be dangerous, too.

"I'm a Marshal and I'm armed. Show yourself," she called into the dark, trying to sound full of authority and not like she was about to collapse. Her voice was far higher than it should be, and sounded weak even in her own ears.

A figure detached from the dark, coming into the light from her torch. An ordinary-looking human man, dressed in dark, casual clothing. Someone she wouldn't look twice at on the street.

But he wasn't on the street. He was here. Standing at the edge of an underground amphitheatre, not that far from a sleeping Strump and under the guard of her shotgun. He looked faintly familiar, and she remembered the group that Faddei had led out of the arena, and the one who had looked back. It might be the same man.

She remembered, too, the dark-clothed man who had been watching her earlier in the day, when she had been checking out the second crime scene. He had been too far away for her to be sure, but the height and build looked about right for this man. Her skin prickled. Had he been following her?

"Marshal Ortis," he said, sending another chill through her. He knew her name. He was definitely not here by chance. "You do find yourself in the most interesting places."

"Do I know you?" Max asked, keeping her gun levelled on him. A tranquilliser round would do some serious damage to a human.

He smiled, and ice formed around her heart. She had seen that expression many times before on predators.

"We've never been formally introduced," he said.

He was familiar. Max just had no idea where from. If he hadn't drawn attention to himself by coming back to the underground chamber, she might never had noticed him or remembered him. For a moment, she wondered if he had been one of the bystanders on the street with the Keliotrope. But that made no sense, as he would have had to get ahead of the Marshals on their way down here.

Then she remembered one of the people in the amphitheatre saying that other people had left. The Marshals hadn't met anyone else in the tunnel. Which meant that there must be at least one more way in and out. That made sense. Even Grayson Forster wouldn't want to bring illegal creatures through his bar.

"How did you get in here?" Max asked. The edges of her vision were hazy, but she kept her gun focused on the unnamed man. He was dangerous. She wanted to shoot him. The temptation was there, her trigger finger ready. But he hadn't actually threatened her. And Marshals avoided shooting humans if at all possible.

A babble of excited voices and bright lights in the distance cut off whatever he might have said. The scientists were on their way, doubtless ecstatic to have the chance to study a Strump up close.

When Max looked back at the man, he had gone. Vanished into the dark. She spat a curse and took a step forward, cursing again as her leg almost gave out under her. The fresh blood was softening up the hard cast of the bandage and it was losing its structure. She braced herself, sweeping her light in a slow, steady arc. Nothing. No one apart from the scientists, with their over-sized torches and chatter.

"Max," one of the figures at the front of the group said. After a moment, she recognised Raymund. That was bad. She should have recognised him right away. "Are you alright? Your leg-"

Max didn't hear whatever else he might have had to say as the ground rose up to meet her, darkness swallowing her whole.

The lights around her were muted, gentle on her stinging eyes as she opened them. Everything was hazy for a moment, then her sight cleared enough to recognise that she was not where she had been. She was in some kind of treatment room, covered in white sheets, with a cool numbness spreading along her leg.

"Oh, good, you're awake," a familiar voice said. Glenda, the nurse practitioner, appeared in Max's line of sight and smiled. "You're in the clinic. It's late afternoon. The Marshals' medical team brought you in early this morning. We had to cut off your trousers, I'm sorry, but we've cleaned out and dressed the wounds in your leg. Twenty-eight stitches. All the important bits and pieces are intact and the muscles will heal in time. You'll need more antibiotics and to take it easy for at least a few days, but you're going to be fine."

Max blinked, trying to take in all the information. She opened her mouth and found a straw placed between her lips.

"Drink. It's supposed to be cherry flavoured. It's basically water with some more healing and rehydration in it," Glenda told her, in the same cheerful voice.

Max took a sip, and her eyebrows lifted. It did, in fact, taste like cherries. It slid down her throat, making her realise how dry her mouth was, and she took another sip, then tried to sit up. Bruises woke up all along her back. She remembered hitting a car at some point in the long night.

"Give me a second," Glenda said, taking the cup and straw away. She pressed a button on the side of the bed and it lifted so Max was sitting more upright. "There, that's better. Here, you can have this," she said, pressing the cup and straw into Max's hands. "We had to give you some strong painkillers to clean out that wound, so you're probably feeling a bit fuzzy-headed."

"Understatement," Max said. She'd drunk most of the liquid in the cup and her senses were slowly settling back down. "The others?"

"Apparently, everyone else is fine. A few bruises, nothing major. There was another creature loose, but they managed to contain it. You're the only one they brought in," Glenda said. She was telling the truth, as far as Max could tell. Relief coursed through her. No one else had been seriously hurt. She hadn't let the people around her down. This time, at least.

"What-" Max started to ask.

The door slammed open and a small, blonde storm front surged into the room.

"Get out," Ruutti snapped at Glenda.

"You need to let the Marshal rest, detective," Glenda began, facing the smaller woman.

"Out. Now," Ruutti said, baring her blunt, human-shaped teeth.

"It's alright," Max said to Glenda. With Ruutti's arrival, Max's memories snapped back into place. "I have things to say to the detective as well."

"If you're sure," Glenda said. She put a small device into Max's hand. "That's a call button. Let me know if you need anything."

"Thank you," Max said.

Ruutti waited until Glenda had left, shutting the door behind her, before rounding on Max.

"What in hells were you thinking? You had no right to go to that bar."

Max stared at Ruutti for a long moment, conscious of a curious feeling of disappointment. She had expected better of the detective, somehow. "So, you did know about the arena."

"It's been there for a hundred years at least," Ruutti said, waving her hand in dismissal. "It's never been a problem before now."

"I'm sorry, what?" Max asked, trying to sit up straighter and having to fall back on her pillows as the bruises twisted again. "An illegal fighting arena where supernatural creatures are pitted against each other. It's never been a problem? Are you serious? Did you miss the illegal part or the creature part?" she asked, voice rising.

"No one ever got hurt until you decided to interfere," Ruutti yelled back. There were bright spots of colour on her cheeks, and she wasn't quite meeting Max's eyes.

"The Keliotrope and the Strump had already escaped before I got there," Max snapped, keeping watch on the other woman. "But I'll be sure to let Faddei know that the police force doesn't consider a supernatural fighting arena in the heart of the city to be a problem. Or something that they should have warned the Marshals about."

"You would have shut it down," Ruutti said, folding her arms over her stomach.

"Yes, we would. And we will," Max said. She didn't need to check with Faddei to know that.

"They are just creatures," Ruutti muttered, the words sounding forced. Like something she had been told, over and over.

"They are creatures, that's true. And most of them could kill a dozen people in moments. There's a reason why we have a barrier to the Wild," Max said, all the fight draining out of her. "So, if you knew about the fights, is that why you didn't want me at the Sorcerer's Mistress?"

Ruutti stared back at her, expression reminding Max of a surly child. "You would have shut it down," she said again.

"It will be shut down," Max stated, voice flat. She knew Faddei well enough to make that confident prediction. "Do you know if any of our victims went to the fights?" she asked.

Ruutti's brows lifted, the sulky expression vanishing. "Why? Do you think there's a connection?"

"We still don't know how the killer is finding or choosing his victims," Max said, "and I came across someone tonight." She paused, trying to think of the right way of describing the nondescript, dangerous man she had seen in the underground.

"Well, Jessica Walsh would certainly have been at the fights. The Five Families have been sponsoring them for years," Ruutti said, and her lip curled in distaste. Ah. So she wasn't quite as comfortable with the pit as she had first appeared. Max filed that information away as Ruutti went on. "Quietly, of course, but all the main players in the Families would know about them."

"You talked to Jessica's family?" Max asked.

"I didn't talk. The chief and councilman did," Ruutti corrected, sounding bitter. The biggest case of her career, most likely, and her boss had intervened. "I was there, though."

"What did the Walsh Family say?" Max asked.

"Their first thought was that she'd been killed by one of the other families, although they didn't know which one," Ruutti said, shoving a hand through her hair in an uncharacteristic fidgeting gesture. "Apparently, she was a bit of a wild child and prone to telling lies. She told one of her younger cousins that she'd been into the underworld. She seemed to be trying to scare him. No one apart from the cousin believed her. He was five at the time," Ruutti added. She stopped, tilting her head. "Oh. Wait. Our killer is trying to make a connection with the underworld. Is that why Jessica was targeted?"

Max took a drink, trying to think of a way to answer that didn't give away her own knowledge.

Ruutti didn't wait for Max to speak, though, beginning to pace the room. "So, Jessica may have been a target because she had boasted about the underworld, and we know at least one of the other victims liked to talk it up, too. Maybe that's the connection. Maybe that's how the killer is choosing them."

"If he's picking victims on the basis of their tall tales, he has a large potential victim pool," Max commented. "A lot of wannabe magicians boast about things they couldn't possibly have done."

"That is true," Ruutti agreed. Her eyes were bright, though, expression determined. "But I'm thinking it's a more specific brag. There can't be all that many people who boasted about being in the underworld."

Max kept her mouth closed, not all that surprised that Ruutti had latched on to that possible connection. She had always known that the detective was smart. But that wasn't the only possible link. "See if the others went to the fights, too," Max said, as Ruutti headed for the door.

Ruutti paused, turning back. "Why? Oh. Right. You said you met someone there. Who? What did they look like?"

Max tried to shift position on the bed and stopped, hissing as pain ran through her leg. "Human. Male. Ordinary looking. Nothing special to look at."

"That doesn't help at all," Ruutti complained.

"I'm sure I've seen him before, though. He might have been following me in the city. I'm not sure about that. But he was definitely part of the group in the arena. He seemed familiar with the space," Max added. Familiar enough that he had either left with Faddei and come back in another entrance, or never left at all.

"He sounds boring. Why did you mention him?" Ruutti asked.

"Because he came back when the others had all fled, and didn't seem worried when I had a gun pointed at him. There was something about him," Max said, her skin crawling in memory. "And he knew who I was."

"It's not much to go on," Ruutti said. "Can you give a better description?"

"Human. Male. Pale skin. Unremarkable features. Mid brown hair cut short," Max answered, closing her eyes briefly to try to recall his face. "About my height. He was wearing dark clothes. No logos or badges that I saw. Well-spoken. He sounded like he was a city boy. No accent or slang. Maybe in his thirties," Max finished.

Ruutti made a noise as Max opened her eyes. The detective was looking less than impressed. "It's not much," she said again.

"I know. But honestly, I wouldn't have noticed him in a crowd," Max said.

"Well, I'll keep an eye out for the most boring man alive," Ruutti said, nose wrinkling, "and see if the other victims went to the fights."

Before she could say more, the door opened again and Faddei stepped into the room. He stayed in the doorway, blocking Ruutti's exit.

"Detective," he said, voice clipped.

"Marshal," Ruutti said, equally terse.

"I've just been speaking with your chief," Faddei said.

"Oh?" Ruutti said, lifting her chin.

"A hundred years at least," Max said, sounding exhausted even in her own ears. "That's how long the arena has been there, apparently."

"So I've been learning," Faddei said, face tight as he stared at the detective. "It won't be operating any longer."

Ruutti was paler than she had been, but she just nodded. "Did you need me for anything else, Marshal?" she asked.

"No," Faddei said, stepping aside to let Ruutti leave.

"Wait," Max said, before Ruutti could storm out. "I know why the killer chose those particular spots for the rituals. They are on ley line intersections."

Ruutti stared back at Max, brows lifted. "Did you hit your head as well?" the detective asked slowly. "Ley lines? A child's story."

"No," Max said. "I went to the games court. There's something there. Underneath."

"It doesn't tell us where he's going to go next," Ruutti said, frowning. Max could tell that the detective didn't believe her.

"I agree, but it might help narrow it down," Max said, voice rasping in her dry throat. She took another sip of the drink. "We don't have to believe it. He believes it," she added. Ruutti's frown cleared and she nodded.

"Alright. I'll see what I can find out," Ruutti told Max, and left the room, shutting the door with a careful click behind her.

"You didn't have to come and visit," Max said to Faddei, heat rising under her skin. He went to visit all the Marshals if they ended up in hospital. It was one of the things that made him a good boss. But she hated being vulnerable. And lying on a treatment bed swathed in blankets was more vulnerable than she had been for a long time.

"You took a hard hit," Faddei said, voice mild. "And I thought you'd want to know that Zoya has woken up. She's going to be fine."

"Oh, that's good news," Max said, relief coursing through her, along with renewed guilt. The other Marshal had been badly wounded when Max was supposed to be keeping watch.

"We've had a bad couple of weeks for injuries," Faddei said. Max remembered the last time she had been in the clinic, with Glenda removing the crow spider stinger from her shoulder. There had been something happening that night involving not just the Marshals but the Order as well. Faddei took a seat on the guest chair, and abruptly looked like he had aged a decade. "We had a tribe of Seacast monkeys in the city green the other week. Took all of us, plus some of the Order, to bring them down."

Max flinched involuntarily. That definitely explained why there had been an injured Guardian in the clinic when she had last been here. She had encountered Seacast monkeys a few times over her years as a Marshal. In ones or twos only. A tribe was five or more, and far more dangerous. The creatures were about the size of a large human, seemingly built entirely of muscle and temper, and had a fondness for destruction. They mostly stayed in the Wild, but were clever enough to take advantage of any breaches to make their way through from time to time.

"We thought they came through the breach in the Wild," Faddei said, scrubbing his hand across his head. "But there were more than a few empty cages under the arena."

"You think that Grayson Forster and his people had kept Seacast monkeys for the pit?" Max asked.

"I'm going to ask the question, at least. If that's the case, then he and his people owe the city for the damage and the loss of life. No, not any of ours. But three civilians were killed before we managed to contain the situation."

Max closed her eyes briefly, all too easily able to imagine the destruction. The city green was a long, sinuous stretch of open land that stretched through the heart of the city, curving along the banks of an artificial river, complete with a lake at one end. The green was full of mature trees, stretches of open grassland and a huge variety of plant and animal life that the city's council deemed safe for the heart of the city. It was the closest most city dwellers got to open countryside, and it was busy day or night. Any creatures loose in the green, whether Seacast monkeys or Keliotropes, could have created a blood bath.

"At least the breach is sealed," Faddei said, voice heavy. "And we've put a stop to the fights."

"Assuming that we're allowed into the city to keep a watch on things," Max said slowly, remembering the challenges to her authority from earlier in the night.

"What have you heard?" Faddei asked, gaze sharp.

"Nothing official. But I had two different people tell me that Marshals don't have any authority in the city," Max said, frowning.

"Oh, that old yarn," Faddei said, waving a hand. "It comes up every now and then in the council. I just tell them that they're perfectly welcome to police their own streets. We've got more than enough to do keeping the city limits creature-free."

Max choked on an unexpected laugh. She might have known that Faddei was ahead of the rumour. And she could very easily imagine him standing, in his battered leathers, in front of the clean-cut, suit-wearing members of the city council and telling them, as bluntly as he had spoken to her, that they could see to their own safety.

"Yes," Faddei said, a gleam of mischief in his eyes. "Oddly enough, the prospect of clearing out crow spiders and Seacast monkeys or whatever other thing makes its way past our guard doesn't find favour with the council."

Max laughed, then hissed as the movement jolted her bruises and sent a fresh wave of pain down her leg.

"We've got Cas and Pol helping Raymund and his team with the new arrivals. There were nineteen other creatures in the cages under the arena," Faddei said, voice shading to a darker tone. "A lot of them are in a bad way. A lot of old wounds that haven't healed properly. Raymund is assessing which ones we can release back to the Wild. Some of them might need to stay with us for a while. It's going to be a busy few days."

He wasn't exactly asking permission to make use of her hounds. But Max knew enough about injuries to know that she'd be out of the field for at least a handful of days. Far better for her dogs to be doing something useful while she healed, even if she would miss them. The dogs liked to work, and lazing around with her would drive them to find other, destructive, ways of entertaining themselves. They had torn apart an entire three-seater sofa one afternoon when she had left them alone.

"I'm sure Cas and Pol will like spending a bit more time around Leonda," Max said, managing a smile. It was perfectly true.

"The clinic wants to keep you here overnight at least," Faddei said. "When you're ready to leave, let us know and we'll bring your vehicle across for you.

It's back at headquarters getting serviced," he added. Max winced slightly. The vehicle's service was long overdue, but she'd never managed to find time to get it done.

"Thanks," Max said. As grateful as she was for the attention to her vehicle, she wasn't used to anyone else looking after her, and it felt strange.

"The doctors here are recommending a couple of weeks' rest and light duties before you can get back out into the field," Faddei added. "You are owed time off, so if you want to take it, that's fine. If not, there's a mountain of paperwork." There was more than a hint of humour in his face at the end.

Max bit her lip against a smile. None of the Marshals liked paperwork. Spending some time at home seemed like a good option right now. But she knew she might feel differently in a day or two.

"I'll let you get some rest. Just keep in touch, won't you?" Faddei said, putting a hand on her arm where it was swathed in blankets before he headed out.

Leaving Max alone with her eyes stinging at the rough affection in Faddei's voice, the wounds on her leg sending fresh waves of pain through her body, and an empty drinking cup in her hands.

She must have fallen asleep, because she woke up to the soft sound of the door closing.

The room was almost completely dark, only the lights from various instruments showing. She could sense enough to know she was still in the clinic, still propped up in the treatment bed. She even still had the empty cup and call button in her hands.

"Did you send that nice young detective looking for me?" a voice said out of the dark. The tone of it sent a chill over her skin.

It took Max a moment to place the voice. She couldn't remember any features of the man's face, but she remembered him standing in the light from her torch, seemingly uncaring that he was under guard of her shotgun.

"You caught my interest," Max said, trying to remember what was around the bed. Nothing she could use as a weapon, she was quite sure. She pressed the button in her hand and heard nothing. It might not even work. There might not be anyone around to hear it.

"How flattering," the voice said. A dark shape moved in the room, coming closer to the side of the bed. She couldn't make out any features, just knew it was a man, and every sense she possessed was telling her that he was dangerous. "But you really shouldn't have involved the detective, you know."

"What have you done to her?" Max asked, mouth dry. She couldn't move. Something was holding her still. Some pressure on her body. And she didn't have any weapons to hand. Her pulse was thumping in her neck, breath too hard and too fast, harsh in the quiet room. She was alone with a dangerous predator. All alone. With no means of defending herself.

Her heart squeezed as she wished Cas and Pol were with her. There was no possible way that this creature would have dared to approach her if the shadow-hounds were with her.

"The detective is fine, Marshal Ortis. You should be more worried about yourself," he said.

"What? Why?" she asked, the words heavy and sluggish in her mouth.

"I knew you would find your way to the bar and to the pit. Although it took you longer than I had thought," he told her, voice low and too close to her. "But you did make it eventually. And now here we are."

Panic coursed through Max. He'd been waiting for her? She struggled to move and couldn't, her whole body weighted to the bed.

There was a faint hissing noise and the world went black again.

Chapter Twenty-Four

Max woke with a foul taste in her mouth, lying on her back with a hard, unyielding surface beneath her. Cool air brushed over her skin, making her realise she was wearing a sleeveless t-shirt, and cotton shorts and nothing else. She blinked, trying to clear her sight, and saw the night sky high overhead, with the faintest traces of false dawn appearing. She tried to sit up, to move, and found she could not.

A sound escaped her throat. Frustration and fear mixed together.

"Oh, you're awake. Good."

It was the voice from the clinic room and the underground space. The nondescript, dangerous man.

Movement beside her made her flinch and try to turn her head. Nothing but her eyes moved. Her whole body was frozen in place, not under her control.

The man was wearing coveralls of the sort used by crime scene techs, his face covered by a clear plastic shield.

And all at once, Max knew where she'd seen him before.

"You. Work. With. Police," she said, each word an effort to force out between her frozen lips and tight throat. Breathing was difficult.

"Very good, Marshal. Or may I call you Max?" he said, and crouched down beside her, a pleased smile on his face. "It's been so much fun watching you and the detective run around trying to work out what I'm doing."

He had been at every crime scene, Max realised, skin prickling. She had seen him at the first scene Ruutti had called her to. The tech who had handed Ruutti the inventory. Calm and professional. Just one of a number of anonymous faces doing the detailed, painstaking work of recording the crime scene and gathering evidence. Except that no evidence had been found. Not one piece of skin or strand of hair. Nothing. Looking at the man dressed head-to-toe in his coverall, his hands gloved and face protected by the plastic shield, Max realised why. He knew exactly what the crime scene techs were looking for. And knew how to avoid detection. There would be no physical evidence to link him to any of the crimes. And even if some trace was found, he would be able to say, with perfect truth, that he had been there as part of the investigation team.

"Why?" she asked. One word at a time seemed to be all she could manage.

"Why, she asks," the man said. His face was set in a smile, but there was no humour in it. "When you don't even know my name. When no one knows my name. Just another worker drone. Not worthy of attention. But that's going to change. The dark lord Himself has recognised me. And soon everyone will know my name."

He sounded quite mad. Max tried to form more words and made another sound of frustration.

"Don't worry, I haven't poisoned you. Just used a little bit of crow spider venom. Not enough to kill you, but it will keep you quiet and still while I work."

"How?" Max managed. She didn't remember being injected with anything. But then, she had been sleeping.

"It's quite ingenious, really," he said, apparently pleased by her question. He picked up what looked like an aerosol can and held it where she could see it. It was just a silver can. "I made it into a spray. Very effective in a closed space. Oh, don't worry, I've taken the antidote. I'm fine. And the venom won't kill you," he repeated.

No, Max thought. The venom wouldn't kill her, because he wanted to do that himself. She wondered if any of the other victims had endured this. Being unable to move, trapped in their own bodies, while the madman talked over their heads, celebrating his own cleverness. Her mind gave her a picture of Jessica Walsh, her pink hair spilling around her head. The girl had died of an asthma attack and had been unable to move or do anything about it. Had she lain there being forced to listen to this madman boast while she suffocated?

Even as Max wondered that, she knew what the answer would be. Whoever this individual was, he would not have been able to resist boasting of his achievements. All of his victims would have heard about his plans. She wondered if he had continued with his cheerful-sounding, awful monologue while he had cut into them to draw their blood and realised that, unless she did something about it, she would find out for herself soon enough. A sound lodged in her throat and she struggled to swallow it. She didn't want him to see how frightened she was. Not for as long as she could help it.

"Where?" she managed to ask. Her lips were moving more freely. Perhaps the venom was wearing off. Perhaps he had got the dose wrong, and she would be able to move soon. Escape.

"Oh, you haven't figured it out yet? Why I chose all the spots? Where we are just now?" he asked, voice hardening. "I thought you were cleverer than that, Marshal."

"Intersections," she said, struggling to complete the word. The venom hadn't worn off that much.

"Ah," he said, drawing out the word, the gleeful tone back in his voice. "So you did work it out. Yes, indeed. Clever Max. We're at another intersection of the land's power lines." He smiled behind the plastic shield and patted her arm before getting up and moving away. She had felt the warmth of his gloved hand on her skin, the touch making her want to move away.

Max shivered. Or, rather, her body tried to shiver. Nothing happened, the shiver translating instead into the sensation of little rivers of ice travelling along her skin. Power lines. Ley lines. She had been right.

And she was on another one of the intersections now. Wherever she was.

She still couldn't move her head, but she could listen. There was no traffic she could hear. No music. No human activity at all. That meant they were no longer in the city itself. The ground was rough and hard beneath her. He would need a solid surface to paint the runes, which ruled out any grassland or areas with planting. So she was likely on a road surface or possibly a parking lot.

Max closed her eyes for a moment, trying to remember the layout of the maps she had seen, and the prints she had made. There was a supposedly powerful intersection of ley lines within an old industrial site. It would have had a large concrete area for the vehicles arriving and departing. It was likely she was there. The buildings themselves had long since been abandoned and robbed of anything useful.

Movement beside her made her open her eyes again. He was back, and this time was carrying a long, wickedly sharp knife, along with a clear plastic pot with what looked like a paintbrush in it. The pot was empty. Ready to be filled with her blood, Max realised.

She made another low, incoherent sound.

"You should be honoured, you know," he said, standing over her with the knife in one hand and pot in the other. "You could be the key that's needed to open the Grey Gates and bring Him to the surface."

He didn't know, Max realised. He was guessing. He had been guessing all along.

"Why me?" she asked, managing the two words with barely a pause between.

"I could smell your blood," he said, smiling again. He knelt by her side and her dominant arm. "It smelled delicious."

"Blood," Max said, and struggled to find another word. He was human. He shouldn't have been able to smell her blood in the underground space.

"It called to me," he said, still with that smile on his face.

He'd been in touch with the underworld, Max remembered. He'd managed to break through the barriers and get a message - *keep looking*. And she had actually been to the underworld. Her blood would still carry a trace of it, all these years later. Enough that he had recognised it despite his blunt human senses, even if he still didn't know what it actually meant.

"It's a shame you've lost so much blood. But the clinic would have given you some fluids, so you should have enough. Well, let's hope so anyway. I'm getting close. I can feel it," he said.

Max was so distracted by his chatter that the first sting of the knife against her skin was a shock. It was simply cold for a moment, the blade extraordinarily sharp, and then he moved on, travelling up her arm, cutting again and again and again and the stinging started. The sting grew to a fire burning in her flesh, white hot agony making her scream before he had even reached her shoulder.

The fire reminded her of the underworld. It was too much. Too hot. Too intense. Too blinding. She wanted to run. To get up and move away. Then grab the knife out of his hand and turn it against him.

But her body wouldn't move. It just lay there, a dead weight on the ground.

As she couldn't run in the world, Max ran in her mind. She turned and fled from what was being done to her, diving into her mind, trying to find somewhere that was safe. Free from pain. Free from the happy chatter of the man who was cutting into her. Away. Far away. To a place inside where she wasn't paralysed by spider venom. Where she wasn't bleeding. Where she wasn't terrified, facing death and unable to do anything about it. To a place where she could move. Could sit up, gather her legs under her, reach out and grab the wrist of the killer so hard that he dropped the knife and then twist his arm until he cried out in pain and scrambled away from her, open-mouthed and astonished.

The feeling of hard, cold concrete under her feet snapped her back to the here and now. She was on her feet, swaying, blood trailing down her arm, dripping onto the ground. Her injured leg was numb rather than painful, holding her steady.

The killer was standing a few paces away from her, open-mouthed behind his protective face shield. He was holding the pot in one hand. It was no longer empty, the inside coated with her blood. His other hand was empty. He had dropped the knife.

Max looked down and found the knife by her feet, the blade stained with her blood, a faint metallic smell reaching her nose. She bent to pick it up without thinking, her movements smooth and unhindered by spider venom.

"You-" the man said. He took another step back, his foot knocking against something metallic on the ground. The spray canister. "You should not be able to move," he said, bending to pick up the canister. "But we can fix that. Yes, we can."

Before he could do anything with the canister, Max charged at him, knife held in front of her.

He dropped the canister, bringing his arm up to defend against her charge. The knife sank into his arm, grating against bone, the momentum of Max's run ramming the knife all the way through and into the man's chest.

They tumbled to the ground, the man making no attempt to stop his fall, his head smacking into the ground with a crunch, Max landing on top of him. The pot with her blood in it spilled, splashing her legs as she scrambled off the man, trying to pull the knife out. The hilt slipped from her grasp. Only one of her hands was working, and she couldn't get enough of a grip on the knife to use it.

The man made a low, dark sound. Pain and fury combined. He moved, trying to grab hold of her.

Max scrambled to get away, one of her feet sliding on the blood-slick concrete, and looked around for something - anything - she could use as a weapon. The spray canister was next to her and she picked it up. It was cold and awkward in her hand. It would do, though.

The killer sat up. His head was an odd shape, skull partly dented, skin extraordinarily pale. He looked like one of the bodies in the mortuary, only he was moving, the sight of it sending chills across Max's skin. He should be dead. With a head wound like that, he should be dead. He looked down at the knife sticking out of his arm and took hold of the handle, pulling it out with seemingly little effort. The blade made a sticky sucking sound as it left his flesh, blood pouring out of the wound until he frowned at it and the bleeding stopped. He was dead. And yet he wasn't.

"What are you?" Max asked, mouth dry, pulse hammering in her throat again. She had assumed he was human. He hadn't looked or felt like anything other than human until he had hit the ground.

He looked up at her and his lips peeled back from his teeth in what might have been a smile. It made Max want to run as far away as possible.

"He has accepted my sacrifices," the man said, voice high pitched and full of glee. "And He has rewarded me with new life." He got to his feet, movements stiff and oddly uncoordinated, as if he wasn't quite sure what to do with the body he was wearing.

"Sacrifice?" Max asked. "You mean the people you killed?"

"Sacrificed," he corrected her, a frown forming on his face.

"Killed," Max countered. He didn't seem to have much emotional self-control. Perhaps she could provoke him into making a mistake. She took a step to the side, looking around to see if there was anything more useful than the canister she was holding. There was what looked like a leather wrap lying on the ground not far from where she had been. It looked like the sort hunters used to store their tools.

She took another step towards it. The killer seemed more interested in his newly undead state than her for the moment.

She reached the leather wrap and nudged it open with her foot. It unrolled easily, revealing another pair of knives. He had brought extra knives. Of course he had.

Max tucked the canister under her useless arm and grabbed up the leather roll. The knives looked as sharp as the one he had used on her, and was even now holding in his hand. The wrap itself had a long strap, which she slid over her head, trying not to think about how many people he had killed with the knives. Good. Now she had weapons she could use.

He was still standing where she had left him, staring at his own hands, turning them over in the growing light.

"I'm alive," he said. He seemed to have forgotten she was there. For the moment, at least.

"No, you really aren't," Max said, mentally reviewing what little she knew about the walking dead. It wasn't much. There were enough problems in the world without walking corpses. He wasn't a vampire. He wasn't a corpse animated by magic. He seemed to have retained his personality and memories. It was just his body that was dead.

Fire, she thought. When she didn't have enough bullets, fire usually killed things quite effectively.

She drew the longest knife out of the leather wrap, its blade gleaming in the first rays of sunlight. Adding fire to metal was a complicated spell at the best of times, but it was the only idea she had.

He looked across at her as she lifted the blade, lips peeling back in what might have been another smile. "It seems you were the right sacrifice after all. Look what a mess you've made. We'll have to start again," he said, and took a step towards her. As if she was going to simply let him put her back on the ground and cut into her with his knives.

Max raised the blade in her hand and focused, trying to draw on what little power she had. The spell for fire sang in her mind and she opened her mouth to speak the words.

Flames burst into light along the blade, blinding white, the heat making Max take an involuntary step back. The heat, and the flames, came with her.

The man followed, eyes on the blade and its flames.

"Nice trick," he said. "You can teach me that before you go."

"I don't think so," Max said, shoving aside the truth that she didn't know how she had made the knife burn in the first place. She hadn't completed the spell. Instead, she faced the killer and thrust the blade forward. The flames left the knife and travelled across to the walking corpse, licking across his clothing, setting everything alight.

He burned. White and yellow and orange flames cascaded over him, burrowing into his dead flesh, the pillar of fire rising impossibly high into the night as it consumed him. He didn't scream, his face set in a startled expression, as if he couldn't believe what was happening to him. But he didn't speak or moan or make any sound at all. That was almost worse than anything else, Max thought, swaying as she stood and watched him burn. The quiet. The heat of the fire seared her skin, but she didn't move. She needed to be sure. Needed to see him die.

Eventually, it was done. He folded to the ground, blackened and crumbling into chunks of ash.

Max took a few paces away before her legs gave out and she crumpled to the ground in turn, managing to stay in a sitting position, her wounded leg stretched out in front of her at an awkward angle, her other knee drawn up.

She should move. She should get up, try to find a phone or some other signalling device, and call the Marshals' office. Call Ruutti, too, to let her know that the killer was dead.

It all seemed like far too much effort.

Far easier to just sit in the growing sunlight and breathe. That, she could manage. Everything else would have to wait.

Chapter Twenty-Five

After a while, she felt a vibration in the ground, and then heard the faint sound of a vehicle approaching. She looked up and only then did she notice a sleek city car parked a short distance away. That must be the killer's car, she realised. He might have a phone in there. Or something to eat and drink. And perhaps a blanket. She was getting cold.

That meant she would need to get up and move. And that seemed like a lot of effort right now. She was tired. So tired.

Before she could do anything more, another sleek vehicle rolled into view. This one was large and black and looked like it could crush the killer's car. It also bore the resonance of familiar magic. She frowned, wondering why the Order was here.

The vehicle stopped a short distance away. She watched as the driver's door opened and a familiar figure stepped out. Bryce. Naturally, her inner voice said. It couldn't possibly be anyone else, could it? The Order had a hundred warriors at least, and she didn't know all of them. But no, the one who arrived here was Bryce. Who had recognised her and spoken her old name.

She kept silent and watched as he took a look around the scene, then at her. He moved to the back of the vehicle, opening it and picking up something from the inside before coming across to her with steady strides. He was moving slowly, she realised. As if he was trying not to frighten her.

That struck her as extraordinarily funny and she choked on a laugh.

He stopped a couple of paces away and crouched down so he could meet her eyes.

"What are you doing here?" she asked, before he could speak.

"Marshal Faddei said one of his people was missing. Asked for the Order's help to search. I saw smoke coming from here," Bryce answered, surprising her with a clear, direct response. He glanced at the charred remains nearby. "Your work?" he asked.

"Burned him," Max said, hoping that he wouldn't ask her how. She wasn't quite sure how she had managed that. She didn't remember creating the spell, just thinking about it, and the magic had burst forth on its own. Something she had never been able to do. Her teeth rattling together distracted her. She hadn't realised she was so cold until she started speaking.

"Here," Bryce said, and opened up the object in his hands. A blanket. And not just any blanket, but one of the Order's feather-light, impossibly warm blankets. He rose to his feet and came closer. Her pulse jumped in her throat. She was all but defenceless. He was looming over her. Not trying to threaten her, she told herself. He could have hurt her, or killed her, without coming close to her. She forced herself to stay still while he draped the blanket around her.

As the warmth started returning to her skin, she started shivering in earnest. The ground was freezing cold under her. How had she not noticed that?

Bryce took a step back and crouched in front of her, taking something out of one of his pockets. A plain bottle of water. He loosened the cap for her and held it out. Not a threat, she reminded herself. He was offering her help. She took the bottle, managing to stutter out some thanks, and took a drink. The water felt warm in her mouth, and sliding down her throat. That was a bad sign, she knew.

While she took a drink, Bryce was typing something on his phone.

"Just letting the others know to stop searching. Do you want to call the Marshals?" he asked, offering the phone to her.

She put down the water and had to grab at the blanket as it slid from her shoulder. She anchored the blanket under her arm, only then realising that she was getting blood all over the Order's blanket. Still, Bryce had given it to her knowing she was injured. She could try to clean it later, when she had healed. She accepted the phone, dialling the Marshal's main number from memory. She knew that number better than her own.

"What?" Therese answered.

"It's Max," Max said, through chattering teeth. "I need a medical pick up and back-up and a clean-up crew. I don't know the address," she said.

Bryce held out his hand for the phone. She handed it across and he gave Therese the precise location, then blinked and looked at the phone.

"She hung up," he said.

"She does that," Max said, picking up the water again and taking another sip.

Bryce looked at her for a long moment. She couldn't tell what he was thinking, and she didn't like that. Not one bit.

"The warriors sent with you didn't die easily, did they?" he asked her in a quiet, serious voice, surprising her into meeting his gaze. She had no idea what had made him say that, or why that had been on his mind. But he was crouched across from her, looking like he was prepared to wait for her to answer. And, more surprisingly, looking as if he would listen to whatever she had to say.

She ducked away from that look. It seemed to bore into her, wanting to draw out things that she had kept hidden for a long time. She had no idea how he had reached that conclusion. It twisted a long-dormant wound in her chest. Kitris had outright accused her of using the warriors as a shield. She had been so shocked that she hadn't been able to defend herself. Not then, anyway.

And here was Bryce giving her an opportunity to put the record straight. With him, at least. The memories rose too close to the surface and she shoved them away. She had grown used to being held in contempt by the Order. Or so she told herself. And she didn't want to think about the underworld or the warriors dying, one after the other, around her.

"No," she answered after too long a pause, when her silence had probably given him the answer he needed.

"You were injured. Back then, I mean," he said.

For a moment, she wanted to ask him what he meant. She had a bandage all around one thigh and fresh cut marks over one arm. Fresh and obvious injuries. How had he seen the older ones? Then she realised she had been sitting in a tank top and shorts, most of her skin exposed in the early morning light. He would have been able to see the old scars and burn marks on her arms and legs. And he was a warrior. He would be able to tell that they were old wounds, the physical injuries long since healed.

It hadn't been a question, so she didn't answer it.

"Why did Kitris tell us that you had failed?" he asked.

A direct question. A hundred possible answers crammed her throat. She had not failed, no matter what Kitris had said. But Kitris' word was law in the Order. If he said she had failed, then that was the truth of the matter so far as the Guardians and warriors of the Order were concerned. Not one of them would go against their leader's word. "You'll need to ask him," she said at length. It was the best answer she could give, however unlikely it was that anyone in the Order would ask Kitris a direct question. He did not encourage questions.

Bryce did not look satisfied with that reply. But to her surprise, he didn't press the matter. Instead, he glanced to one side, hesitating slightly as if trying to decide what to say. She didn't think she had ever seen him hesitate and could not imagine what had caused it now.

He looked back at her, face serious. "I remember throwing you against a wall in training class," he said to her.

A bark of laughter escaped her before she could check it. Of all the things he might have said, that was perhaps the most unexpected. "I remember that, too. At least the wall was padded," she said.

He was frowning now. "Why were you in that class?" he asked.

"What do you mean?" she asked. Her body was slowly warming up, the knife cuts on her arm stinging enough to make her eyes water. Her brain was still sluggish, though, not understanding what he was asking or why.

"That was an advanced unarmed combat class," he explained. There was no anger or irritation in his voice, he was just stating a plain fact. "It's not somewhere I'd expect to see an apprentice."

"Oh," she said. She remembered the humiliation of turning up for the next class and not even being allowed into the room. "Is that why you didn't let me back in the day after?"

"Yes, of course," he said. "You weren't ready for that level of training. It would have been dangerous for you to continue."

"Oh," she said again. "Well, I was told to go to your class by the senior apprentice at the time. Did you think I just turned up?" she asked.

"No," he said, a smile pulling his mouth, surprising her almost as much as his questions had. "You were always a diligent and careful student. I knew someone had to have sent you."

Max opened her mouth, but no sound came out. All those years before, she had been doing her best to learn the lessons that were being taught to her, and constantly failing. She had thought she had been invisible to everyone apart from her tormentors, but it seemed that one person, at least, had noticed her. It shouldn't have meant so much to her, but more warmth spread through her body and she could not help smiling.

She wanted to ask him more, but there were more vehicle engines in the distance, quickly drowned out by the sound of a helicopter whirring overhead. The Marshals' medical team was here.

"Is it over?" Bryce asked her, tilting his head towards the charred remains not far away.

The warmth and laughter faded as she stared back at him, trying to frame an answer. The killer was dead. But she still had questions. Such as how he could possibly have risen from the dead. "This part is. For the moment."

Chapter Twenty-Six

The small space of quiet was overtaken by noise and bustle. Bryce stood up and moved away, somehow melting into the background as the medical team arrived. The helicopter landed on the bare expanse of concrete and the same medical team who had treated Zoya rushed across to Max's side with the same professionalism they had used with Zoya. The pair used a lot of words over Max's head including *hypothermia, burst stitches, immediate transfer to hospital* and *dehydration.*

They had stripped her of the leather wrap and silver canister and transferred her to a stretcher before she realised what was happening, cool stings letting her know that there were needles going into her arm. A bag of clear fluid was hung over her head, a bright light shone in her eyes. They wanted to move her to the helicopter.

Out of the corner of her eye, she saw the charred remains of the killer shift on the ground. She had thought he was dead. She had been sure he was dead.

Drowsy with exhaustion, blood loss and now warm from the Order's blanket, which she had refused to let go of, Max said no to being moved. Softly at first, then more forcefully. She was not leaving until more Marshals arrived.

Somewhat to her surprise, the medical team obeyed her and waited in the open with her until a pair of Marshals arrived. Pavla and Yevhen, as luck would have it.

The married pair listened with obvious disbelief as Max told them that the charred remains had risen from the dead once already, and they needed to be extra careful with the corpse. But Pavla and Yevhen had both been Marshals long enough to listen to weird stories. They promised to be careful.

That done, the medical team wheeled her away to the waiting helicopter. In settling her into the helicopter, they put a mask over her face and darkness swallowed her again.

Max woke to a dry mouth and the sensation of being smothered. She opened her eyes to find a great, dark head lying on her chest, another one across her legs.

She must have made a sound, because Cas opened his eyes, his head still on her chest, and stared at her for a long moment before stretching forward and licking her face. Pol woke up from her legs and crawled up the bed to settle at her other side, pinning her under the covers.

The dogs' movement must have set off an alarm somewhere, as the door burst open and a pair of harassed-looking nurses ran in, careening to a halt in the doorway as they saw the dogs.

"You're awake," one nurse said.

"Er, they wouldn't get off the bed when we asked," the other nurse said. "Do you think you can get them to move now?"

"I'll try," Max said, her voice rasping. "Cas. Pol. Get down, please."

The dogs stared back at her. Cas gave her another lick for good measure, then he and Pol slid off the bed in a manner designed to show that they could have stayed - if they had wanted to - but they were choosing to leave. They moved a fraction away from the bed, sitting down next to each other.

Max scrunched up her face. She didn't like being licked, but it was a sign of how worried her dogs had been. They only did it when she was ill or badly hurt. She tried to raise her arm to wipe her face, stopping when she found her limb stiff and unresponsive. Looking down, she saw that one arm was swathed in bandages from shoulder to wrist and the other was tied to the side of the bed with a strip of bandage, a shunt at her elbow leading to a bag of clear fluid on a stand by her bed.

"Sorry about that," the first nurse said, coming around the bed to cut off the bandage. Cas and Pol kept a careful watch on her, but didn't move. "You were restless in your sleep, and we were worried you'd dislodge the drip. But we can take it out now, if you like?"

"Yes, please," Max said. She watched, fascinated and repulsed at the same time, as the nurse expertly disconnected the tube to the bag of fluid and then withdrew a far-too-long needle from Max's arm, pressing a bit of gauze down in its place.

"You'll have a bruise for a few days," the nurse said.

"Alright," Max said. She had plenty of other bruises. One more was not going to make a difference.

Now that she was more awake, she caught a heady, decadent scent in the room and turned her head, looking for the source. There was a vase of deep red roses set on a small shelf halfway up the wall, the scent seeming to grow stronger as Max noticed them.

"Aren't they beautiful?" the second nurse said. "There was a card with them," she added, moving to the shelf and picking up a small envelope next to the vase.

Max took the heavy paper envelope and opened it, pulling out a single piece of card and reading the handwritten note.

I admire someone who can keep their promises. Until the next time. K.

Lord Kolbyr. It could be no one else. Max shivered slightly as she tucked the card away. She had promised to tell him if Ruutti gave her any information about the case. That hadn't happened, and the vampire's telephone number was sitting unused in the glove compartment of her pick-up. She wasn't sure she wanted the ancient vampire to remember who she was, let alone admire her.

A knock at the door caught her attention. There was a wheelchair in the doorway, with Zoya in its seat, and Faddei pushing her.

"Up for some visitors?" Zoya asked, grinning.

"Yes," Max said, even if she wasn't quite sure. Her stomach was turning itself into a knot seeing the other Marshal in a wheelchair.

"We'll leave you to talk," the second nurse said. She pressed a button next to the bed, lifting it up so that Max was almost sitting. Then she pressed a cup with a straw into Max's free hand. "You probably have a dry mouth. Try to take little sips only. And don't stay too long," she added, with a stern frown to Faddei and Zoya.

"Of course," Faddei said, sounding respectful. He wheeled Zoya into the room and closed the door behind the nurses.

All at once the space felt crowded with the two dogs and three humans. Her throat was sore, so she took a sip from the drink the nurse had left and made a face. It was bitter. There was probably some kind of medicine in it. At least it took the raw edge off her throat.

"How are you?" she asked Zoya.

"I'll be out of here in a day or so," Zoya answered, smiling. She stood up out of the chair and took a slow turn. "See. I'm all better, really. They're just being careful."

"I'm sorry," Max said, throat tightening. It had been her job to look after Zoya.

"It would have been one of us," Zoya said, with a one-shouldered shrug, settling herself back in the wheelchair. "If you're going to blame anyone, blame the kid for breaching the wards."

"The Order has extended its concern for the events," Faddei said, eyes gleaming. "Apparently even they realised that sending partly trained apprentices out to the Wild was not the best idea."

"Is that why they were helping you look for me?" Max asked.

"Yes. How much do you remember?" Faddei asked, eyes on her face.

"Most of it, I think. The killer came to the clinic. Oh, is everyone alright? I'm sure I pressed the call button, but no one came."

"Yes, they're fine," Faddei said. "John Smith had dosed them with the spray as well. It takes a while to wear off. He didn't hurt any of them."

"That's something, at least," Max said. "John Smith? That's his actual name?"

"That's the name on his employment record, at least. No, I don't believe it any more than you do. He joined the police's technical division about two years ago. He must have passed their security checks, but there doesn't seem to be any record of him before that time. I've asked the Librarian to look into it." Faddei's face was tight.

And if anyone could find the truth of John Smith and his actual identity, it would be the Librarian, Max thought. "He'd been working there for two years? Any idea what happened to make him start killing?" she asked.

"No one is sure. There's a lot of shouting going on at police headquarters, and in the council rooms. The Walsh clan are furious that someone within the police killed one of their number."

Yes, Max thought. That would be the thing they worried about. The killing of a member of the Five Families. Not the other victims. Not the reason why John Smith had been killing. None of that would matter in comparison to the insult.

Faddei took a seat next to Zoya and let out a long breath.

"You sound tired, boss," Zoya said, putting her hand on his knee. "Perhaps we should get you a bed in here, too?"

Faddei rubbed a hand over his face, then put his hand over hers. "And have to eat hospital food? No thanks."

Zoya grinned and turned back to Max. "The whole place has been buzzing. Did you really burn that man?"

"I did," Max confirmed, shivering at the memory. "I'm not really sure how," she added, before either of them could ask.

"You were right to be concerned, though," Faddei said, all humour gone from his face. "Audhilde said she saw signs of repair beginning in his tissues when she got him to the mortuary. Apparently, they had to apply a special treatment of some kind."

"He's definitely dead, though?" Max asked.

"Yes. Audhilde confirmed it. She said she'd send you a certificate as well." Faddei's brow lifted. "It's already waiting for you at headquarters."

Max's eyes prickled with unexpected tears. She would not have expected the ancient vampire to understand, but it seemed that Audhilde had known without needing to be told that Max needed to be absolutely sure that John Smith was dead.

"So, that's it then," she said, blowing out a breath. "The killer is dead. He never succeeded in his rituals. The city is safe from the underworld again." At least for now, she added in the quiet of her own mind. The dark lord had never been content to simply rest in his realm. He would be trying to escape again soon enough.

Before she could dwell on that too much, Faddei leant forward a fraction.

"And I had a most interesting meeting with the council yesterday," he said, that gleam of humour back in his face. Max eyed him warily. She had an idea that she was not going to like whatever he had to say. "They've agreed to stop the underground fights at the Sorcerer's Mistress," he said.

Max turned the words over in her mind. Faddei's words had been very precise, and he had one of the sharpest minds she'd ever come across. "But not any other fights that they might have going?"

"Oh, you noticed that, too," Faddei said, the gleam deepening. "After some protesting, they said that the Sorcerer's Mistress was the only venue currently active. I've told them to make sure no other fights take place."

"You enjoyed yourself a bit too much," Zoya said, grinning again.

"I have to take these little wins where I can," Faddei said.

"I'm not following," Max said. "What win?"

"Because the council admitted knowledge of the illegal fights, I offered them a deal. The council and each of the Five Families could pay a fine to the Marshals, or we'd drag this into the public eye," Faddei said.

From the gleam in his eye, whatever fine he had managed to levy on the council and the Five Families would be a significant boost to the Marshals' resources.

"And if they do anything that stupid again, I will be going public," Faddei added. "I've left copies of the evidence in various places around the city. And let the council know that, too." The gleam of mischief was still in his eyes. Max could only imagine how much fun he was going to have watching the council and the Five Families try to find his hiding places.

That was Faddei's concern, though, and she would back him against the Five Families.

For now, she was pleasantly warm and numb from head to toe, the killer was dead, and the city was safe for the moment. It was a win. She would take it.

THANK YOU

Thank you very much for reading *Outcast*, The Grey Gates - Book 1. I hope that you've enjoyed meeting Max and getting a bit of insight into her world as much as I enjoyed spending time with her.

It would be great, if you have five minutes, if you could leave an honest review at the store you got it from. Reviews are really helpful for other readers to decide whether the book is for them, and also help me get visibility for my books - thank you.

Max's story continues in *Called*, The Grey Gates - Book 2, which you can also find on Amazon.

Meantime, if you want to be kept up to date with what I'm working on, and get exclusive bonus content, you can sign up for my newsletter at the website: www.taellaneth.com

CHARACTER LIST

(Note: to avoid spoilers, some names may have been missed, and some details changed)

Alexey T'Or Radrean - human, male, twin to Sandrine and apprentice to Radrean

Arkus - dark lord, lord of the underworld

Audhilde (Hilda) - vampire, medical examiner

Bethell - lady of light

Bryce - partly human, male, one of the warriors of the Order

Cas - one of Max's dogs

Connor Declan Walsh - human, male, head of one of the city's most powerful families

David Prosser - human, male, councilman for one of the city districts

Ellie Randall - human, female, senior police officer in the city

Evan Yarwood - human, male, chief of detectives in the city

Faddei Lobanov - human, male, head of Marshal's service

Forster - family name of one of the powerful families in the city

Gemma - human, female, one of the warriors of the Order

Glenda Martins - human, female, nurse at the city clinic the Marshals use

Grandma Parras - human, female, Leonda's grandmother

Grayson Forster - human, male, owns the Sorcerer's Mistress, member of Forster family

Hop - partly human, male, one of the warriors of the Order

Jessica Walsh - human, female, niece of Connor Declan Walsh
Killan - partly human, male, one of the warriors of the Order
Kitris - male, magician, head of the Order of the Lady of the Light
Kolbyr - vampire, male, master of dark magic
Leonda Parras - human, female, chief armourer for the Marshals
Malik - male, owns the Hunter's Tooth
Max Ortis - female, Marshal
Nico - human, male, magic user
Orshiasa - human, male, Guardian in the Order
Pol - one of Max's dogs
Pavla Bilak - human, female, one of the Marshals, wife to Yevhen
Queran - outwardly a human male
Radrean - human, male, Guardian in the Order
Raymund Robart - human, male, lead researcher and scientist for the Marshals
Ruutti Passila - female, detective
Sandrine T'Or Radrean - human, female, Alexey's twin and apprentice to Radrean
Sean Williams - human, male, police Sergeant
Therese - human, female, dispatcher for the Marshals' service
Vanko Tokar - human, male, one of the Marshals
Walsh - family name of one of the powerful families in the city
Yevhen Bilak - human, male, one of the Marshals, husband to Pavla
Zoya Lipka - human, female, one of the Marshals

ALSO BY THE AUTHOR

(as at February 2024)

The Grey Gates (complete)
Outcast, Book 1
Called, Book 2
Hunted, Book 3
Forged, Book 4
Chosen, Book 5

Fractured Conclave
A Usual Suspect, Book 1 – expected to release early May 2024

Ageless Mysteries (complete)
Deadly Night, Book 1
False Dawn, Book 2
Morning Trap, Book 3
Assassin's Noon, Book 4
Flightless Afternoon, Book 5
Ascension Day, Book 6

The Hundred series (complete)
The Gathering, Book 1
The Sundering, Book 2

The Reckoning, Book 3
The Rending, Book 4
The Searching, Book 5
The Rising, Book 6

The Taellaneth series (complete)
Concealed, Book 1
Revealed, Book 2
Betrayed, Book 3
Tainted, Book 4
Cloaked, Book 5

Taellaneth Box Set (all five books in one e-book)
Taellaneth Complete Series (Books 1–5)

ABOUT THE AUTHOR

Vanessa Nelson is a fantasy author who lives in Scotland, United Kingdom and spends her days juggling the demands of two spoiled cats, two giant dogs and her fictional characters.

As far as the cats are concerned, they should always come first. The older dog lets her know when he isn't getting enough attention by chewing up the house. The younger dog's favourite method of getting her attention is a gentle nudge with his head. At least, he would say it's gentle.

You can find out more information at the following places:

Website: http://www.taellaneth.com

Facebook: https://www.facebook.com/Taellaneth

Printed in Great Britain
by Amazon